Guy Newell Boothby

The Beautiful White Devil

Guy Newell Boothby

The Beautiful White Devil

ISBN/EAN: 9783337339364

Printed in Europe, USA, Canada, Australia, Japan

Cover: Foto ©Andreas Hilbeck / pixelio.de

More available books at **www.hansebooks.com**

BY

GUY BOOTHBY

AUTHOR OF A BID FOR FORTUNE, DR. NIKOLA,
THE MARRIAGE OF ESTHER, ETC.

NEW YORK
D. APPLETON AND COMPANY
1897

COPYRIGHT, 1896,
BY D. APPLETON AND COMPANY.

CONTENTS.

THE BEAUTIFUL WHITE DEVIL.

CHAPTER I.

HOW I COME TO HEAR OF THE BEAUTIFUL WHITE DEVIL.

THE night was sweltering hot, even for Hong Kong. The town clock had just chimed a quarter-past ten, and though the actual sound of the striking had died away, the vibration of the bells lingered for nearly half a minute on the murky stillness of the air. In spite of the exertions of the punkah coolie, the billiard-room of the Occidental Hotel was like the furnace-doors of Sheol. Benwell, of the Chinese Revenue cutter *Y-Chang*, and Peckle, of the English cruiser *Tartaric*, stripped nearly to the buff, were laboriously engaged upon a hundred up; while Maloney, of the San Francisco mail-boat, and I, George De Normanville, looked on, and encouraged them with sarcasm and utterly irrational advice. Between times the subdued jabbering of a group of rickshaw coolies, across the pavement, percolated in to us, and mingled with the click of the billiard balls and the monotonous whining of the punkah rope; then the voice of a man in the verandah upstairs, singing to the accompaniment of a

banjo, drifted down, and set us beating time with our
heels upon the wooden floor.

The words of the song seemed strangely out of place
in that heathen land, so many thousand miles removed
from Costerdom. But the wail of the music had quite
a different effect. The singer's voice was distinctly a
good one, and he used it with considerable ability :

> " She wears an artful bonnet, feathers stuck all on it,
>   Covering a fringe all curled ;
>   She's just about the neatest, prettiest, and sweetest
>   Donna in the wide, wide world.
>   And she'll be Mrs. 'Awkins, Mrs. 'Enry 'Awkins,
>   Got her for to name the day.
>   We settled it last Monday, so to church on Sunday,
>   Off we trots the donkey shay.

> " Oh, Eliza ! Dear Eliza ! If you die an old maid
>   You'll only have yourself to blame.
>   D'ye-hear Eliza—dear Eliza !
>   Mrs. 'Enry 'Awkins is a fust-class name."

Half a dozen other voices took up the chorus, and
sent it rolling away over the litter of sampans alongside
the wharf, out to where the red and blue funnel boats
lay at anchor half a mile distant. The two players
chalked their cues and stopped to participate.

> " Oh, Eliza ! Dear Eliza ! If you die an old maid
>   You'll only have yourself to blame.
>   Oh, Eliza ! Dear Eliza !
>   Mrs. 'Enry 'Awkins is a fust-class name."

The music ceased amid a burst of applause.

" Sixee, sixee—sevenee-three," repeated the marker
mechanically.

"Give me the rest, you almond eyed lubber," cried Peckle with sudden energy ; "we'll return to business, for I'll be hanged if I'm going to let myself be beaten by the bo'sun tight and the midshipmite of a bottle-nosed, unseaworthy Chinese contraband."

Maloney knocked the ash off his cigar on his chair-arm and said, by way of explanation, "Our friend Peckle, gentlemen, chowed last night at Government House. He hasn't sloughed his company manners yet."

Benwell sent the red whizzing up the table into the top pocket, potted his opponent into the right-hand middle, by way of revenge, and then gave the customary miss in baulk.

"A Whitechapel game and be hanged to you," said Peckle contemptuously. "I'll bet you a dollar I—— Hullo! who's this? Poddy, by all that's human! Watchman, what of the night? Why this indecent haste ?"

The newcomer was a short podgy man, with a clean-shaven red face, white teeth, very prominent eyes, large ears, and almost marmalade-coloured hair. He was in a profuse perspiration, and so much out of breath that for quite two minutes he was unable to answer their salutations.

"Poddy is suffering from a bad attack of suppressed information," said Benwell, who had been examining him critically. "Better prescribe for him, De Norman-ville. Ah, I forgot, you don't know one another. Let me introduce you—Mr. Horace Venderbrun, Dr. De Normanville. Now you're acquent, as they say in the farces."

"Out with it, Poddy," continued Peckle, digging him

in the ribs with the butt of his cue. "If you don't tell us soon, we shall be sorrowfully compelled to postpone our engagements to-morrow in order to witness your interment in the Happy Valley."

"Well, in the first place," began Mr. Venderbrun, "you must know——"

"Hear, hear, Poddy. A dashed good beginning !"

"Shut up, Peckle, and give the minstrel a chance. Now, my Blondel, pipe your tuneful lay."

"You must know that the *Oodnadatta*——"

"Well—well, Skipper—Perkins, martinet and tee-totaller ; chief officer, Bradburn, otherwise the China Sea Liar ! What about her ? She sailed this evening for Shanghai ?"

"With a million and a half of specie aboard. Don't forget that ! Went ashore in the Ly-ee-moon Pass at seven o'clock. Surrounded by junks instantly. Skipper despatched third officer in launch full steam for assistance. Gunboat went down post haste, and, like most gunboats, arrived too late to be of any use. Apologies, Peckle, old man ! Skipper and ten men shot, chief officer dirked, first saloon passengers of importance cleaned of their valuables and locked up in their own berths. The bullion room was then rifled, and every red cent of the money is gone—goodness knows where. Now, what d'you think of that for news ?"

"My gracious !"

"What junks were they ?"

"Nobody knows."

"The Ly-ee-moon Pass, too ! Right under our very noses. Criminy ! Won't there be a row !"

"The Beautiful White Devil again, I suppose ?"

"Looks like it, don't it?　Peckle, my boy, from this hour forward the papers will take it up, and—well, if I know anything of newspapers, they'll drop it on to you gunboat fellows pretty hot."

"If I were the British Navy I'd be dashed if I'd be beaten by a woman."

"Hear, hear, to that.　Now for your defence, Peckle."

"Go ahead; let me have it.　I'm down and I've got no friends; but it's all very well for you gentlemen of England, who sit at home in ease, to sneer.　If you only knew as much as we do of the lady you wouldn't criticise so freely.　Personally, I believe she's a myth."

"Don't try it, old man.　We all know the Lords Commissioners will stand a good deal, but, believe me, they'll never swallow that.　They've had too many proofs to the contrary lately."

I thought it was time to interfere.

"Will somebody take pity on a poor barbarian and condescend to explain," I said.　"Since I've been in the East I've heard nothing but Beautiful White Devil—Beautiful White Devil—Beautiful White Devil.　Tiffin at Government House, Colombo—Beautiful White Devil; club chow, Yokohama—Beautiful White Devil; flagship, *Nagasaki*—Beautiful White Devil; and now here.　All Beautiful White Devil, and every yarn differing from its predecessor by miles.　I can tell you, I'm beginning to feel very much out of it."

Each of the four men started in to explain.　I held up my hand in entreaty.

"As you are strong, be merciful," I cried.　"Not all at once."

One of the silent-footed China-boys brought me a

match for my cigar, and held it until I had obtained a light. Then, throwing myself back in the long cane chair, I bade them work their wicked wills.

"Let Poddy tell," said Peckle. "He boasts the most prolific imagination. Go on, old man, and don't spare him."

Venderbrun pulled himself together, signed for silence, and, having done so, began theatrically: "Who is the Beautiful Devil? Mystery. Where did she first hail from? Mystery. What is her name, I mean her real name, not the picturesque Chinese cognomen? Mystery. As far as can be ascertained she made her first appearance in Eastern waters in Rangoon, July 24, 18—. Got hold of some native prince blowing the family treasure and blackmailed him out of half a million of dollars. A man would never have come out of the business alive, but she did, and what is more, with the money to boot. Three months later the *Vectis Queen* went ashore, when forty-eight hours out of Singapore, junks sprang up out of nowhere, boarded her in spite of stubborn resistance on the part of the ship's company, looted her bullion room of fifty thousand pounds and her passengers of three thousand more."

"But what reason have you for connecting the Beautiful White Devil with that affair?"

"White yacht hanging about all the time. Known to be hers. Signals passed between them, and when the money was secured it was straightway carried on board her."

"All right. Go on."

"Quite quiet for three months. Then the Sultan of Surabaya chanced to make the acquaintance in Batavia of an extraordinarily beautiful woman. They went about a good deal together, after which she lured him on board a steam yacht in Tanjong Priok, presumably to say good-bye. Having done so, she coaxed him below, sailed off with him there and then, kept him under lock and key until he had paid a ransom of over four hundred thousand guilders, when he was put ashore again. Two months later, Vesey—you know Vesey—of Johore Street, probably the richest man in Hong Kong, met a woman staying at this very hotel. She pretended to be just out from home, and no end innocent. Well, Vesey was so awfully smitten that he wanted to marry her— bad as all that. She took him in hand, and one day got him to take her for a cruise in his yacht. Of course he jumped at the chance, and off they sailed. Out at sea they were met by a white schooner. I believe Vesey was in the middle of protesting his undying love, and all that sort of thing, you know, when my lady clapped a revolver to his head, and bade him heave-to. A boat put off from the stranger, and both lady and friend boarded her. The long and the short of it was, when Vesey was released he had signed a cheque for fifty thousand pounds, and, by Jove, the money was paid on the nail. Chinese Government have a score against her for abducting a Mandarin of the Gold Button. They tried to catch her but failed. English cruiser went after her for two days and lost her near Formosa. Silence again for three months, then new Governor and wife, Sir Prendergast Prendergast, were coming out here on the *Ooloomoo*. Her ladyship, whom you know was mixed up in that Belleville business, had her famous diamonds with her —said to be worth thirty thousand pounds. There was

also eighty thousand in gold going up to Shanghai. It
is supposed that the purser must have been bribed and
in the business ; at any rate when they arrived at Hong
Kong both bullion, diamonds, and purser were mysteriously missing. Couldn't find a trace of 'em high or low.
Whether they went overboard in a fog, whether they
were still stowed away on board, nobody ever knew.
They were gone, that was enough. The Governor was
furious, and worried the Admiralty so with despatches
that two cruisers were sent off with instructions to look
for her. They pottered about, and at last sighted and
chased her to the Philippines, were they lost her in a
fog. Those are the principal counts against her, I believe. Rum story, ain't it ? "

"Extraordinary. Has anybody ever seen her ? "

"I should just think so. Sultan of Surabaya, Vesey,
Native Prince, and all the people staying at this house
when she was here."

"What description do they give of her ? "

"Quite a young woman—eight-and-twenty at most.
Tall and willowy. Beautiful features, clear cut as a
cameo—exquisite complexion and rippling golden hair—
a voice like a flute, figure like Venus, and eyes that
look through yours into the uttermost depths of your
soul."

"Bravo, Poddy! The little man's getting quite
enthusiastic."

"And isn't she worth being enthusiastic about? By
Jove! I'd like to know her history."

"And do you mean to tell me that with the English,
American, French, German, Chinese, and Japanese fleets
patrolling these waters, it's impossible to catch her ? "

"Quite—up to the present. Look at the facts of the case. She's here to-day, and gone to-morrow. White yacht seen near Singapore to-day—copper-coloured off Macassar on Thursday—black with white ports near Shanghai the week following. The police and the poor old Admiral are turning gray under the strain."

"By Jove! I'd like to see her."

"Don't say that or you will. Nobody ever knows where she'll turn up next. It is certain that she has agents everywhere, and that she's in league with half the junk pirates along the coast. Glad I'm not a man worth abducting."

"But in spite of what you say, I can hardly believe that it's possible for a woman to carry on such a trade. It's like a romance."

"It's not *like* it, it *is* a romance, and a pretty unpleasant one too. Sultan of Surabaya and poor old Vesey were glad enough to see the final chapter of it, I can assure you. You should just hear the latter's description of the yacht and its appointments. He used to make us creep when he told us how this woman would sit on deck, looking him through and through out of her half closed eyes till he began to feel as if he'd have to get up and scream, or sit where he was and go mad. He saw two or three things on board that boat that he says he'll never forget, and I gathered that he doesn't want any more excursions in the lady's company."

"He must be a man without imagination."

"He's a man blessed with good sound common sense. That's what he is."

"All the same, as I said before, I'd like to see her."

" Well, I shouldn't be surprised if your wish is gratified before long. They're simply bound to catch her ; the wonder to me is that they haven't done so months ago."

"It seems incredible that she should have escaped so long."

Peckle took up his cue again.

" Hear, hear, to that. And now, Benwell, my boy, if you don't want to go to sleep in that chair, turn out and finish the drubbing you've begun. I must be getting aboard directly."

Benwell rose, and went round the table to where his ball lay under the cushion. The imperturbable marker called the score as if there had been no pause in the game, and the match was once more getting under way, when the swing doors opened and an elderly man entered the room. He was dressed in white from top to toe, carried a big umbrella, and wore a broad-brimmed solar topee upon his head. Once inside, he paused as if irresolute, and then, looking round on its occupants, said politely :

" Forgive my intrusion ; but can you tell me where I can find a gentleman named De Normanville ? "

" I am that person ! " I said, rising from my chair.

"I hope you will not think me rude," he continued, "but if you could allow me the honour of five minutes' conversation with you I should be obliged."

" With pleasure."

I crossed the room to where he stood, and signed him to a seat near the door.

" Pardon me," he said, " but the business about which I desire to consult you is of a highly important and confidential nature.   Is there any room in the hotel where we can be alone ? "

"Only my bedroom, I'm afraid," I answered.   "We shall be quite free from interruption there."

"That will do excellently.   Let us go to it."

With that we went upstairs.   All the way I was puzzling my brains to think what he could want with me. The man was so mysterious, and yet so palpably desirous of pleasing, that I was becoming quite interested.   One thing was certain—I had never seen him before in my life.

Arriving at my room, I lit a candle and pushed a chair forward for him ; having done so I took up my position beside the open window.   Down in the street below I could hear the subdued voices of the passers-by, the rattle of rickshaws, and the chafing of sampans alongside the wharf.   I remember, too, that the moon was just rising over the mainland, and to show how unimportant things become engraved upon the memory, I recollect that it struck me as being more like the yolk of a hard-boiled egg than ever I remember to have thought it before.   Suddenly I remembered the laws of hospitality.

"Before we begin business, may I offer you some refreshment?" I asked—"B. and S. ?   Whisky ? "

"I am obliged to you," he answered.   "I think I will take a little whisky, thank you."

I put my head out of the door.   A servant was passing.

"Boy, bring two whisky pegs."

Then returning to my guest, I said : "Do you smoke ? I think I can give you a good cigar."

He took one from the box and lit it, puffing the smoke luxuriously through his nose. Presently the pegs were forthcoming, and when I had signed the *chit* I asked his business.

"You are a stranger in Hong Kong, I believe, Dr. De Normanville?" he began.

"Not only in Hong Kong, but you might say in the East generally," I answered. "I am out on a tour to study Asiastic diseases for a book I am writing."

"You have achieved considerable success in your profession, I believe. We have even heard of you out here."

I modestly held my tongue. But so pitiful is the vanity of man that from this time forward I began to look upon my companion with a more friendly air than I had hitherto shown him.

"Now, forgive my impertinence," he continued, "but how long do you contemplate remaining in the East?"

"It is very uncertain," I replied; "but I almost fancy another six weeks will find me upon a P. and O. boat homeward bound."

"And in that six weeks will your time be very importantly occupied?"

"I cannot say, but I should rather think not. So far as I can tell at present my work is accomplished."

"And now will you let me come to business. To put it bluntly, have you any objection to earning a thousand pounds?"

"Not the very least!" I answered with a laugh. "What man would have? Provided, of course, I can earn it in a legitimate manner."

"You have bestowed considerable attention upon the treatment of small-pox, I believe?"

" I have had sole charge of two small-pox hospitals, if that's what you mean."

" Ah ! Then our informant was right. Well, this business, in which a thousand pounds is to be earned, has to do with an outbreak of that disease."

" And you wish me to take charge of it ? "

" That is exactly what I am commissioned to negotiate."

" Where is the place ? "

" I cannot tell you ! "

" Not tell me ? That's rather strange, is it not ? "

" It is all very strange. But with your permission I will explain myself more clearly."

I nodded.

" It is altogether an extraordinary business. But, on the other hand, the pay is equally extraordinary. I am commissioned to find a doctor who will undertake the combating of an outbreak of small-pox on the following terms and conditions : The remuneration shall be one thousand pounds ; the doctor shall give his word of honour not to divulge the business to any living soul ; he shall set off at once to the affected spot, and he shall still further pledge himself to reveal nothing of what he may have heard or seen when he returns here again. Is that clear to you ? "

" Perfectly. But it's a most extraordinary proposition."

" I grant you it is. But it is a chance that few men would care to let slip."

" How is the person undertaking it to find the place ? "

" I will arrange that myself."

" And how is he to return from it again ? "

"He will be sent back in the same way that he goes."

"And when must he start?"

"At once, without delay. Say twelve o'clock to-night."

"It is nearly eleven now."

"That will leave an hour. Come, Dr. De Normanville, are you prepared to undertake it?"

"I don't really know what to say. There is so much mystery about it."

"Unfortunately, that is necessary."

I paced the room in anxious thought, hardly knowing what answer to give. Should I accept or should I decline the offer? The thousand pounds was a temptation, and yet, supposing there were some treachery lurking behind it, that, in my innocence of the East, I could not fathom—what then? Moreover, the adventurous side of the affair, I must own, appealed to me strongly. I was young, and there was something supremely fascinating about the compliment and the mystery that enshrouded it.

"Look here," I said at length. "Pay me half the money down before I start, as a guarantee of good faith, and I'm your man!"

"Very good. I will even meet you there!"

He put his hand inside his coat and drew out a pocket-book. From this he took five one hundred pound Bank of England notes, and gave them to me.

"There, you have half the money."

"Thank you. Really, I must beg your pardon for almost doubting you, but——"

"Pray say no more. You understand the conditions

thoroughly. You are not to divulge a detail of the errand to any living soul now or when you return."

"I will give you my word I will not."

"Then that is settled. I am much obliged to you. Can you arrange to meet me on the wharf exactly at midnight?"

"Certainly. I will be there without fail. And now tell me something of the outbreak itself. Is it very severe?"

"Very. There have already been nearly a hundred cases, out of which quite fifty have proved fatal. Your position will be no sinecure. You will have your work cut out for you."

"So it would appear. Now, if you will excuse me, I will go out and endeavour to obtain some lymph. We shall need all we can get."

"You need not put yourself to so much trouble. That has been attended to. To prevent any suspicion arising from your asking for such a thing, we have laid in a stock of everything you can possibly need."

"Very well, then. I will meet you on the wharf."

"On the wharf at twelve o'clock precisely. For the present, adieu!"

He shook me by the hand, picked up his hat and umbrella, and disappeared down the staircase, while I returned to my room to pack.

CHAPTER II.

AN EVENTFUL VOYAGE.

THE last stroke of twelve was just booming out on
the muggy night when I stepped on to the landing-
stage to await my mysterious employer. The hotel
servant who had carried my bag put it down, and having received his gratuity left me. The soft moonlight
flooded everything, threw quaint shadows upon the
wharf planks, shone upon the sleeping sampans beside
it, and gurgled in oily wreaths on the placid water in
the depths between them. Very few people were
abroad, and those who were had no attention to spare
for me. The Sikh policeman, who passed and repassed,
alone seemed to wonder what a white lord could be
doing in such a place at such a time. But doubtless he
had had experience of the curious ways of Sahibdom,
and, being a wise man, if he possessed any curiosity, he
refrained from giving me evidence of the fact.

Suddenly the patter of naked feet behind me caught
my ear. A Chinese chair, borne by two stalwart
bearers, was approaching. Very naturally I settled it
in my own mind that it contained the man whom I was
to meet, and turned to receive him. But when the
conveyance was set down, it was not the respectable
Englishman I had seen before who stepped out of it,
but a portly Chinaman of considerable rank and dignity.

He was gorgeously clad in figured silk ; his pigtail reached halfway to his heels and was adorned with much ornamentation ; and I noticed that he wore large tortoiseshell spectacles which, while they completely hid his eyes, gave a curious effect to his otherwise not unhandsome countenance. Having descended from his equipage, he dismissed his bearers, and began to stump solemnly up and down the landing-stage, drawing closer and closer to me at every turn. Presently he summoned up courage enough to accost me. To my surprise he said:

" What for you come here one piecee look see ?"

Not being an adept at pigeon English, I simply answered—

" I'm afraid I don't understand you."

" What for you come here look see ? "

" I'm waiting for a friend."

" Your friend allee same Engleesman ?"

" Yes, I believe he's an Englishman."

" You go 'way look see chop-chop ?"

" You'll excuse me, but that's my own affair, I think."

" Allee same smallee pox, I think !"

" You may think what you please."

" S'posing you say, smallee poxee, allee same one piecee thousan' pound ?"

" I'm afraid I can't continue this conversation. Good evening."

I turned on my heel, and was about to leave him, when he stopped me by saying in excellent English:

" Thank you, Dr. De Normanville. I'm quite satis-fied."

" Good gracious, what's all this ?"

"Why, it means that I have been trying you, that's all. Forgive the deception, but the importance of our mission must be my excuse. Now we must be going. Here is the boat."

As he spoke, a large sampan shot out from among its companions and came swiftly towards the wharf.

"Two cautions before we embark. The first— remember that I am a Chinaman, and speak only pigeon English. The second—if you are armed, be careful of your revolver. The men who work the junk we are going down to meet are not to be trusted ; hence my disguise."

He left me and descended the steps. The sampan by this time had come alongside ; a woman was rowing and a vigorous conversation in Chinese ensued. When it was finished my companion beckoned to me, and picking up my bag I went down to him. Next moment I was aboard and stuffed away in the little pokey rat-hole of a cabin amidships. My friend took his place beside me, a small boy took the helm, and we pushed off. Not a word was spoken, and in this fashion for nearly an hour we pursued our way down the harbour, passed a flotilla of junks, threaded a course between the blue and red funnel boats, and finally swept out into the clear space that stretches away from Port Victoria as far as Green Island.

For hours we seemed to be imprisoned in that stuffy little cabin. Like most sampans, the boat smelt abominably, and as we could only see the mechanical rowing of the women in the well forrard, and hear the occasional commands of the tiny boy steering aft, our enjoyment may be placed on the debit side of the account without any fear of miscalculation.

At length my companion, who had not uttered a word since he stepped aboard, began to show signs of impatience. He rose from his seat and peered out into the night. Presently he appeared to be a little relieved in his mind, for he reseated himself with a muttered "Thank goodness," and gave himself up to a careful consideration of our position. Through a slit in the tarpaulin I could just see that we were approaching a big junk, whose ample girth almost blocked the fairway. Her great, square cut stern loomed above us, and round it our coxswain steered us with a deftness extraordinary.

As we came alongside one of the women rowing drew in her oar and said a few words to my companion. In answer he stepped out of the shelter and called something in Chinese. A voice from the junk replied, and the answer being evidently satisfactory we hitched on and prepared to change vessels. A rope was thrown to us, and when it had been made fast my guide signed to me to clamber aboard. I did so, and the next moment was on the junk's deck assisting him to a place beside me.

Two or three men were grouped about amidships watching us, and one, the owner, or skipper of the boat I presumed, entered upon a longwinded conversation with my conductor. As they talked I heard the sampan push off and disappear astern. Then our crew fell to work—the great sails were hoisted, a hand went aft to the tiller, and within five minutes we were waddling down the straits at a pace that might possibly have been four knots an hour. All this time my companion had not addressed me once. His whole attention seemed to be concentrated upon the work going on around him.

He treated me with the contemptuous indifference gener-ally shown by Chinamen towards barbarian Englishmen, and this I was wise enough not to resent.

I will not deny, however, that I was nervous. The mysterious errand on which I was bound, the emphatic, but not reassuring, warning of my astute companion, and the company in which I now found myself, were calculated to have this effect. But as we left the land behind us and waddled out to sea, my fears began in a measure to subside, and I found myself gazing about me with more interest than I should at any other time have thought possible.

The junk was one of the largest I had ever seen, and, like most of her class, appeared to be all masts, sails, and stern. The crew were as usual very numerous, and a more evil-looking lot no one could possibly wish to set eyes on ; the face of one little pock-marked fellow being particularly distasteful to me. That this indi-vidual, for some reason, bore me no good will I was pretty positive, and on one occasion, in passing where I stood, he jolted against me in such a fashion and with such violence that he nearly capsized me. At any other time I should have resented his behaviour, but, bearing in mind my companion's advice, I held my peace.

By this time it was nearly two o'clock. The wind was every moment freshening and a brisk sea rising, The old tub began to pitch unpleasantly, and I found repeated occasion to thank my stars that I was a good sailor. Sharp dashes of spray broke over her decks at every plunge, soaking us to the skin, and adding con-siderably to the unpleasantness of our position. Still, however, my companion did not speak, but I noticed that he watched the men about him with what struck me as increased attention.

Seeing that I had had no sleep at all that night it may not be a matter of much surprise that I presently began to nod. Stowing myself away in a sheltered corner, I was in the act of indulging in a nap when I felt a body fall heavily against me. It was my companion who had dropped asleep sitting up, and had been dislodged by a sudden roll of the ship. He fell clean across me, his face against my ear. Next moment I knew that the catastrophe was intentional.

"Keep your eyes open," he whispered as he lay; "there is treachery aboard. We shall have trouble before long."

After that you may be sure I thought no more of sleep. Pulling myself together I slipped my hand into the pocket that had contained my revolver, only to find, to my horror and astonishment, that it was gone. My pocket had been picked since I had come aboard the junk.

My consternation may be better imagined than described, and as soon as I could find occasion I let my companion know of my misfortune.

"I gave you fair warning," he replied calmly, " now we shall probably both lose our lives. However, what can't be cured must be endured, so pretend to be asleep and don't move, whatever happens, until you hear from me. That little pock-marked devil haranguing the others forrard is Kwong Fung, the most notorious pirate along the whole length of the coast, and if we fall into his hands, well, there will not be two doubts as to what our fate will be."

He tumbled over on to his side with a grunt, while I shut my eyes and pretended to be asleep. It was growing cold; the wind was rising and with it the sea. Already the stars in the East were paling preceptibly, and in another hour, at most, day would be born.

It's all very well for people to talk about coolness and presence of mind in moments of extreme danger. Since the events I'm now narrating took place, I've been in queerer quarters than most men, and though I've met with dozens who could be brave enough when the actual moment for fighting arrived, I've never yet encountered one who could lie still, doing nothing, for three-quarters of an hour, watching his death preparing for him, and not show some sign of nervousness. Frankly, I will admit that I was afraid. To have to lie on that uncomfortable heaving deck, a big sea running, and more than a capful of wind blowing, watching, in the half dark, a gang of murderous ruffians plotting one's destruction, would try the nerves of the boldest of men. Small wonder then that my lower limbs soon became like blocks of ice, that my teeth chattered in my head, and that an indescribable sinking sensation assumed possession of my internal regions. I could not take my eyes off the group seated frog fashion on the deck forrard. Their very backs held an awful fascination for me.

But, as it soon turned out, my interest in them was almost my undoing. For had I not been so intent upon watching what was before me I should perhaps have heard the rustling of a human body outside the bulwarks against which I had seated myself. In that case I should have detected the figure that had crawled quietly over and was now stealing along the deck towards where I lay. In his hand he carried a thin cord at the end of which was a noose just capable of encircling my head.

Suddenly I felt something touch my throat. I lifted my head, and at the same instant the truth dawned upon me. *I was being strangled.* How long a time elapsed between the cord's touching my neck and my losing consciousness I could not say, but brief as was the interval, I can recollect seeing my companion half raise himself. Then came a flash, a loud report, a sudden singing in my ears, and I remember no more.

When I recovered my wits again my companion was bending over me.

"Thank God," he said piously, "I began to think the brute had done for you. Now pull yourself together as fast as you can, for there's going to be serious trouble."

I looked round me as well as I could. By my side lay the body of the man, with the cord still in his hand, and from the way in which one arm was stretched out and the other doubled under him, I gathered that he was dead. Amidships the crew of the junk were assembled, listening to the excited oratory of the little pock-marked devil against whom my companion had warned me. He held in his hand a revolver—mine, I had no difficulty in guessing—and, from the way in which he turned and pointed in our direction, I understood that he was explaining to the others the necessity which existed for exterminating us without delay. I turned to my companion and warmly thanked him for the shot that had saved my life.

"Don't mention it," he answered coolly. "It was fortunate I saw him coming. You must remember that besides saving you it has put one of our adversaries out of the way, and every one against odds like this counts. By the way, you'd better find something to lay about you with—for from all appearance we're in for a big thing."

Under the bulwarks, and a little to the left of where I sat, was a stout iron bar some two feet six in length. I managed to secure it, and having done so, felt a little easier in my mind.

As I crawled back to my station another report greeted my ears, and at the same instant a bullet bedded itself in the woodwork, within an inch of my left temple.

"That's the introduction," said my imperturbable friend with a grim smile. "Are you ready? He's got the only weapon among them and five more cartridges left in it. Keep by me and give no quarter—for remember if they win they'll show you none."

Bang! Another bullet whizzed past my ear.

Bang! My companion gave a low whistle and then turned to me.

"Grazed my forearm," he said calmly, and then raising his pistol shot the nearest of our assailants dead. The man gave a little cry, more like a sob, and with outspread arms fell on his face upon the deck. The next roll of the vessel carried him into the lee scuppers, where for some time he washed idly to and fro. Never in my life before had I seen anything so coolly deliberate as the way in which he was picked off. It was more like rabbit shooting than anything else.

" Two cartrides gone!" said my comrade.

As he spoke a bullet tore up the deck at my feet, while another grazed my right shoulder.

"Four. Keep steady ; he's only two left. Look out *then*, for they'll rush us to a certainty ! I wish I could get another shot at them first."

But this wish was not destined to be gratified. The scoundrels had had sufficient evidence of his skill as a marksman, and being prudent, though precious, villains they had no desire to receive further proof of it. They therefore kept in shelter.

Minute after minute went slowly by, and everyone found the night drawing further off the sky, and the light widening more perceptibly. But still no sign came from those in hiding forrard. To my mind this watching and waiting was the worst part of the whole business. All sorts of fresh horrors seemed to cluster round our position as we crouched together in the shelter aft.

Suddenly, without any warning, and with greater majesty than I ever remember to have observed in him before or since, the sun rose in the cloudless sky. Instantly with his coming, light and colour shot across the waters, the waves from being of a dull leaden hue became green and foam-crested, and the great fibre sails of the junk from figuring as blears of double darkness, reaching up to the very clouds, took to themselves again their ordinary commonplace and forlorn appearance.

Our course lay due east, and for this reason the sun shone directly in our faces, dazzling us, and for the moment preventing our seeing anything that might be occurring forrard. I could tell that this was a matter of some concern to my companion, and certainly it was not to remain very long a matter of indifference to me,

The sun had been above the sky line scarcely a matter of two minutes when another shot was fired from forward, and I fell with a cry to the deck. Next moment I had picked myself up again, and, feeling very sick and giddy, scrambled to my companion's side. He was as cool and apparently as unconcerned as ever.

"The other was the prologue—this is going to be the play itself. Keep as close to me as you can, and above all things fight to the death—accept no quarter, and give none."

The words were hardly out of his mouth before we heard a scampering of bare feet upon the deck, and a succession of shrill yells, and then the vessel paying off a little on her course showed us the ruffians climbing on to the raised poop upon which we stood. To my horror —for, strangely enough, in that moment of intense excitement, I was capable of a second emotion—I saw that they were six in number, while a reinforcement, numbering three more, waited upon the fo'c's'le head to watch the turn of events.

As the head of the first man appeared my companion raised his pistol and pulled the trigger. The bullet struck the poor wretch exactly on the bridge of the nose, making a clear round hole from which, an instant later, a jet of blood spurted forth. A second bullet carried another man to his account, and by this time the remaining four were upon us.

Of what followed in that turmoil I have but a very imperfect recollection. I remember seeing three men rush towards me, one of whom I knew for Kwong Fung, the little pock-marked rascal before mentioned, and I recollect that, with the instinct of despair, I clutched my bar of iron in both hands and brought it down on the head of the nearest of the trio with all my force. It caught him on the right temple, and crushed the skull in like a broken egg-shell. But the piratical scoundrels had forgotten the man lying on the deck. In their haste to advance they omitted to step over his body, caught their feet and fell to the ground. At least, I am wrong in saying they fell to the ground, for only the pock-marked rascal fell ; the other tripped, and would have recovered himself and been upon me had I not sprung upon him, thrown away my bar, caught up his companion's knife, which had fallen from his hand, and tried my level best to drive it in above his shoulder-blade. But is was easier said than done. He clutched me fiercely and, locked hard and fast, we swayed this way and that, fighting like wild-cats for our lives. He was a smaller man than I, but active as an acrobat, and in the most perfect training. Up and down, round and round we went, eyes glaring, breath coming in great gasps, our hands upon each other's throats, and every moment drawing closer and closer to the vessel's side.

Though the whole fight could not have lasted a minute it seemed an eternity. I was beginning to weaken, and I saw by the look in his hateful almond eyes that my antagonist knew it. But he had bargained without his host. A heavy roll sent the little vessel heeling over to the port side, and an instant later we were both prone upon the deck rolling, tumbling, fighting again to be uppermost. From the manner in which I had fallen, however, the advantage now lay with me, and you may be sure I was not slow to make the most of it. Throwing myself over and seating myself astride of him,

3

I clutched my adversary by the throat, and, drawing back my arm, struck him with my clenched fist between his eyes. The blow was given with all my strength, and it certainly told. He lay beneath me a bleeding and insensible mass. Then staggering to my feet I looked about me. On the deck were four dead bodies; two on the break of the poop lying faces down, just where they had fallen, one at my feet, his skull dashed in and his brains protruding, a horrible sight,— another under the bulwarks, his limbs twitching in his death agony, and his mouth vomiting blood with automatic regularity. My companion I discovered seated astride of another individual, admonishing him with what I knew was an empty revolver to abstain from any further attempt to escape.

"I think we have got the upper hand of them now," he said as calmly as if he were accustomed to going through this sort of thing every day of his life. "Would you be so good as to hand me that piece of rope? I must make this slippery gentleman fast while I have him."

"Surely it's the leader of the gang," I cried, at the same time doing as he had asked me. "The man you pointed out to me, Kwong Fung?"

"You're quite right. It is."

"And now that you have him, what will his fate be?"

"A short shrift and a long rope, if I have anything to do with the matter. There! That's right, I don't think you'll get into much mischief now, my friend."

So saying he rose to his feet, rolled the man over on to his back, and turned to me.

"My goodness, man, you're wounded," he cried, spinning me round to find out whence the blood was dripping.

And so I was, though in my excitement I had quite forgotten the fact. A ball had passed clean through the fleshy part of my left arm, and the blood flowing from it had stiffened all my sleeve.

With a gentleness one would hardly have expected to find in him, my friend drew off my coat and cut open my shirt sleeve. Then bidding me stay where I was while he procured some water with which to bathe the wound, he left me and went forrard. I did not, however, see him return, for now that the excitement had departed, a great faintness was stealing over me. The sea seemed to be turning black, and the deck of the junk to be slipping away from under me. Finally, my legs tottered, my senses left me, and I fell heavily to to the ground.

When I came to myself again I was lying on a pile of fibre sails under the shelter of an improvised awning. My companion, whose name I discovered later was Walworth, was kneeling beside me with a preternaturally grave expression upon his usually stolid face.

"How do you feel now?" he inquired, holding a cup of water to my lips.

I drank eagerly, and then replied that I felt better, but terribly weak.

"Oh, that's only to be expected," he answered reassuringly. "We ought to be glad, considering the amount of blood you must have lost, that it's no worse. Keep up your heart. You'll soon be all right now."

"Has anything happened?"

"Nothing at all! We're the victors without doubt. As soon as you can spare me I'm going forrard to rouse out the rest of the gang, and get the junk on her course again. We've no time to waste pottering about here."

"I'm well enough now. Only give me something to protect myself with in case of accident."

"Here's your own revolver, of which I relieved our pock-marked friend yonder. I've refilled it, so, if you want to, you can do damage to the extent of six shots— two for each of the three remaining men!"

After glancing at his own weapon to see that it was fully charged, he picked his way forrard and called in Chinese to those in hiding to come forth, if they wished to save their lives. In response to his summons three men crawled out and stood in a row. After he had harangued them, I noticed that he questioned them eagerly in turn, and was evidently much perturbed at the answers he received. When he had said all that he had to say he searched for something, and, not finding it, left them and came back to me. Before making any remark he turned over the bodies on the deck, and, when he had done so, seemed still more put out.

"What's the matter?" I inquired. "Are we in for any more trouble?"

"I'm afraid so. That rascally captain, seeing how the fighting was going, and dreading my vengeance, must have jumped overboard, leaving no man save myself capable of navigating the junk. Added to which the food and water supply—which, had this trouble not occurred, and we had got further upon our way, would have been ample for our requirements—will only last us, at most, two more meals. However, it's no good crying over spilt milk; we must do our best with what we've got, and having done that we can't do more. Let us hope we'll soon pick up the boat of which we're in search."

"And what boat may that be?"

"Why, the vessel that is to take us to the island, to be sure. What other could it be?"

"I had no idea that we were in search of one."

"Well, we are; and it looks as if we shall be in search of her for some time to come. Confound those treacherous beggars!"

As he said this he assumed possession of the tiller, the vessel's head was brought round to her course, and presently we were wobbling along in a new and more westerly direction.

Hour after hour passed in tedious monotony, and still we sailed on. The heat was intense—the wind dropped toward noon, and the face of the deep then became like burnished silver—almost impossible to look upon. But no sign of the craft we were in search of greeted our eyes; only a native boat or two far away to the eastward and a big steamer hull down upon the northern horizon.

It was not a cheerful outlook by any manner of means, and for the hundredth time or so I reproached myself for my folly in ever having undertaken the voyage. To add to my regret my arm was still very painful, and though, to a certain extent, I was protected from the sun by the awning my friend had constructed for me, yet I began to suffer agonies of thirst. The afternoon wore on—the sun declined upon the western horizon, and still no wind came. It looked as if we were destined to spend yet another night upon this horrible junk, the very sight of which had become beyond measure loathsome to me. As darkness fell, it seemed peopled with ghosts, for though the bodies of those killed in the late affray no longer defaced the deck with their ghastly presence, I could not drive the picture they had presented from my brain.

When the sun disappeared below the horizon, a great peace fell upon the deep, broken only by the groaning of our timbers and the ill-stepped masts. Little by little darkness stole down upon us, a few stars came into the sky, followed soon after by multitudes of others. But there was no wind at all, and by this time my thirst was excruciating. About seven o'clock my companion brought me a small cup of water, hardly sufficient to wet my lips, but more precious than any diamonds, and held it while I drank.

"I'm sorry to say that's all we have," he said solemnly when I had finished it. "Henceforward we must go without."

His words seemed to toll in my ears like a death knell, and I became thirsty again immediately. I suppose I must have been in a high state of fever; at any rate I know that I have never spent such another night of pure physical agony in my life.

I was asleep next morning when the sun rose, but his heat soon woke me to the grim reality of our position. My companion was still at the tiller, and from where I lay I could see that we were still sailing in the same direction. He called to me to know how I felt, and to show him that I was better, I endeavoured to rise, only to fall back again in what must have been a dead faint.

I have no recollection of what followed immediately upon my recovering myself, except a confused remembrance of craving for water—water! water! water! But there was none to be had even if I had offered a hundred pounds for a drop.

Towards evening our plight was indeed pitiable. We were all too weak to work the boat. Friends and foes mingled together unmolested. Unable to bear his agony one of the men jumped overboard, and so ended his sufferings. Others would have followed his example, but my companion promised that he would shoot the next man who attempted it, and so make his end still more certain.

About half-past seven the sun sank beneath the horizon, and with his departure a welcome breeze came down to us. Within an hour this had freshened into a moderate gale. Then, just before darkness obscured everything, a cry from one of the Chinamen forrard brought my companion to his feet. Rushing to the side he stared towards the west.

"Yes! Yes it is! We're saved, De Normanville— we're saved. As he says, it is the schooner!"

Then for the fourth time during that eventful voyage my senses deserted me!

CHAPTER III.

THE BEAUTIFUL WHITE DEVIL.

WHEN I opened my eyes again I found myself, to my intense astonishment, lying, fully dressed, in a comfortable hammock beneath a well-constructed awning. The canvas walls of my resting-place prevented me from seeing anything more of my surroundings than my toes, but when I lifted myself up and peered over the side, it was not the junk's evil planks that I saw before me, but the deck of a handsome, well-appointed yacht. My hammock was seemingly swung amidships, and judging from the side upon which I looked—save the man at the wheel and a couple of hands polishing brass-work forrard—I appeared to have the entire deck to myself. Whose boat was she? How had I come to be aboard her? And how long had I been there? But though I puzzled my brains for an answer to these questions I could find none. My memory refused to serve me, and so, feeling tired, I laid myself back again upon my pillow and once more closed my eyes.

I had scarcely done so before I heard a noise on the other side which caused me to look over again. How shall I describe what I saw there? Three years have passed since then, but I have the recollection of even the minutest detail connected with the picture that was before me at that moment just as plainly engraved upon my memory as if it had occurred but yesterday.

Seated in a long cane chair, one elbow balanced on the arm-rest and one tiny hand supporting her dimpled chin, was the most beautiful woman—and I say it advisedly, knowing it to be true—that I had ever or have ever beheld, or shall ever behold, in my life. Though she was seated, and for that reason I could not determine her exact height, I was convinced it was considerably above the average ; her figure, as much as I could see of it, was beautifully moulded ; her face was exquisitely shaped ; her eyes were large, and of a deep sea-blue ; while the wealth of rippling hair that crowned her head was of a natural golden hue, and enhanced rather than detracted from the softness of her delicate complexion. As if still further to add to her general fairness, she was dressed entirely in white, even to her deck shoes and the broad Panama hat upon her head. Only one thing marred the picture. By her side, presenting a fitting contrast to so much loveliness, crouched, his head resting between his forepaws, a ferocious white bulldog, who ever and anon looked up with big blood-shot eyes into her face as if to make quite sure that there was no one within reach whom she might wish him to destroy.

She was evidently absorbed in her own thoughts, and presently the hand that was hanging down beside the chair found the dog's head, and began softly to stroke his tulip ears. Then her eyes looked up, caught mine, and seeing that I was no longer asleep she rose and came towards me.

"So you are awake at last, Dr. De Normanville?" she said with a smile. And as I heard her it struck me that her voice was even more beautiful than all her other attributes put together. "You have had a long sleep. Twelve hours!"

"Twelve hours?" I cried in amazement, at the same time gazing at her with admiration only too plainly written on my face. "You don't mean to say that I've been twelve hours asleep? I can hardly believe it. Why it seems only a few minutes since we were aboard that rascally junk. And what has happened since then? Is this the vessel we left Hong Kong to meet?"

"Yes. This is the boat. We were just beginning to grow anxious about you when the junk was sighted. I am afraid, from your companion's account, you must have had a desperate time on board her."

"I should not care to go through it again, certainly," I answered truthfully. "One such experience is enough to last a man a lifetime. By the way, how *is* my companion? I hope he is none the worse for his adventures."

"You need have no fear on that score; he is accustomed to that sort of thing and thrives on it, as you may have noticed. He is below at present, but as soon as he comes on deck I will send him to you. Now you had better lie down again and try to get some more sleep. You must remember that your strength is of the utmost value to us."

"I don't think I quite understand. But before we go any further will you tell me what yacht this is and to whom I am indebted for my rescue?"

"This yacht is called the *Lone Star*," she answered, "and I am the owner." As she said this she looked at me in rather a queer sort of a way, I thought. But I let it pass and asked another question.

"I am very much afraid you will think me pertinacious, but is it permissible for me to know your name?"

"You may certainly know it if you wish to!" she answered with a short and, I could not help thinking, rather bitter laugh; "But I don't think you will be any too pleased when you hear it. My real name is Alie, but by the benighted inhabitants of this part of the globe I am called by another and more picturesque cognomen."

She stopped, and I almost caught my breath with excitement. A light was breaking upon me.

"And that is——" I said, trying in vain to keep my voice down to a steady level.

"The Beautiful White Devil," she answered, with another of her peculiar smiles, and then, calling her bulldog to her, she bowed to me, turned on her heel, and went slowly aft along the deck.

I laid myself back in my hammock, my heart—why, I could not say—beating like a piston-rod, and tried to think the situation out. So my thoughtless wish was gratified after all: I had now seen the Beautiful White Devil face to face, and, what was more to the point, I was likely to be compelled to see more of her than I should consider necessary for my own amusement. Like the Sultan of Surabaya and Vesey of Hong Kong, I was now her prisoner. And by what a simple ruse I had been caught! By all that was reasonable in woman, however, what possible advantage could she hope to gain by abducting me? At the very most, I could not lay my hands on more than three thousand pounds, and what earthly use could that be to a woman who was known to deal in millions? But perhaps, I reflected, it was not money she was after ; perhaps she had some other desperate game to play—some other move in that wonderful life of hers in which my science could be of use to her and the nature of which I could not be expected to fathom. Situated as I was, she could compel me to do her bidding if she pleased, or make it extremely awkward for me if I felt it my duty to refuse. .

You will doubtless have noticed that I had quite abandoned the idea of the small-pox epidemic. The notion of that island with the raging pestilence probably only existed in the fertile brain of the man who had been sent to induce me to leave Hong Kong. But in that case—and here the original argument wheeled back upon me—what possible advantage could accrue to her through abducting me ? There were hundreds of richer men in Hong Kong. Why had not one of them been chosen ? But as the more I thought it out, the farther I seemed to be from getting at the truth of it, I gave the problem up and turned my thoughts in another direction.

As I did so I heard somebody coming along the deck. This time it was a man's footstep, so I looked out to see who it might be. It was Walworth, the individual who had visited me in Hong Kong and enticed me away. He was dressed in European habiliments now, and carried a cigarette in his hand. Seeing that I was aware of his presence he came across to the hammock and held out his hand.

" Good morning, doctor ! " he said cheerily enough. " I'm glad to see you're better. All things considered you've had a nasty time of it since you said good-bye to the Victoria Hotel—haven't you ? "

"A pretty cheeky way of putting it, considering he was the cause of it all," I thought to myself. "However, I'll give him a Roland for his Oliver! He shall not think I'm wanting in pluck."

"You have certainly contrived a good many stirring adventures for my entertainment, I must say," I answered aloud. "But will you tell me one thing? Why did you not let me know in Hong Kong who my hostess would turn out to be?"

"Because in that case you would probably have informed the police, and we should not then have been able to give ourselves the pleasure of your company and assistance."

"Well, all I can say is, I am sorry you didn't try for higher game while you were about it. For even with that five hundred you gave me, your leader will only get a sop for her pains. You can't force blood out of a stone, can you?"

He seated himself in the chair she had occupied, and lit a fresh cigarette. Having done so, he continued:

"I don't know that I quite follow you!"

"Well, I don't think I could make it much plainer without being absolutely rude. The long and the short of it is, Mr. Walworth, if it's money you're after—why not have gone in for a pigeon better worth plucking?"

"But then we're not after the money, you see. Why should I have paid you that five hundred else? No! Dr. De Normanville, you need have no fear on that score—our motive was perfectly honest. We are on our way to the island now where the small-pox exists, and believe me, when your work is accomplished, you will be conveyed safely back to your hotel. I can't say more than that.   Play fair by us and we'll play fair by you.   In the meantime we shall hope to make your stay with us as pleasant as possible."

I breathed freely again.   I was not abducted.   I was only wanted in my professional capacity after all. Well, that was a relief.   I was in a unique position, for it was evident I was not only to be permitted the opportunity of making the Beautiful White Devil's acquaintance, but I was to be well paid for doing so.   In the first freedom from anxiety I began to look forward with almost pleasure to what lay before me.

"Don't you think you could get up for a little while?" Walworth said, when he had finished his smoke; "it would do you good.   Let me help you."

With his assistance I scrambled out of the hammock into a cane chair alongside the companion hatch.   I was still very weak, and incapable of much exertion.   There could be no doubt that I had lost a good deal more blood than I had at first imagined.

Once seated in the chair I looked about me.   I was now permitted a full and uninterrupted view of the vessel, and was able to make good use of my eyes. Roughly speaking, that is to say as far as I could tell, not being a nautical man, she must have been a topsail schooner of about three hundred tons burden, with auxiliary steaming power, for I could see the funnel, which was not in use just then, lying along the deck. In what part of the world she had been built I could not tell; but wherever it was, she did credit to her designer, for her lines were perfection, and nothing short of it.   If ever a boat were built for speed she was that one, and I said as much to my companion, who laughed.

"There can be no doubt about that," he answered. "But then, you see, no other boat but the fastest built would suit her ladyship. Believe me, there are times when even the *Lone Star* is pretty well put to it to throw dust in her enemies' eyes. If you feel strong enough, shall we take a walk round and examine her?"

There was nothing I should have liked more, so, taking the arm he offered me, we set off. The first thing that attracted my attention was the spotless neatness and cleanliness prevailing. The decks, which were flush fore and aft, were as white as curds ; the brasses on the wheel, capstans, masts, skylights, belaying pins, shone till you could see your face in them. Not a detail seemed to have been overlooked. Even the great sheets of canvas, bellying into balloons above our heads, appeared at first sight to have been lately washed, while the very ropes were white and, when not in actual use, flemish-coiled upon the decks. She carried six boats, an unusually large number for a craft of her size ; two were surf-boats, I found on inspection ; two were uncollapsible lifeboats ; one was an ordinary ship's gig, while the other was a small steam launch of excellent build and workmanship. For a craft of three hundred tons her spars were enormous : her topmast head must have been a hundred and fifty feet from her deck, if an inch, while from her rig forrard I could guess the amount of extra canvas she was capable of carrying. Walking to the side, I discovered that she was painted white, with a broad gold stripe a little above the water-line ; below this she was sheathed with copper, which shone like gold whenever the water left it.

Inside the bulwarks, and reaching to within an inch

of the scuppers, were some contrivances that caused me a considerable amount of curiosity. At first glance they looked like reversible shop shutters more than anything else, being about six feet long by three wide, and were attached to the rail of the bulwarks by enormous hinges. On my asking for what purpose they were intended, my guide again laughed, and said :

"You must not ask too many questions, my friend, for obvious reasons. In this case, however, and since you have given your word not to tell what you may see, I will explain."

Detaching the catch of one, he lifted it from the deck and threw it over the side, where it hung, just reaching to the top of the copper below water.

"Do you grasp the idea ?" he continued. "The next one fits into that, and the next one into that again, and so on all round the boat. You see, they can be attached in no time, and when they are once fixed, the shape of the masts altered, the funnel differently cased or done away with altogether, the character of her bows and stern changed beyond recognition by another appliance, she can be three different crafts inside of twenty-four hours."

This then accounted for the number of different vessels the Beautiful White Devil was supposed to possess. I began to understand the marvellous escapes more clearly now.

"And whose idea was this ingenious invention ?" I ventured to ask.

"Like most of our things, her ladyship's own," he replied. "And wonderfully successful it has proved."

"And shall I be presuming too much on your good nature if I seek to learn something of the lady herself?"

"Ah ! I'm afraid there I cannot satisfy your curiosity," he answered, shaking his head. "We have strict instructions on that point, and there's not a man aboard this ship who values his life so little as to dream of disobeying. One piece of advice I will give you, however, for the sake of what we went through together yesterday. Take care how you behave towards her. In spite of her quiet demeanour and frank, artless manner, she sees, takes in, and realises the motive and importance of everything you say or do. If you act fairly towards her, she will act fairly by you ; but if you play her false you're a dead man. Remember that. Now you must excuse me if I go to my duties. My absence in Hong Kong has delayed my work sadly. And there goes eight bells."

As the silvery voice of a bell chimed out from the fo'c's'le, he left me and went below. Hardly knowing what to do with myself, I went back to my chair. A tall man with a gray beard close-cropped, sharp glittering eyes, and a not unhandsome face, marred, however, by what looked like a sabre cut extending from the left temple to his chin, resigned the deck to another officer and went below.

While the watch was being changed I had an opportunity of examining the crew ; they were nearly all natives, smart, intelligent-looking fellows, and excellently disciplined. Whether they were Dyaks or Malays, however, I had not sufficient experience to determine, and, for more than one reason, I did not like to ask.

It was a lovely morning; the sea was as blue as the sky, a fresh wind was driving the schooner along at an exhilarating pace, and, looking over the side at the line of foam extending from either bow, I was afforded a very good idea of what an exceptional sailor the *Lone Star* really was.

Being a little tired after my perambulations, I lay back in my chair, and shutting my eyes, fell to ruminating on the queer trick Fate had played me. So far I could hardly accept my position as real. It was difficult to believe that I, George De Normanville, unromantic, plodding student of Guy's,—now M.D., of Cavendish Square, London, whose sole aim in life, a year ago, had been to put a brass plate upon his front door, and collect wealthy hypochondriacal lady patients,—was now medical adviser to a mysterious female, who perambulated Eastern waters in a chameleon craft, blackmailing rajahs, abducting merchants, levying toll on mail boats, and bringing down on her devoted head the wrath of all sorts of nations, principalities, and powers. And then another point struck me. While outwardly so fair, what sort of a woman was she at heart? From Walworth's warning I had gathered that I must be careful in my dealings with her.

But at that moment my reverie was interrupted by the appearance of a neatly-clad steward, who in broken English presented me with an invitation from her ladyship to tiflin in the saloon in half an hour. This was an unexpected honour, and one which, you may be sure, I did not hesitate to accept. I wanted, however, to make a suitable toilet first, but where to do it puzzled me, for so far as I knew no cabin had yet been apportioned to me. I placed my difficulty before an officer who was standing near me. He said something in native dialect to the steward, who replied, and then turned again to me.

"Your traps have been placed in a cabin next to Mr. Walworth's, he says, and if you will follow him he will conduct you to it."

I followed the steward down the main companion (I afterward discovered that the one aft was sacred to her ladyship) as requested, and found myself in a large mess-room, in which three officers were seated at lunch. On either side a number of fair-sized berths were situated. The one set apart for me was nearest the companion, and contained a bunk, a small settee and locker combined, a wash-hand basin, and a place for hanging clothes. The first operation was to shave, a bath followed, to which another steward conducted me, after which I returned to my berth, dressed my wound, and, having selected a clean suit of white ducks, attired myself and repaired on deck.

Punctual to the stroke of two bells (one o'clock) I was summoned to the after-saloon by my first messenger. I followed him, and descending the companion, the scantling of which was prettily picked out in white and gold, found myself in her ladyship's own quarters. There was no one present, and I must own I was glad of that, for I wanted an opportunity to look about me. In the small space I can allot to it, it would be difficult to do adequate justice to the cabin in which I found myself, but for the better understanding of my story I must endeavour to give you some description of it. In the first place, you must understand that the companion-ladder opened directly into the saloon itself. This otherwise commonplace effect, was, however, rendered most artistic by a heavy pile of carpet which covered the steps, and by the curtains which draped the entrance and the portholes. More of the same noiseless carpet covered the floor, while light was supplied from ports on either side, and from a richly decorated skylight in the deck above. The effect of the thick butt of the mainmast was entirely taken away by a number of artfully contrived and moulded Japanese mirrors, which, besides fulfilling their original purpose, gave an additional air of light and elegance to the room. The walls, which were exquisitely panelled and moulded in ivory and gold, were loaded with bric-a-brac of every description, including much china and many pictures of rare value, while deep chairs and couches, Turkish and Indian divans, piles of soft cushions and furs were scattered about here and there, as if inviting the cabin's occupants to an existence of continual repose. A grand piano stood in one corner, firmly cleated to the deck; on the bulkhead above it was an exquisitely inlaid Spanish guitar, and a Hungarian zither, while above them again were several fine specimens of the old Venetian lute. Altogether a more luxurious and beautifully furnished apartment it has never been my good fortune to behold, and I settled myself down in a comfortable chair prepared to spend a really critical and enjoyable time. Then a daintily-bound volume, open on a cushion near where I sat, attracted my attention. I took it up to find that it was a volume of Heine's poems in the original.

"So my lady understands German, and reads Heine too, does she?" I said to myself. "I must——"

But I was prevented saying what I would do by the drawing aside of a curtain that covered a door at the further end of the saloon, and the entrance of my hostess herself. If she were capable of such a weakness, my astonishment must have flattered her, for, prepared as I was to see a beautiful woman, I had no idea she would prove as lovely as she looked then. She had discarded the close-fitting white dress she had worn earlier in the day, and was now attired in some soft clinging fabric of a dark colour, which not only brought out all the lines of her superb figure, but rendered her even more attractive than before. There must have been a quantity of jet scattered about the costume, for I was conscious of a shimmering sensation which accompanied her every movement. She carried herself with a truly regal air, and I had a better opportunity permitted me now of seeing what a beautiful face it really was, and how exquisitely her head was set upon her shoulders. Her hands and feet were very small, so was her mouth, while her ears were like shells tucked into fragrant nests against her head. But the glory that eclipsed all others was the wealth of golden hair that crowned her. Such hair I have never seen before or since. It seemed to have caught all the sunshine of the world and to be jealous of dispersing it again.

Once more, as if to afford as great a contrast as possible to so much loveliness, the same ferocious bulldog followed at her heels, and, when she approached me, stood regarding me with calmly scrutinising eyes.

"Welcome to my cabin, Dr. De Normanville," she said, coming over to me and holding out her tiny hand with a frank gesture. "I am delighted to see that you are looking so much better."

"I'm feeling quite strong again, thank you," I answered, completely carried away by the charm of her manner. "I cannot think what made me break down in that undignified fashion. I'm afraid you will despise me for giving such an exhibition of weakness."

She seated herself in a deep chair beside me and slowly fanned herself with a black ostrich plume, at the same time stroking the dog's ugly head with her little foot.

"I don't really see why I should," she said seriously, after a moment's pause. "You must have had a terrible time on that horrible junk. I feel as if I was personally to blame for it. However, I shall have more to say on that subject later ; in the meantime let us be thankful that you came out of it as safely as you did. I do not like the Chinese ! "

I saw a little shudder sweep over her as she said this, so to turn the conversation into a pleasanter channel, I commented on the sailing qualities of her schooner. The subject evidently pleased her, for her eyes sparkled with a new light.

"There is no boat like her in the wide, wide world," she cried enthusiastically. "I had her built for me on my own lines, and I have tried her on every wind, and in every sea, till I have come to know her better than a rider knows his horse. She is the most beautiful and the swiftest craft in the world. And there are times, Dr. De Normanville,"—here she sank her voice a little, and it seemed to me it trembled,—"when it is of the utmost importance to me that I should move quickly. She has saved my life not once, but a hundred times. Can you wonder, therefore, that I love her? But I'm afraid you are too prejudiced against me to have much sympathy in my escapes."

"I hope you will not think so. I——"

" Forgive my interrupting you. But don't you think it would be better if we sat down to table instead of discussing my unfortunate self ? "

She pressed an electric bell in the woodwork by her side and ordered tiflin. When it was served we went over to the table and the meal commenced.

I am not going to tell you what we ate, for, to confess the honest truth, within half an hour I had forgotten what it was myself. I only know that it was admirably cooked and served. As it proceeded we chatted on various minor matters, literature of all nations, music and painting, and it was not until we had finished, and the cloth had been removed and we were alone together, that my hostess touched upon the reason of my presence on board.

" You know, of course, Dr. De Normanville," she said, ensconcing herself in a big chair when we had left the table, " why I sent for you ? "

" It was explained to me by your messenger. But I must confess I do not quite understand it yet. He said something about an island."

" And he was quite right. An outbreak of small-pox has occurred on the island which I make my depot. Where that island is, I cannot of course tell you. But you will see it for yourself soon enough. In the meantime I may inform you that the havoc wrought by the disease has been terrible, and it was only when I found that I could make no headway against it myself that I determined to send to Hong Kong for assistance. To get hold of you was a piece of good fortune I did not expect."

I bowed my acknowledgment of the compliment she

paid me, and asked if she herself had been much among the cases.

"Why, of course!" she answered. "My poor people call me their mother, and naturally turn to me for assistance in their trouble. It went to my very heart not to be able to help them."

"But were you quite wise, do you think, to run so much risk?"

"I did not think of myself at all. How could I? Do you think of the risk you run when you are called in to an infectious case?"

"I take all proper precaution, at least. When were you vaccinated last, may I ask?"

"In Rome, in June, 1883."

"Then, with your permission, I'll do it again, and at once. You cannot be too careful."

Receiving her assent I went off to my cabin, where I had noticed that a large portion of my medical outfit had been stored, and having obtained what I sought, returned with it to the saloon. Alie, for by that name I must henceforward call her, was waiting for me, her arm bared to the shoulder. Never, if I live to be a hundred, shall I forget the impression that snow-white arm made upon me. It seemed like an act of basest sacrilege to perform even such a simple operation upon it. Beelzebub, the bulldog, evidently thought so too, for he watched me attentively enough during the whole of the time it took me. However, it had to be done, and done it accordingly was. Then, when I had put my paraphernalia back into its case, I bade her good-bye, and turned to go. She stopped me, however, and held out her hand.

"Do you know, Dr. De Normanville, I want to make you like me. I want you to forget, if you can,—while you are with us, at any rate,—the stories you have heard about me. Some day, perhaps, I will attempt to show you that I am not altogether as bad as people have painted me."

For the moment I was so completely carried away by her outburst of girlish frankness that I hardly knew what to say.

"'Pon my soul, I really don't believe you are!" I blurted out, like a schoolboy.

"Thank you for that, at least," she said, smiling at my earnestness ; and then, making me a little curtsey, she turned and disappeared through the door by which she had first entered the saloon.

Putting my case into my pocket, I looked round the room once more, and then went up on deck, not knowing what to think. It seemed impossible to believe that this frank, beautiful girl, whose eyes were so steady and true, whose voice had such a genuine, hearty ring in it, could be the notorious criminal of whom all the East was talking. And yet without a shadow of a doubt it was so. And if it came to that, what was I, staid, respectable George De Normanville, doing, but aiding and abetting her in her nefarious career? True, I might salve my conscience with the knowledge that I had been drawn into it unconsciously, and was only acting in the interests of humanity, but it was nevertheless a fact, and one that I could not have disputed if I had wanted to, that I was the paid servant of the Beautiful White Devil.

It was just two bells in the first dog watch when I

came on deck, and hard upon sundown. The great round sun, which had been so busy all day long, now rested in a bed of opal cloud scarcely a hand's breadth above the edge of the horizon. The breeze had moderated, since midday, and now the water around us was almost without a ripple, but glorified with flakes and blotches of almost every colour known to man. Near at hand it was a mixture of lemon and silver, a little further almost a lilac-purple, further still a touch of pale heliotrope meeting salmon-pink and old gold, while under the sun itself a blotch of red, fierce as a clot of blood, worked through the cloud till it got back to gold, then to salmon-pink, then through purple up again to the lemon and silver sky. It was a wonderful sunset, and a fitting termination to an extraordinary day.

After dinner, of which I partook in the officer's mess-room, I returned to the deck. It was nearly eight o'clock, and as fine a night as I had seen since I came into the East. Lighting a cigar I walked aft, and, leaning upon the taffrail, scanned the quiet sea. Situated as I was, it is not to be wondered at that a variety of thoughts thronged my brain. I tried to think what my dear old mother would have said could she have seen the position my over-rash acceptance of a tempting offer had placed me in. From my mother, who, with my father, had been dead nearly five years, my thoughts passed on to other relatives—to a girl whom I had once thought I loved, but who had jilted me in favour of a brother student. The old heartache was almost gone now, but it had been a most unfortunate affair; since then, however, I flattered myself, I had been heart-whole, and I deluded myself with the notion that I was likely to remain so.

Since dinner the breeze had freshened, and the schooner, with all sail set, was now slipping swiftly through the water. I turned, and, leaning against the rail, looked aloft at the stretch of canvas which seemed to reach up almost to the stars, then back again at the wake and the wonderful exhibition of phosphorised water below the counter.

Suddenly I became aware of someone standing by my side, and turning my head, I discovered it was none other than the Beautiful White Devil herself. She was still dressed in black, with a sort of mantilla of soft lace draped about her head.

"What a supreme fascination there is about the sea at night, isn't there?" she said softly, looking down at the sparkling water. I noticed the beauty of the little white hand upon the rail as I replied in appropriate terms.

"I never can look at it enough," she continued almost unconsciously. "Oh, you black, mysterious, unfathomable depths, what future do you hold for me? My fate is wrapped up in you. I was born on you; I was brought up on you; and if my fate holds good, I shall die and be buried in you."

"At any rate, you need give no thought to that contingency for very many years to come," I answered bluntly. "Besides, what possible reason can you have for thinking you will end your days at sea?"

"I don't know, Dr. De Normanville. It would puzzle me to tell you. But I feel as certain of finding my grave in the waves as I am that I shall be alive to-morrow! You don't know what the sea has been to me. She has been my good and my evil genius. I love her in every mood, and I don't think I could hope for a better end than to be buried in her breast. Oh, you beautiful, beautiful water, how I love you—how I love you!"

As she spoke she stretched her arms out to where the stars were paling in anticipation of the rising moon. In any other woman such a gesture would have been theatrical and unreal in the extreme. But in her case it seemed only what one might expect from such a glorious creature.

"There is somebody," she continued, "who says that 'the sea belongs to Eternity, and not Time, and of that it sings its monotonous song for ever and ever.'"

"That is a very beautiful idea," I answered, "but don't you think there are others that fully equal it? What do you say to 'The sea complains upon a thousand shores'?"

"Or your English poet Wordsworth, 'The sea that bares her bosom to the wind'?"

"Let me meet you with an American: 'The sea tosses and foams to find its way up to the cloud and wind.' Could anything be finer than that? There you have the true picture—the utter restlessness and the striving of the untamed sea."

> "'Would'st thou,' so that helmsman answered,
>   'Learn the secret of the sea?
> Only those who brave its dangers
>   Comprehend its mystery!'"

"Bravo! That caps all."

For some seconds my companion stood silent, gazing across the deep. Then she said, very softly:

"And who is better able to speak about its dangers than I, whose home it is? Dr. De Normanville, I think if I were to tell you some of the dangers through which I have passed you would hardly believe me."

"I think I could believe anything you told me."

"I rather doubt it. You see, you have no idea what an extraordinary existence mine is. Why! my life is one long battle with despair. I am like a hunted animal flying before that hell-hound, man. Do you know how near I was to being caught once? Let me tell you about it, and see if it will convey any idea to you. It was in Singapore, and I was dining at the house of a prominent police official, as the friend of his wife. I had met her some months before under peculiar circumstances, and we had become intimate. During the meal my host spoke of the Beautiful White Devil, and commented on her audacity. 'However, we have at last received a clue concerning her,' he said. 'She is not far away from Singapore at the present moment, and I have every reason to believe that in forty-eight hours she will be in our hands.' I had a full glass of champagne in my hand at the moment, and it is a compliment to the strength of my nerves to say that I raised it to my lips, before answering him, without spilling one drop."

"And did he never suspect?"

"No, indeed. To tell the truth, I doubt if he knows to this day how close the Beautiful White Devil really was to him. Yet one moment's hesitation might have cost me my life. Another time I attended a Viceregal ball in Colombo in the capacity of an heiress from England. In the middle of the evening the partner with whom I was dancing, a young inspector of police, apologised for having to leave me. He said he had received information concerning the Beautiful White Devil, who was known to be in the town. During supper he had been telling me about his prospects, and the girl who was coming out from England to marry him when he got his step. 'It will be a good thing for you if you catch this woman, won't it?' I inquired. 'It will get me promotion, and that will mean the greatest happiness of my life—my marriage!' he answered. 'Won't you wish me luck?' I did wish him luck, and then went off to dance the lancers with His Excellency the Governor."

"Do you think it wise to run such awful risks?" I asked, amazed at her audacity.

"Perhaps not; but in that particular case I could not help myself. I stood in need of some important information, and could trust nobody to obtain it but myself."

"It must have been a terrible five minutes for you."

"Yes; I almost fainted after the dance. His Excellency apologised profusely for the heat of the room."

As she finished speaking, the moon lifted her head above the horizon, and little by little rose into the cloudless sky. Under her glamour the sea became a floor of frosted silver, till even the spangled glory of the phosphorus was taken from the curdling wake.

"I expect you have been told some very curious stories about me, Dr. De Normanville?" my companion said, after a little while. "I wish I could induce you to tell me what you have heard. Believe me, I have a very good reason for wanting you to know the truth about me."

"That is easily told," I answered. "I have heard a

great many variations of the same story, but knowing how news travels out here, I have placed very little credence in any of them."

"You have heard, perhaps, about the Sultan of Surabaya?"

I intimated that I had.

"At first you must have thought that rather a cruel action on my part. And yet, if you knew all, your blame would probably turn to admiration. You do not know, perhaps, what a character that man bore in his own state, the life he led, his excesses, his constant crimes, his tyranny over his unfortunate subjects. I tell you, sir, that that man was, and is, one of the greatest scoundrels upon the face of this earth. I had heard over and over again of him, and when I discovered that his people could obtain no redress for their grievances, I determined to meet him on his own ground. I arranged my plans accordingly, abducted him, made him disgorge a large sum of money, half of which I caused to be anonymously distributed amongst the poor wretches he had robbed, and at the same time told him his character for the first and only time in his heathen existence, promising him as I did so that if he did not mend his ways, I'd catch him again and silence him for ever. Punishment was surely never more fitly earned. Then there was a merchant in Hong Kong, by name Vesey. I expect you have heard of him and the trick I played him? Well, that man made an assertion about me in a public place to the effect that I was—— But never mind what it was. It was so vile that I cannot repeat it to you, but I made a vow I would be revenged on him for it, sooner or later. I *was* revenged, and in the only way he could be made to feel—that is, through his banker. He will never forgive me, of course. Now, what else have you heard?"

"Pardon my alluding to it," I said, "but—the *Vectis Queen*—the *Oodnadatta*."

"So you have heard of those affairs? Well, I do not deny them. I must have money. Look at the expenses I have to meet. Look at this boat—think of the settlement I maintain, of the hundreds of pensioners I have all through the East, of the number of people whose services it is necessary for me to retain. And, pray do not misunderstand me. To you it may seem that such transactions make me neither more nor less than a thief —a common cheat and swindler. In your eyes I may be that, but I must own I do not look upon it in the same light myself. I am, and have been all my life, at war with what you call Society—the reason I may perhaps explain to you some day. I know the risk I run. If Society catches me, in all probability my life will pay the forfeit. I know that, and I am naturally resolved not to be caught. One thing is certain, I prey only on those who can afford to lose, and, like the freebooters of romance, I make it my boast that I have never knowingly robbed a poor man, while, on the other hand, I have materially assisted many. There are those, of course, who judge me harshly. Heaven forbid that they ever find themselves in the position in which I am placed! Think of it! I am hunted by all men—every man's hand is against me; I am cut off from country and friends; a price is put upon my head, and for that reason I am obliged to distrust everyone on principle. Think of having the knowledge continually before you that if you are not constantly on the watch you may be caught. And then——"

"And then ?"

I heard her grind her little white teeth viciously.

"There will be no *then*, Dr. De Normanville, so we need not talk of it; while I live they will never catch me, and when I am dead it cannot matter who has possession of my body. Good-night !"

Before I could answer she had left me and vanished down the companion ladder. I turned to the sea and my own thoughts. The ship's bell struck four (ten o'clock), the lookout at the fo'c's'le-head cried, "All's well !" silence reigned, a wonderful quiet broken only by the humming of the breeze in the shrouds, and the tinkling of the water alongside. I leant against the rail and considered the life of the Beautiful White Devil as I had heard it from her own lips.

CHAPTER IV.

THE sun next morning had scarcely made his appearance when I awoke to a knowledge of the fact that the yacht was stationary. Such a circumstance could have but one meaning: we had arrived at our destination. As soon, therefore, as this idea became properly impressed upon my mind, I sprang from my bunk, made for the port-hole, and, drawing back the little curtain that covered it, gazed out upon the world. And what a picture met my eager eyes! What a scene to paint in words or pigments! But oh, how difficult! If I were a literary craftsman of more than ordinary ability, I might possibly be able to give you some dim impression of what I saw. But being only an amateur word-painter of the sorriest sort, I very much fear it is a task beyond my capabilities. However, for the sake of my story, I suppose I must try.

To begin with, you must endeavour to imagine a small harbour, at most half a mile long by three-quarters wide, having upon the side towards which I looked a wide plateau extending almost to the sands that fringe the water's edge. Picture this tableland, or plateau, as I have called it, backed by a tall, forest-crowned hill, almost a mountain, which soars up and up a couple of thousand feet or more into the azure sky; while peering out of the jungle that ornaments its base may be seen the white roofs of houses, with, here and there, the thatch of a native hut of the kind usually met with on the west coast of Borneo and the islands thereabout.

So strikingly beautiful was the view, and so great was my curiosity to examine for myself this home of the Beautiful White Devil, for such I could not help feeling convinced it was, that I dressed with all possible speed and repaired on deck.

From this point of vantage the prospect was even more pleasingly picturesque than it had been from the port-hole of my cabin.

All round us the water was smooth as green glass, and so wonderfully transparent that, on leaning over the starboard bulwark, I could plainly discern the flaking of the sand at the bottom and the brilliant colours of the snout-nosed fishes as they swam past, at least a dozen fathoms below the surface.

To my surprise the harbour was entirely landlocked, and, though I searched for some time, I could discern no opening in the amphitheatre of hills through which a vessel of even the smallest size could pass in from the sea. But being more taken up with the beautiful scenery of the bay than its harbour facilities, I did not puzzle over this for very long.

So still was the morning that the smoke of the huts ashore went up straight and true into the air, the pale blue contrasting admirably with the varied greens of the foliage out of which it rose. Overhead, and around us, flocks of gulls, of kinds hitherto unknown to me, wheeled and screamed, while at intervals gorgeously-plumed parrots flew across our bows from shore to shore. Once a small green bird, apparently of the finch tribe, settled on the foreyard foot-rope, and a little later a tiny sand-piper came aboard, and hopped about the fo'c's'le as calmly as if he had been doing nothing else all his life.

When first I came on deck, with the exception of the cook in his galley, not a soul was to be seen. But presently, while I was watching the antics of the bird I have just described, my old acquaintance Walworth joined me at the rail, and laid himself out for conversation.

"Doctor," he said, "I want you to tell me candidly, if, in all your experience of the world, you have ever looked upon a fairer scene than that you have before you now?"

"No; I don't think I have," I answered. "It is marvellously beautiful, but all the same, I must own one or two things about it rather puzzle me."

"And what are they?"

"Well! in the first place, since I can see no opening in the hills, how did we get in here?"

"Ah! you have been thinking about that, have you? Well, to save you any further trouble on that score, let me tell you that if you were to look for a hundred years from where you stand now you would not be able to discover it. And, unless her ladyship gives permission, it would be as much as my life is worth for me to tell you. Now for your second question?"

"Well, I can see, say, a dozen huts, all told, over yonder," I answered. "Surely they don't constitute the settlement of which you spoke to me?"

"No; they do not. Those you see over there are only the outlying portions of the village, meant to deceive the crew of any vessel who might land and find their way in here ; the real place itself lies five miles inland, round that hill, through the gap you can just make out alongside that bit of terra-cotta coloured cliff yonder."

"I see ! And now, to change the subject. With regard to that lymph you procured for me in Hong Kong, where is it ?"

"It has already been sent to your bungalow with the rest of the medical paraphernalia we brought with us."

" And her ladyship ? "

" Went ashore as soon as we came to anchor. If I mistake not that's her boat coming off to us now."

As he spoke, a large white surf-boat put off from the beach, and, under the sturdy arms of her crew, came swiftly across the stretch of blue towards us. As she ranged alongside, I carefully examined the men rowing. They were of medium size, and evidently of the Dyak race, being taller than the average Malay, and inclining more to the build of the Solomon Islander than to any other class I could think of. They were bright, intelligent-looking fellows, and evidently well cared for. As soon as they had hitched on to the gangway, the coxswain came aboard, and said something in native to my companion, who, in reply, pointed to me.

Thereupon the man drew a note from his turban, and handed it to me with the confidence and easy bearing of one gentleman rendering a service to another. It was addressed in Alie's handwriting.

Though a considerable time has elapsed since my receipt of that little note, I can plainly recall the thrill that went through me as I opened it. It ran as follows :

DEAR DR. DE NORMANVILLE :

I beg you will forgive my not remaining on board to welcome you to my home, but as you will readily imagine I was most anxious to see for myself, at once, how things were progressing ashore. Unfortunately, however, I have nothing favourable to report. Will you come and breakfast with me immediately on receipt of this ? My coxswain will show you the way. Then, afterward, I could take you, myself, round the settlement.

With very kind regards,

Believe me, truly your friend,

ALIE.

I thrust the note into my pocket, and having told Walworth what I was about to do, went below to my cabin to prepare for my excursion. Then returning to the deck I descended into the boat alongside, and we set off for the shore. As we rowed I was able to look back and observe, for the first time, the proportions and symmetry of the beautiful craft I had just left.

Indeed, a prettier picture than the *Lone Star* presented at that moment could not possibly be imagined. Her tall masts and rigging showed out clear-cut against the blue sky, while her exquisitely-modelled hull was reflected, with mirror-like distinctness, in the placid water around her ; the brasswork upon her binnacle and wheel shone like burnished gold, and so clear was the water, that the whole of her bright copper sheathing, and even the outline of her keel, could plainly be distinguished.

Within five minutes of leaving her, our coxswain had deftly brought us alongside a small, but neatly-constructed, wooden jetty. Here I disembarked, and, escorted by that amiable individual, set off at once on our journey to the dwelling of my mysterious hostess.

Leaving the white, sandy foreshore of the bay, we passed by a well made track through the forest in a due northerly direction. And such a forest as it was! Such wealth of timber, such varieties of woods, shrubs, creepers, orchids, and flowers. On one hand, perhaps, an iron tree of imperial growth would tower above us ; on another an enormous teak, with here and there the curious leaves and twisted outline of a gutta-percha—all mixed up with pipa palms, camphor trees, canes and bamboos of every possible hue and description. From tree to tree, across our path, birds of all kinds, including paddi birds, green pigeons, flycatchers, barbets, and sunbirds flew with discordant cries, while not once, but more often than I could count, hordes of monkeys swung themselves wildly from branch to branch overhead, chattering and calling to each other as if the whole wide world were there to applaud their antics. Our path was indeed a varied one ; one moment we were surrounded on all sides by the forest, the next we were out on the bare face of the hill looking down upon the tops of trees. The bright sunshine flooded everything ; while the fresh breeze from the sea was just cool enough to make the exertion of walking pleasant. Indeed, so enjoyable was it, that I was almost sorry when we left the forest for the last time and emerged on to a small plain, bounded by the scrub on one side and by the mountain on the other. On this I could discern a collection of huts and houses to the number of perhaps three hundred. But what struck me as most remarkable about them was the fact that they were arranged in streets, and that the majority of them were built on European lines; also in almost every case—and I was able to verify this later on—each one possessed a well-kept and apparently productive garden, varying in extent from a quarter up to as much in some cases as an acre. On the other side of the village furthest from where I stood, the forest began again, and ran in an unbroken mass up to the high mountain land before referred to. On the right side of this mountain, and distinctly visible from every part of the village, was a fine water-fall, perhaps a couple of hundred feet high, from which rose continually a heavy mist, catching in the sunlight every known colour of the rainbow. Altogether, a more picturesque little place could not have been discovered. It was quite in keeping with the woman, the yacht, the forest, and the harbour. And to think that this was the home of the Beautiful White Devil, the home of that mysterious woman whose so-called crimes and acts of daring were common gossip from Colombo to the farthest Saghalien coast.

Leaving the village on our left, we ascended the mountain side for a short distance by a well-worn track, then turning sharply to our left hand, wound round it to where another large plateau began. Reaching this, midway between the village and the waterfall, we saw before us a high and well-made picket fence in which was a gate. Through this gate we passed, and after carefully closing it behind us, followed a short track along a lovely avenue of Areca palms and india rubber trees towards a house we could just discern through the foliage ; then, having ascended a flight of broad stone steps, flanked with quaint stone gods and images, we stood before the dwelling of the Beautiful White Devil.

I fear, deeply as the memory of it is impressed upon my mind, it is hardly in my power to convey to you any real impression of the building I had come so far to see, and in which I was destined to spend so many hours. Suffice it that it was an *adobe* construction—one story high, and designed on somewhat the same plan as an Indian bungalow; the walls were of great thickness, the better to withstand the heat, I suppose; the rooms presented the appearance of being lofty and imposing, while one and all opened by means of French windows on to the broad verandah which ran round the house upon every side. This verandah, and indeed the whole house, was embowered in dense masses of different-coloured creepers, which in the brilliant sunshine presented a most charming and novel effect. From the verandah on the left, or south, side, another broad flight of stone steps, similarly adorned with stone carvings, conducted one to the garden, while to the right, and scarcely more than a couple of hundred yards distant, crashed the waterfall I had seen from the hill, with a roar that could have been heard many miles away, down into the black pool two hundred feet below.

At the foot of the first steps my guide left me and returned to the harbour by the road along which he had come. I paused to recover my breath and watched him out of sight, then turning to the house ascended the flight of steps. Just as I reached the top, and was wondering how I might best make my presence known to those inside, I heard the rustling of a dress in the verandah; next moment Alie herself, clad in white from tcp to toe, as was her custom, came round the corner, followed by her enormous bulldog, and confronted me. I can see her now, and even after this lapse of time can feel the influence of her wonderful personality upon me just as plainly as if it were but yesterday I stood before her. Seeing me she said something to the dog,—who had uttered a low growl,—and stretched out her hand.

"Good-morning, Dr. De Normanville," she said, smiling as no other woman could ever do; "you received my note, then? I am glad to see you, and I make you welcome to my home."

"A Garden of Eden I should be inclined to call it," I answered, looking about me. "How many of us would be glad to dwell in it!"

She looked at me for a moment, and then asked somewhat bitterly:

"Pray is that pretty speech meant for Alie or the Beautiful White Devil? There is a difference, you know."

Then, not permitting me time to answer, she changed the subject by saying:

"Breakfast is on the table, I believe. Let us go in to it. Will you give me your arm?"

I did so, and together we passed from the creeper-covered verandah into a room straight before us.

In the previous chapter I have described to you Alie's cabin on board the *Lone Star*, and, in doing it, almost beggared myself of language; now I can only ask you to believe that rich as that cabin was in its appointments, in its arrangements, its curios and articles of *vertu*, the room which we entered now eclipsed it in every particular. Indeed, such another I never remember to have seen. From floor to ceiling it was filled with curiosities and articles of the greatest beauty and value. Rich Persian, Indian, Chinese, and Japanese hangings covered the walls, interspersed with such articles of pottery, silver, and china, as made me break the Tenth Commandment every time I looked at them. Native weapons of all kinds and of every nationality, some with plain, others with superbly jewelled, hilts ; Indian, Cinghalese, Burmese, Siamese, Japanese, and Chinese bric-a-brac ; two large cases of mineral specimens, comprising many precious stones ; quite a dozen pictures of rare value, one looking suspiciously like a Titian ; while fully a couple of hundred books, a grand piano, and at least half-a-dozen other musical instruments, including a harp and a guitar, helped to complete the furniture.

In the centre of the room stood the breakfast table, covered with an exquisitely embroidered white linen cloth, on which was displayed such a collection of beautiful gold and silver ware as I had never seen on a table before. Three heaps of fruit, consisting of durians, pisangs, bananas, mangoes, mangosteens, and custard apples were piled upon three lovely Sèvres dishes in the centre, flanked by two quaintly-shaped decanters filled with wine.

We seated ourselves at either end of the table, and my hostess struck a tiny silver gong by her side. Breakfast was instantly served by the same impassive servant who had waited upon us on board the yacht. If he felt any surprise at my presence on this occasion, he did not show it ; indeed, it would almost have seemed as if he were not aware that I was the same person.

And now a word as to the *déjeuner* itself. It has been my good fortune to have breakfasted at most of the famous restaurants in Europe, that is to say, in London, Paris, Rome, and Vienna, but I am prepared to state, and I put it forward believing it to be true, that the meal of which I partook that morning in the Beautiful White Devil's bungalow excelled any I had ever partaken of before. From beginning to end it was perfect in every way. The fish, evidently but lately caught, could only have been called a poem of culinary art, the omelets were Parisian in their daintiness and serving, the cutlets were of the right size and done to a turn, the wine (for the meal was served after the French fashion) was worthy of imperial cellars, and the fruit had evidently been in the garden less than half an hour before. My hostess noticed the surprise with which I regarded these things; for extraordinary it certainly was to sit down to such a breakfast on an island in the North Pacific.

"You are evidently wondering at the civilisation of my surroundings," she said, as the man servant poured her out a glass of Tokay.

"Indeed, yes!" I answered. "I must own I had no notion I should find anything in any way approaching it in these seas. Your cook must be a wonder."

"Well, perhaps he *is* rather extraordinary!" she continued. "But I doubt if you will deem it so wonderful when I tell you that he is a Frenchman of the French, who was once in the service of Victor Emanuel. How I came to obtain the benefit of his skill is, of course, another matter."

"And will he stay with you, do you think? Are you

not sometimes afraid that your servants will want to leave you, and return to civilisation again ?"

"My servants never leave me," she answered, with an emphasis there was no mistaking. "And for the best of reasons. No! I certainly have no fear on that score."

"You are able to place implicit trust in them, then ?" I asked, amazed at the confidence with which she spoke.

"The most implicit trust," she said. "My servants are carefully chosen. They give their services cheerfully, and, like my dog there, they would obey me at any cost, however great, to themselves. Would you like an example ?"

"Very much, if you will favour me," I answered.

"Then watch me closely. In the first place you must understand that, next to myself, my bulldog's greatest friend and companion is my butler—the man who has just left the room. Well, I will ring for him."

She did so, and, as soon as the bell had stopped ringing, called the dog to her side and said something to him in the same curious language she had employed before. Thereupon he went over to the door, and, laying himself down about a yard from it, watched it intently. He had not been there a half minute before the door opened, and the servant stood upon the threshold.

Immediately the dog saw him he rose to his feet, every bristle erect, showing all his teeth, and growling savagely. At first the man did not know what to make of this behaviour. Then he spoke to the animal, and at the same time attempted to pass him. But this the beast would not permit. His upper lip drew further back, and he showed unmistakably that if the man advanced another step he would bite, and bite severely. All this time his mistress lay back in her chair, toying with a spoon upon the table, and watching the pair out of half-closed eyes, according to her peculiar habit. Then she spoke to the man.

"I have told the dog," she said in English, for my benefit, I suppose, "to seize you by the throat if you attempt to enter the room. You know that he will do what I tell him. Very well then, come in !"

Dangerous as was his position, so great was the influence the Beautiful White Devil exercised over her dependents that the man did not hesitate or wait to be bidden twice, but at once complied with her order. He had not advanced two steps, however, before the dog had sprung into the air, and had his mistress not called to him in time, would have taken the unfortunate domestic by the throat. As it was he stopped midway in his spring, and a moment later was back again crouching at her side. Then having addressed some words of explanation to the frightened man, she turned to me and said :

"Are you satisfied with that practical proof, Dr. De Normanville, or do you want another? You are satisfied? I am glad of that, for I tell you just as that man obeyed my orders, regardless of the consequences, so would every other man in my employ, from my chief officer down to the little native lad who pulls the punkah."

"It is very wonderful !"

"On the contrary, it is very simple."

"I'm afraid I do not quite understand ?"

"Then I'm sorry to say I must for the present leave you in your ignorance. Some day I may afford you another example which will perhaps enlighten you more fully."

For a few moments she sat wrapped in thought, looking at a flower she had taken from a vase ; then she lifted her eyes again and addressed me with an air of authority that sat well upon her.

" We have finished our breakfast, I think," she said. "Now I imagine you will be anxious to inspect your patients. Well, if you will wait ten minutes while I transact a little legal business, I will accompany you."

So saying she led me out into the verandah, where we seated ourselves in long cane chairs. A tall native was in waiting, and when she had said something to him he withdrew.

"Now you will have an opportunity of witnessing a little piece of retributive justice," she observed ; " and also of observing how I treat those who misconduct themselves in my domains."

She had hardly spoken before the tramp of feet sounded from round the corner, and next moment two stalwart natives appeared escorting a young man, also an islander, whose bright attractive countenance won my regard from the first. Behind this party came the complainant, an elderly native, whose puckered and wrinkled face was about as unprepossessing as the other's was pleasing. Seeing their ruler before them they prostrated themselves with one accord, and remained in that position until they were told to rise. When they had done so, Alie narrated the features of the case to me in English. The old man, it appeared, had a young wife ;

the prisoner was her cousin, and, if the complainant could be believed, had shown himself fonder of her than was comfortable for the husband's peace of mind. Age proving jealous, and at the same time suspicious of the motive of Youth's cousinly affection, had trumped up a charge of stealing gardening implements against him, and had brought sworn testimony to prove that the stolen articles had been found in his possession. But it so happened that Alie had been aware for some time past that the real object of the youth's affection was one of her own domestics, a comely enough damsel, employed in the house. The upshot of it all was that the charge was dismissed; the old man had to listen to a short homily on jealousy; the young couple were married there and then, and given a hut in the township for their own use, while the old man was ordered, by way of compensation for the false accusation he had brought, to provide them, that self-same day, with certain goods and chattels necessary to their housekeeping. As for the three false witnesses, who had placed so small a value upon their reputations for veracity as to allow themselves to be suborned against an innocent man, their case was somewhat harder; they were taken to the rear of the house, where they received ten strokes of the rod apiece, well laid on, as a warning to them against future dealings in unsound evidence.

This case finished, Alie made another sign to one of her men, who instantly disappeared. Then she settled herself in her chair, and I noticed that a harder look came into her face.

"You have witnessed how I conduct one side of my court," she said. "Now you shall see the other."

Again the tramp of feet was heard, and once more guards and prisoner made their appearance round the corner. To my surprise, the latter was none other than my old acquaintance Kwong Fung, the notorious Chinese pirate. But though he must have remembered me, his sullen, evil face betrayed no sign of surprise. He only stood between his guards watching my hostess and waiting for her to speak. Presently she did so, in Chinese, and once, only once, did he answer her. During the harangue I glanced at her face, and was amazed at the change in it. The old soft expression was completely gone, and in its place had come one that, to tell the honest truth, even frightened *me*. Never before or since have I seen such a perfect exhibition of self-contained, but all-consuming, rage. Once more she spoke to the prisoner, who refused to answer. She instantly addressed herself to the escort. The man in command was in the act of replying when the prisoner, by some means which I shall never be able to explain, raised his right arm before his guards could stop him. In the palm of his hand lay a knife, somewhat resembling a Malay krise, but with a shorter and straighter blade. With the swiftness of thought the hand seemed to drop back and instantly resume its upright position. The impetus thus given sent the weapon flying along the verandah toward us, and if I had not thrown my left arm before her, there could be no doubt that it would have found a scabbard in Alie's breast. As it was it stuck in the sleeve of my white jacket, passing through the fabric without even scratching the flesh. Unnerving as the incident was, the Beautiful White Devil did not show the slightest sign of fear, but simply said " Thank

6

you!" to me, and then resumed her instructions to the guard. Kwong Fung was immediately led away.

For some seconds after his departure neither of us spoke, then, noticing that her face was regaining its old expression, I took courage enough to inquire my enemy's fate.

"Death," she answered. "I have forgiven that man times out of number; I have helped him when he was in distress, and once I rescued him when he was within an ace of being executed. But since he has murdered one of my bravest subjects in cold blood, and cannot respect the orders I have given, but must needs attempt the lives of those I have sworn to protect, he must be prevented from doing any more harm by the safest means we can employ."

She was silent again for a few moments, then picking up the dagger, which had fallen on the floor, she looked me steadily in the face, and said:

"Dr. De Normanville, I owe you my life. If ever the opportunity arrives you will not find me ungrateful. It was a near escape, was it not? I shall have to change my servants if they cannot see that their prisoners are unarmed."

I was about to reply, but was interrupted by the arrival of a second batch of litigants, who were followed by a third. They were all natives, for, as I discovered later, there was not one single instance on record, in the history of the island, of the white population having found it necessary to resort to law to settle their differences. A more peaceable, happy, and law-abiding community could not be found. One thing was very noticeable in each of these cases, and that was the pacific

reception of, and the resignation with which, the decisions
of their ruler were received. She spoke to them, chided
them, sympathised with them, and smoothed down their
ruffled feathers just as if they had in reality been what
she had called them—her children. And as a result, in
each case plaintiff and defendant went off together,
their differences settled and their former animosity
quite forgotten. When the last case was concluded,
Alie put on her large white hat, which throughout the
legal business had been lying beside her, and we were
in the act of setting out for the village, accompanied by
the dog, when an incident occurred which was fraught
with as much interest to me, in my study of her extraordinary position and character, as anything else I had
so far met with during my stay in the island.

We were descending the long stone steps before
described, when a young and attractive native woman
hove in sight, carrying in her arms a bundle, which on
her nearer approach proved to be a baby. Arriving at
the steps she halted and knelt at Alie's feet, kissing the
hem of her dress, and at the same time saying something to her in the soft native tongue I have so repeat-
edly admired.

When she had finished Alie turned to me and said :

"Doctor, this is your first case ; and a sad one. Will
you tell me if you can do anything for this poor creature's child ?"

Turning to the woman I signed to her to let me look
at the infant. The poor little thing was in the last
stage of confluent small-pox, and presented a sickening
appearance.

"Is it a hopeless case?" Alie asked, with almost an

entreaty in her voice, a note that had certainly not been there a quarter of an hour before, when she had sent Kwong Fung to his doom.

"Quite hopeless," I answered ; "but I will endeavour to make death as painless as possible. Will you tell the poor soul to bring the child to me in half an hour in the village ?"

Alie translated my speech and must have given the mother some encouragement, for she fell at my feet, and in the deepest reverence kissed my boots. Then with an obeisance to my companion she passed down a side path and disappeared among the trees.

Alie turned to me and said, with a deep sigh :

"Now, Dr. De Normanville, if you are ready we will set off on our tour of inspection."

I agreed, and accordingly we passed through the gate and went down the path towards the settlement.

CHAPTER V.

LEAVING the house behind us we made our way by means of a circuitous path, round the base of the majestic waterfall before described, down towards the buildings on the plain. The route chosen was a perfect one in every way, not only for observing the excellent placing of the township on the plateau, but for noting the beauties of nature along the path. As in the jungle through which I had passed to approach the house, lovely creepers twined from tree to tree, orchids gaped from every crevice, some of them almost human in their quaintness; while mixed up with them in marvellous profusion were palms, ferns, shrubs, and bamboos of every known hue and description. Butterflies and beetles, of colourings so glorious that my fingers positively itched for my collecting box, fluttered from flower to flower, while parrots (*Palædinis longianda*), Nikobar pigeons, and the darter, or snake bird, were so frequently met with as to lose all their charm of novelty. Sometimes we would be in places where the wealth of greenery shut out all view of the sky; a moment later we could look through the leaves at the great mountain pushing its head up into what seemed the azure vault of heaven itself. But beautiful as all this was, not the least lovely part of it was the mysterious woman walking by my side.

As we made our way down the path we talked on many subjects, European politics, of which her knowledge was extensive, the beauties of the East, literature and art; but, somehow or another, however far we might wander from it, the conversation invariably came back to the epidemic that was the occasion of my presence in the settlement.

At last we left the jungle and prepared to descend the precipitous hillside by means of a long flight of wooden steps, which ended at the commencement of the main street. In the brilliant sunlight the township looked a pretty enough little place, with its well laid-out and nicely planted thoroughfares, neatly built European houses, and picturesque native huts. It was hard to believe that, clean and healthy as it all looked, it had lost more than a quarter of its population by the ravages of one of the most awful pestilences human flesh is heir to. Indeed, so much impressed was I with its beauty that for a moment or two I stood watching it, unable to say a word. Then I looked at my companion. She, like myself, had been very silent for the last hundred yards, and now, as she looked down at her kingdom, I saw her beautiful eyes fill with tears.

"Dr. De Normanville," she said, as we arrived at the bottom of the steps, "if you will allow me, some day, when we are a little better acquainted, I will tell you the story of this place and the influence it has had upon my life. Then you will be able to understand how it is that I am so much affected by my people's sufferings."

I murmured an appropriate reply and we entered the village. Our arrival had been anxiously expected, and at the gate of the first house we were met by an old man, who was evidently a person of considerable importance in the place. He had a white skin and a slightly Scandinavian cast of countenance, and, though he spoke Chinese and the native tongue with unusual fluency, was evidently more than half an Englishman. On seeing my companion he raised his hat politely and waited for her to speak.

"Mr. Christianson," she said, holding out her hand, "this is Dr. De Normanville, who has been kind enough to come to our assistance from Hong Kong. I don't think it is necessary for me to assure him that you will give him your entire assistance in this terrible crisis, in the same manner as you have hitherto given it to me."

The old man bowed to me, and then addressed my companion.

"We have done our best in your absence," he said sorrowfully; "but it seems as if Fate were against us. There are at the present moment one hundred and thirty cases all told, of which eighty-four are men, twenty-three women, and the remainder children. Yesterday there were eighteen deaths—among them your old coxswain, Kusac, who died at seven in the morning, and Ellai, the wife of Attack, who followed him within an hour. The Englishman, Brandon, died at midday, his wife during the afternoon, and their only child this morning, scarcely an hour ago. Doctor, is there any hope at all of our being able to stop this awful plague?"

I assured him we would do our best, and he agreed that no man could ask or expect us to do more. By the time our conversation was finished I had taken a decided fancy to the old fellow, and with Alie's permission enrolled him there and then as my second in command.

"Now," I said, turning to her, "before we commence our work let me exactly understand my position. With what powers am I invested?"

"With full and complete authority," she answered promptly. "Whatever you may deem best for my unfortunate people, please do without consulting any-one. Believe me, no one will attempt to dispute your right."

"That is as it should be, and I thank you," I said. "Now, will you tell me where my own abode is to be? It should be as far removed from the centre of the infected district as possible, yet, at the same time, central enough to be convenient for all the inhabitants."

"I thought that house on the mound at the foot of the hill," she answered, pointing with her beautiful hand to a neat weather-board structure about a couple of hundred yards from the place where we were then standing; "in fact, I have even gone so far as to give orders that it should be prepared for you. Shall we go and examine it?"

Accordingly, accompanied by the old man, we set out for it, eagerly watched by a crowd of natives, who, from the expressions on their faces, had come quite to look upon me as their deliverer.

The house proved to be a most commodious little place of four rooms, and, from the luxury with which the two living apartments were furnished, it was evident that considerable trouble and care had been bestowed upon them. When we entered, an intelligent native lad was called from an inner room and informed in English that I was his new master, and that he was to see that I wanted for nothing. It is only fair to add that during my stay in the island no man could have desired a better and more trustworthy servant.

From the bedroom and sitting-room we passed on to the room at the end of the verandah, which I found had been set apart for, and equipped as, a surgery. Neatly arranged round the walls, on shelves, were enough drugs of all sorts and descriptions to stock half a dozen chemists' shops, while my instruments, cases, and other paraphernalia were spread out upon the table in the centre. Altogether the arrangements were most satisfactory and complete, and I intimated as much to Alic, who stood watching me from the window.

"It is all Mr. Christianson's doing," she said. "You must thank him."

I did so, and then proposed that we should set about our work at once.

"In the first place, Mr. Christianson," I began, "have you had any symptoms of the disease yourself?"

"Not one! Since it started I have been as well as I remember ever to have been in my life."

"When were you vaccinated last?"

I put the question with some little timidity, for I feared lest by so doing I might wake some unpleasant memory in the old man's mind. But, whatever his past may have been,—and there were few men in the settlement, I afterwards found, who had not more or less of a romantic history,—he answered without hesitation :

"I was vaccinated in Liverpool, twelve years ago next March."

"Then, with your permission, I'll do it for you again.

After that we'll call up the heads of the village and I'll operate on them."

So saying, I unpacked my things, and, having done so, vaccinated my second in command. When this was accomplished, he gave me a list he had prepared of the half-dozen principal inhabitants. They were immediately sent for, and as soon as they arrived my position was explained to them in a short speech by Alie.

"Now, gentlemen," I said, when her address was finished, "in view of the serious nature of our position and the necessity for a well-organized attack upon the disease which has so decimated your population, I propose to enrol you as my staff. You will each of you have special duties assigned to you, and I need not say that I feel sure you will fulfil them to the very best of your ability. Before we go any further, as I hear none of you have taken the disease, I propose vaccinating you all, as I have just done Mr. Christianson. When that has been accomplished we will get properly to work."

In half an hour or so this was done, and I was free to enter upon my next course of action.

"We will now," I said, after a little consultation with Alie, "assemble the healthy folk of the village on the green yonder."

This was soon done, and, at the word of command, the entire population able to get about assembled themselves on the open space before my verandah— blacks and whites, yellow and copper colour, all mixed up, higgledy-piggledy, in glorious confusion. From a cursory glance at them they appeared to come from all countries and from all parts of the globe. I could distinguish Englishmen, Frenchmen, Germans, Swedes,

Italians, Portuguese, Spaniards, Russians, Hindóos, Malays, Dyaks, and even Chinamen. The dusky population, however, predominated.

The first business to be performed, when they were all before me, was to separate the men from the women, and, as soon as this was accomplished, to carefully examine each in turn ; after that I singled out those who were skilled in carpentering and hut-building, and kept them on one side. Fortunately, I was able to procure nearly thirty who were in some degree efficient. All of these—I mean of course those who had not had the disease—were forthwith vaccinated and despatched, under the leadership of one of my six lieutenants, to a site I had chosen on the hillside for the hospital. There they were employed erecting huts with all possible despatch.

When the remainder had undergone the necessary operation, volunteers were requested to enrol themselves for the work of nursing the sick, and for this duty no less than twenty held up their hands, eight of whom had themselves been victims of the pestilence.

Long before I had completed my work of vaccination, the sun had disappeared behind the hill, and it was time for the evening meal. But tired as we all were, it was useless to think of stopping, so after we had broken our fast, the work of hut-building and vaccination proceeded again by torch and lamp light, until long after midnight. By the time my last patient was dismissed I was utterly worn out. But this was not the case with Alie, who throughout the day, and up to the very last moment at night, had never abated one jot of her energy. Encouraging the women, cheering the men, weighing out stores, and measuring cloth, she had been occupied without ceasing. Her enthusiasm was like a stimulant, and it had the effect of one upon all concerned. When my arms ached and my brain seemed fagged out beyond all recouping with plotting, planning, and giving advice, it was like a breath of new life to see her moving about among her people, taking no thought of herself, or of the danger she was running, thinking only of the terror-stricken wretches who turned to her in their hour of trouble for sympathy and help. And certainly as she passed about among them, Beelzebub, the bulldog, slouching along at her heels, it was wonderful to see how their faces would brighten, and the light of fear for the moment die out of their eyes. Nothing in my science had the power to do as much for them.

As I put down my implements and received Christianson's report that the fourth hut was ready for occupation, the clock on the mantelpiece of my sitting room struck a quarter to one. Bidding him good-night, and warning him to be early astir on the morrow, I took my hat, and prepared to accompany Alie on her homeward journey.

Following the path behind my house, we ran it round the foot of the falls, and up through the jungle to her gate. By the time we reached the spot where I had first looked down at the settlement that morning the moon was sailing high in a cloudless sky, and the whole of our world was bathed in its pale, mysterious light. The scene was indescribably beautiful, and perhaps the exquisite softness of the night, and the thought of the sickness raging in the valley below us, may have had something to do with the silence that followed our arrival at the top. We were standing at the gate, looking down upon the white roofs, showing like flakes of silver through the sea of dark jungle. For some time neither of us spoke. Then it was Alie who began the conversation.

"Dr. De Normanville," she said,—and it must not be thought conceited on my part to repeat it,—"I want to thank you from the bottom of my heart for the way in which you have taken up your work of mercy. I cannot say what I would like to do, because my heart is too full for utterance ; but if you could only realise what a relief it is to me to know that you are here to conduct matters, you would understand something of the gratitude I feel."

I uttered some commonplace reply, all the time watching the wistful look upon her face. Then she said suddenly :

"We have scarcely known each other three days yet, but somehow I feel as if, despite all you have heard of me, you are my friend."

"And you are quite right in so feeling," I said. "Believe me, I have forgotten all the foolish stories I have heard about you."

"No, no ! I don't know that you ought to do that," she continued, "because, you see, a great number of them are true."

"You wish me to remember them, then ?" I cried, in some surprise.

"Yes !" she answered. "I think you ought to get a clue for your own guidance out of them. But in saying that, I wish you to understand why I do so. To do that involves my telling you my history. Are you too tired to listen to it to-night ? "

"Of course I am not," I answered quickly, only too

glad of the opportunity of hearing a story that others would have given anything to have had related to them. "But if it means recalling unhappy memories, why tell it me? I shall serve you just as faithfully without knowing it."

"I do not doubt that for an instant," she said. "But you must surely see, Dr. De Normanville, that being brought into contact with you as much as I am, I want to set myself right with you. I want you to know all about me. Hitherto you have only thought of me, remember, as—well, as a beautiful woman, whose pleasure in life it is to rob and blackmail innocent and unsuspecting folk in this distant portion of the globe. Having seen your kindness and gentleness to my unfortunate people to-day, and honouring you for it as I do, is it to be wondered at that I want you to understand my work in life properly? May I tell you my story?"

"Please do ! It will interest me deeply."

She moved over from the gate to the broad wooden rail that ran along the path side, and which had evidently been placed there to protect foot passengers from the abyss. Leaning on it, she scanned the moonlit valley for some moments without speaking. Then turning her face toward me, she began :

"My father, you must know, Dr. De Normanville, was a typical Englishman ; he came of a good old Yorkshire family, and was an officer in Her Majesty's navy ; he was also remarkable for his great height, strength, and wonderful personal beauty. He was very popular with his fellow-officers and men, and in the early part of his career saw a good deal of active service in various parts of the globe. It was during the time that he was stationed in the West Indies, and soon after he was made commander of his ship, that he met my mother, a beautiful Creole, and married her. From the moment of his marriage the good luck which had hitherto attended his career seemed to desert him ; he lost his ship on an uncharted rock, and, when he was appointed to another, was ordered to a bad station, where he nearly lost his wife and his own life of fever. With his recovery came the most unfortunate part of his career. For just as he was about to be relieved, a charge was preferred against him by the admiral of the station, of so base and wicked a description that all those who heard it refused at first to entertain the notion. He was court-martialled and expelled the service. Since then the charge has been proved to have been entirely without foundation, but by the time that was known my poor father had died in exile. He appealed, but what was the use of that? To a proud, headstrong man, conscious of his innocence, such disgrace was unbearable, and he at length fled from England, resolved to shake its dust for ever off his feet. He went to India, but the result of the trial was known there, and every post was barred to him. He passed on to Singapore, and finally to Hong Kong, but always with the same result. By this time everything that was obstinate and worst in him was roused ; and when the admiral, the same who had brought the charge against him, was transferred to the China station, my father sought him out in Shanghai, decoyed him outside the city, requested him to publicly admit that the charges he had brought against him were false, and on his refusing, produced pistols, invited him to a duel, and shot him dead. Then, while the police were hunting for him, he fitted out a boat, with a large sum of money that had some time before been left him, collected a dozen other men as desperate as himself, tested them thoroughly before he trusted them, and, having bound them to secrecy, set off to find an island where they could lead their own lives unhindered by the outside world. This was the place they came to, and those old houses near the harbour were their first dwellings. Once in every six months my father went off to Hong Kong for supplies, and it was during one of these excursions that he met the man whose destiny it was to recognise him, and so hasten the trouble that lay before him. High words passed between them, and the result was a betrayal, and a fight with the police, in which two men were left dead upon the beach. That was the beginning of the end. The same night a boatload of marines put off to arrest my father, who was in the act of getting his schooner under weigh. When they came within hailing distance they were challenged and asked their business. The officer in charge replied that he held a warrant for my father's arrest. But the latter had no desire to fall into the authorities' hands again, so he bade them stand off. The officer, however, ordered his men to board. Again they were warned not to approach, but they paid no heed; the result may be imagined : a volley was fired from the schooner, and four men out of the six constituting the boat's crew, including the officer in charge, fell dead. Without more ado my father got under weigh, and raced for his life out of the harbour, pursued by three shots from the cruiser in the bay. From that day forward he was a proscribed man. Rewards were offered for his capture in all the principal ports of the East, not only by the English Government, but by the rich residents of Singapore, Hong Kong, and the treaty ports. Considering that it was not their affair, this action on the part of his former friends so enraged my father, that he swore that if ever one of the signatories fell into his hands, he would make him pay dearly for his action. It may interest you to know that Mr. Vesey, the man whom you perhaps remember I abducted, was the chairman of the meeting that offered the first reward for my father, and years afterwards for me.

"Well, months went by, and once more the stores on the island began to run short. It became imperatively necessary that a fresh supply should be obtained. To do this my father repainted and rerigged his boat, disguised himself and his men, and sailed off for Shanghai. Reaching that port, he sent his mate ashore to make the purchases. But suspicion seems to have been aroused, the man was arrested, and had not my father been warned in time and put to sea, he would have shared the same fate. But he was resolved not to be beaten, and at the risk of his life he went back and ashore. By means of a subterfuge, which it would take me too long to explain, he succeeded in rescuing his companion. In the course of the rescue, however, a man was killed, and this closed the treaty ports even more firmly to him than before.

"The matter had become terribly serious now. He could not go into any port for fear of being arrested, and yet stores had to be obtained for the starving island. To a headstrong man like my father, rendered desperate by deliberate injustice, there was only one natural way out of it. He made for Hong Kong, chose a dark night,

7

went down the harbour in a junk, boarded a trading boat, confined the skipper in his cabin, and took possession of his cargo, for which, it is only fair to say, he paid the full market price. The skipper, however, for some purpose of his own, forgot the incident of payment, went ashore in the early morning and proclaimed the fact to the police that he had been robbed of his cargo under the very noses of the cruisers. The description of the robber tallied with that of my father, and the hue and cry began again. Thenceforward he declared himself openly in opposition to society, collected round him all the men who were worth anything, and whose lives were as desperate as his own, and levied toll on the ships of all nations whenever occasion offered. He ran many risks, for often he was sighted and chased by cruisers. It was on one of these occasions that my poor mother died, killed by an English bullet. Three months later my father caught the fever in the Manillas and followed her to the grave, bidding me, a girl of eighteen, keep up this settlement and carry on the war he had begun. Ever since then the island has been my tenderest care. I have watched over it and guarded it as a mother guards her child. But at the same time, as you know, I have not spared my enemies. My first adventure proved successful, my second well-nigh ruined me. My father's death had become known by some mysterious means, and, when it was discovered that I was carrying on his trade, a supreme effort was made by the authorities to capture me. But they have not succeeded yet. The same year I had the *Lone Star*, the boat you found me on, built in Scotland, and began my work in earnest. Ever since then I have had a price upon my head; but, as I

told you on board the *Lone Star*, I can truthfully say
that I have never knowingly robbed a poor man, and as
you have seen for yourself, I have materially helped a
good many. In some cases, too,—the Sultan of Surabaya,
for instance,—I have gone out of my way to assist the
oppressed, and have taught wholesome lessons to their
rulers and oppressors. Now you know my story. It
may be that you take a different view of my life and
would call it by a harsh name. I should be sorry to
think that. I simply remember how my father's life
was ruined by his enemies, and that I have never been
given a chance, even if I would have taken it. The English, French, and Chinese governments are my natural
enemies, as they were my father's before me. If the
innocent suffer by what I do, I am deeply sorry for them.
But do your nations in their wars heed the peasantry of
either side, even as much as I do? I think not. Dr. De
Normanville, most of those white people you saw to-day
have curious histories. Do not suppose for an instant
that I receive anyone here without strict inquiry into
his temperament and antecedents. But, on the other
hand, when I do take him in, I never swerve from my
duty towards him. Now, what have you to say?"

"I can only answer that I think your character has
been grossly maligned."

"No, don't say that, for you are only speaking on the
impulse of the moment; and, besides, you must remember that those who speak against me in that fashion
look upon my actions from their own point of view.
However, you will not think so badly of me for the
future, will you?"

As she said this she came a little closer to me and

looked me in the face. Never before had I seen her look so beautiful.

"No, I can safely promise you I won't," I answered stoutly. "I am your champion for the future, come what may."

"You are very good to me. Now, as we are both tired, had we not better say good-night?"

She held out her little hand, and for some reason. goodness only knows what, I took it and raised it to my lips. Then with another "good-night," she turned away from me and, with the dog at her heels, disappeared through the gate and up the path, among the bushes, that led to her abode.

When she had gone I stood for a few moments looking down upon the lovely panorama spread out before me, then I turned myself about and went down the hill to my residence at the foot. But though I went to bed it was not to sleep. The extraordinary story I had just been told, and the exciting events of the day, were not of a nature calculated to induce repose, and so I tossed and tumbled upon my couch hour after hour, till the first faint signs of dawn made their appearance. Then I had a bath in cool spring water, and, having dressed, went out and began to prepare my work for the day.

As the sun made his appearance above the tree-tops, Christianson and his colleagues, my trusty lieutenants, came up the path towards the house, and five minutes later Alie herself appeared upon the scene, eager to be employed. As she entered the verandah and greeted me I glanced at her face. But there was no trace there of the sadness of the previous night. Indeed, if the truth must be told, there was even a sort of distant haughtiness about her manner towards me, that was as unexpected as it was difficult to account for.

"Good-morning, Dr. De Normanville!" she said, as she put down on the table the parcel she had brought with her. "It is nearly five o'clock; are you ready to commence work?"

"Quite ready," I answered, turning to a man named Andrews. "To begin, sir, will you and your deputies hunt up the builders and continue the work at the huts till breakfast time?" Then turning to another, "Mr. Williams, you might take three men and erect four bed places in each hut. Mr. Christianson, and the remainder of you gentlemen, if you will accompany me, we will make a careful house-to-house inspection of the village."

Having despatched the others to their various employments, I set off, accompanied by Alie, to begin the ghastly work of inspection. It must not be supposed that I in any way induced her to run the risk; to tell the truth, I protested vigorously against it, but without result; her heart was set upon it, and she would not be deterred.

The first house we visited was a small one, built of *adobe* mixture and inhabited by three people, two of whom were down with the disease. There had originally been six in the family, but three had perished. I made my examination, noted their cases in my pocket-book, spoke some cheering words to them, and passed on to the next house. This was of wood, neatly built, and contained one patient who was quite alone, his wife and daughter having both succumbed to the plague. In the next there was no case, nor the next; but in the three following there were eight. Hardly a house was free from it, and in many cases, all the inhabitants being dead, the buildings were quite tenantless. By the time I had finished my inspection it was eight o'clock, and I was quite ready for breakfast. This disposed of, work was at once resumed.

Everyone toiled with a will, and the hut-builders to such good purpose, that by midday twelve fine huts were standing ready for occupation on the slope of the western hill. The real work was now about to commence. Summoning to my assistance those men and women who had volunteered to act as nurses, I had a number of stretchers made, and on these conveyed the sufferers to the hospitals. Four patients went to each hut. The men I sent to those on the right hand of the street, the women to those on the left. By this means forty-eight persons were disposed of, and by five o'clock sufficient huts were at my disposal to contain as many more. By sundown every sufferer in the place had been removed, the nurses were duly instructed in their duties and installed, and the real combating of the disease had commenced. But at this juncture a serious problem was presented for our consideration. Having removed the owners to places of safety, what were we to do with the old houses and their contents? Taking Alie into my confidence, I explained the situation to her, told her how loth I was to destroy so many good buildings, but at the same time pointed out to her how imperatively necessary it was that every dwelling and any article likely to harbour infection should be got rid of. To my satisfaction she met it in the proper spirit.

"If it is necessary for the safety of those who remain,

there can be no doubt at all as to what course we should pursue," she answered. "The houses must go. And that being so, I must endeavour to make it up to the owners when they shall require them again. Will you give the necessary instructions ? "

I did so forthwith, and in less than half an hour no less than eighty houses, with their contents, were blazing on the plain.

And so the week went on, and the next after that, with hardly a break in the routine of work. Out of one hundred cases treated, thirty succumbed in the first eight days, twelve in the remaining six, while fifteen more were added from the township during the same period.

And now I must say something about the care and attention bestowed on these patients by those who had volunteered for the arduous task of nursing. Indeed, I feel justified in saying that no better service could have been obtained in any London hospital. Fortunately, a sincere bond of affection seemed to bind all these people together, and this, taken with the influence exercised by the wonderful woman at their head, made its power thoroughly felt in everything they did. And here I should also like to put on record Alie's wonderful devotion to her people, during that time of awful anxiety. Day in, day out, night and morning alike, accompanied by her dog, she was occupied about the different huts, helping and reproving, chiding and encouraging. Her presence was like a ray of sunlight which seemed to light the place long after she had left it. The convalescent derived new vigour from her touch, the dying were soothed by her voice. Never once throughout the whole of the time did she think of herself ; the path of what she considered to be her duty lay before her, and the Beautiful White Devil, the notorious adventuress, the abductor of rich merchants, the terror of the China seas, trod it without murmur or complaint. It was a wonderful exhibition of womanly gentleness, forbearance, and endurance. And when I saw her, tired and almost dispirited by the results of the struggle, and noted how she put all this aside, assumed a smiling face to speak words of comfort to some sufferer, and then re-membered the accusations and stories to which I had listened in the Victoria Hotel that first evening, I felt almost as mean and contemptible as it was possible for a man to be.

And here, gentle reader, let me make a confession, though I doubt if it will come upon you as a surprise. Already, I expect, you have accused me of being in love with the Beautiful White Devil. I do not deny that I was. Where so many better men had succumbed, who was I that I should go free ? And surely if so many others had fallen captive to her mere beauty, knowing next to nothing of her real merit, I, who had exceptional opportunities of studying her character under every aspect, who saw her grave and gay, passionate and self-sacrificing, imperious and the most humble of any, might claim for my affection that it was based on something more tangible than any mere personal beauty.

Yes ! I *was* in love with Alie, and, what is more, I am in love with her now, as I shall be in love with her on my dying day, and afterwards if that be possible. And this I can say truthfully, that throughout my love for her, my heart has known no unworthy thought. I

have loved her for her beautiful, noble, impulsive, generous self, and, if that be an offence, I can only say that I
am proud to acknowledge it.

But though I was over head and ears in love with her,
seeing no sun in heaven when she was not with me, no
stars at night when I was not by her side, never once
did I allow her to suspect my passion. I did my work
as I had contracted to do it—that is, to the best of my
ability. But hard as I worked, she worked harder. Day
in, day out, she was never idle ; she took her share of
nursing, superintended the erection of huts and houses
for those who had been deprived of them, and cheered
and encouraged everyone with whom she came in contact. Beautiful White Devil, the Chinese called her.
Beautiful White Angel would surely have been a better
and more appropriate name.

CHAPTER VI.

SIXTY-FOUR days exactly after my taking charge of the health of the settlement, the last patient was discharged from the hospital, cured. Out of one hundred and ninety-five cases treated, one hundred and thirty-three had recovered ; the rest lay in the little graveyard on the hillside to the eastward of the town. It had been a weary, harassing time from beginning to end, and the strain and responsibility had had a more severe effect upon me than I should have anticipated. Alie alone, of all the workers, seemed untouched. Her indomitable will would not permit her body to know such a thing as fatigue, and for this reason the last day of our work found her powers as keen and her energy as unabated as they had been on the first.

On the afternoon of the day following the discharge of my last patient, she came into the surgery, and, seating herself in my armchair, looked about her with that interest my medical affairs always seemed to inspire in her.

"Dr. De Normanville," she began, clasping her little white hands together on the arm of the chair ; "I have been watching you lately, and I have come to the conclusion that you are thoroughly tired out. There is but one cure for that—rest and complete change of air and scene."

"And pray what makes you suppose I am worn out?" I asked, wiping a pair of forceps that I had been using on a native boy five minutes before, and putting them back into their case.

"The colour of your face for one thing," she answered, "and the way you move about for another. Your appetite, I have also noticed, has been gradually falling off of late. No, it won't do! My friend, you have been so good to us that we should be worse than ungrateful if we allowed you to get ill. So, without consulting you, I have arranged a little holiday for you!"

"That is very kind of you," I said; "and pray what is it to be?"

"I will tell you. You are an enthusiastic botanist and entomologist, are you not? Very well, then. This island abounds with unclassified flora and fauna. I will have an expedition fitted out to-day, and to-morrow morning we will leave the settlement and plunge into the interior. I expect a week's absence from worry will work a wonderful change in you. At any rate, we'll try it. What have you to say to my proposition?"

"I should like it above all things," I answered eagerly. And, indeed, apart from the scientific chances it would afford me, a trip anywhere in her company could not be anything else than delightful.

Having gained her point, she rose to go.

"I may consider it settled, I suppose?" she said. "At daybreak to-morrow morning we are to mount our ponies in the square down yonder, and set off. You need not bother about rifles or any impedimenta of that kind. I will see that you are well provided."

So saying she withdrew, and I saw no more of her that

day. The rest of the afternoon I spent in preparing my specimen boxes for the trip, and when I sought my couch at night it was to dream of birds and beetles of the most glorious colouring, size, and variety.

True to our arrangement, daybreak next morning found me, booted and spurred, striding towards the village square. Early as I was at the rendezvous, Alie was there before me, mounted on a neat bay pony, and evidently awaiting my coming. She wished me "good morning," and then pointed to the group of pack-horses standing at a little distance in charge of half a dozen men.

"We shall not want for provisions during our travels," she said, with a happy laugh; and as she did so she signed to one of her attendants to lead up a pony she had reserved for my use. "The cook and his staff," she continued, "have gone on ahead of us to prepare our breakfast, so now if you are ready we'll start."

The order to march was thereupon given, and we immediately set off up the mountain track. Within five minutes of starting the settlement lay hidden behind the hill, with all its painful memories and anxieties, and we found ourselves surrounded by the primeval forest. The mysterious silence of the dawn still held the landscape, and all nature seemed waiting for the sun to make his appearance before beginning the business of the day. Here and there in the dips, and upon the pools, heavy mists wreathed and curled themselves, suggestive of malaria and a hundred other unpleasantnesses. Before we have been riding an hour, however, the sun rose in all his majesty; in a trice the forest woke to life and activity; hordes of monkeys leaped from branch to branch above our heads, in many cases racing us nearly a hundred yards before they left us; gigantic swine crashed through the undergrowth, almost under our ponies' noses; while birds of every plumage flew, from tree to tree, across our path. A moment before the world had seemed dead, now it was full and brimming over with vitality.

When the first half-dozen miles were overcome the aspect of the country began to change; it became more open, and we continually emerged from timber on to highly-grassed plains, where pig and deer of many kinds were to be seen feeding placidly. Towards eight o'clock the trend of the country lay upward, and continued so until we had mounted to a considerable elevation, when an extensive panorama was unfolded before us. The island must indeed have been a large one if it could be judged by the extensive views we had presented to us of it; only on the settlement side could I see the sea, while on the other the forest rolled away as far as the eye could reach.

At half-past eight, or between that and nine o'clock, we commenced to descend again, following the course of a pretty stream, until our guides came back to tell us that we were approaching the spot where it had been arranged we should partake of breakfast.

And surely enough, as we reached the bottom of the valley, the smoke of a fire rose above the palms before us, and, a few seconds later, we were permitted a view of an impromptu camp, with a blazing fire, and a white man actively engaged beside it, frying-pan in hand. As I looked at the little scene I could not help thinking of the many picnics I had assisted at in dear old England, and I naturally fell to comparing them with this one, at which I was the guest of so extraordinary a woman, under such novel and exciting circumstances.

Had I been told only half a year before that I should be picnicking on an island in the North Pacific, of which I knew neither the location nor the name, with a woman who had a reputation such as Alie unfortunately possessed, I should certainly have refused to believe it. Yet it was so, and, what was more to the point, I was not only picnicking, but was head over ears in love with that self-same woman, and, what was perhaps still more extraordinary, gloried in the fact.

As soon as breakfast was over we remounted our ponies and pushed on in the same fashion, through the same sort of country, with a brief halt at midday, until nightfall. Towards the middle of the afternoon the view once more began to change ; craggy uplands rose on our right, while the same wonderful forest still continued on our left. What struck me as remarkable was the fact that so far we had seen no villages and encountered no natives. Could the island—if island it really were, and of that I was beginning to have my doubts—be inhabited only by the people of our settlement ? It seemed scarcely probably, but if not, where were the rest of its aboriginal population ?

A little before sundown, Alie informed me that we were close upon our destination. And surely enough, just as the orb of day disappeared behind the tree tops, we saw before us, on a small plateau, four or five large and exceedingly comfortable huts, which the men who had preceded us that morning had erected for our accommodation. They faced towards the east, and the view from the little terrace on which they stood was beautiful in the extreme. Across it, and for a short distance below, the land was open, then the undergrowth began again, gradually rising from small bushes to great trees, and afterwards continuing in one unbroken sea of green, away to where the faint outline of a mountain range peered up, upon the southeastern horizon. It was a picture to see and remember for ever.

Having dismounted from our ponies, we prepared to make ourselves comfortable. The distribution of huts was as follows: Alie took that to the right, I had a large one on the left, while that in the centre was set apart for our dining-room and sitting-room (if we wanted to be indoors, which was unlikely); the fourth was destined for the accommodation of the cook, and from it already resounded the clatter of pots and pans.

Full of curiosity to see in what sort of comfort Alie travelled, I entered my own hut, and was amazed at the completeness of the arrangements. A comfortable bed-place, with mosquito curtains, occupied one side; a square of matting covered the floor, a portable wash-hand stand stood near the bed; while against the opposite wall, neatly arranged in a rack, were my guns and specimen cases. By the time I had washed off the stains of travel, and exchanged my riding costume for a lounge suit, the native gong had summoned us to dinner, and Alie and I, meeting on the terrace, entered the centre hut together.

If I had been surprised at the completeness of the arrangements of my own hut, how much more astonished was I now. Indeed, had it not been for the walls, which were covered with some peculiar sort of tapestry, and the different ceiling, I should hardly have known that we were not in the bungalow at the settlement. The white cloth, the glittering glass and silver, the costly ornaments and the profusion of dishes, were the same; and when the same impassive servant entered to wait upon us, clad in his usual white livery, my astonishment was complete. Alie was in exceptionally good spirits and for this reason the meal proceeded in a most delightful fashion.

When it was over we drew our chairs outside into the gathering gloom, and sat watching the fire-flies dashing in and out amid the tangle of dark forest across the plateau. It was indeed a night to be remembered. Overhead the tropic stars shone in all their beauty; around us were the unfathomable depths of the forest; from the right sounded the tinkling music of a stream; while now and again out of the darkness would come the deep note of some forest animal, or the melancholy hoot of an owl or other night bird.

Later on, by Alie's orders, enormous fires were lit at intervals all round the circle of the camp, and these not only failed to detract from, but succeeded in adding to, the weird picturesqueness of the scene. From the darkness behind us we could catch the subdued voices of our followers, varied now and again by the occasional snorting and stamping of the picketed ponies.

"How beautiful it all is!" said Alie, looking up at the winking stars. Then, as if to herself, "If only we could always be as peaceable as this, how much happier we should be!"

"Do you really think we should?" I answered. "Don't you think it is the wild unrest and turmoil of the world, to say nothing of that constant struggling, which makes existence so sweet to us?"

"Ah! You speak of your own world," she said sadly. "Think what *my* world is? Continual plotting, endless striving, with always the one great dread of capture hanging over me. Oh! Dr. De Normanville, you little know the sort of life I lead!"

"Then why do you go on with it? If only I might——"

I checked myself suddenly. Another moment and the fatal words would have passed my lips. But to see her thus and not to tell her of my love was almost more than I could bear. I kept a tight rein upon myself, however, and crammed the words back into my heart. She had paused, and was looking away towards the dark forest.

"Why do I go on with it?" she answered, a few moments later. "Because I must! Because there is no one else to guide and care for them but me."

"But supposing you were caught? They would have to shift for themselves then."

"I shall never be taken alive. That is, except by treachery. No, Dr. De Normanville, come what may, I can never forsake them. My duty lies before me, and as I have endeavoured to do it in the past, so I must strive to do it in the future. But it is getting late, and we have travelled a long distance to-day. Don't you think we had better bid each other good-night?"

As she spoke she rose, and I followed her example. Then she shook hands, wished me good-night, and disappeared into her own hut, her dog at her heels. When she had gone I reseated myself, lit another cigar, and fell to work upon my thoughts. Away in the darkness

8

beyond the leaping fires, a Sambhur deer, probably disturbed by our lights, was barking to his mate, and in a tree near at hand a night bird hooted dolefully. The first sweetness of the evening had passed, and now an unutterable melancholy seemed to have laid its hand upon it. When my cigar was finished I passed into my hut, glanced at my rifles to see that they were ready to my hand in case of need, and, having disrobed myself, went to bed. Tired as I was, my slumbers were almost dreamless, and it seemed but a few minutes from the time I laid my head upon my pillow before my servant was waking me to the new-born day.

Immediately breakfast was over I took my specimen cases and a light rifle, and, accompanied by Alie and two of our native servants, dived into the forest on collecting thoughts intent. But the profusion of subjects was so vast that it was difficult to know quite where to begin. At every turn some peculiar grass, some plant, some shrub would arrest my attention, while in the air butterflies, beetles, and birds innumerable seemed to call upon me to catch and catalogue them without delay. Alie had quite recovered her good spirits by this time, and having once grasped the general idea, followed her new hobby with the same impassioned ardour that was noticeable in everything she undertook. By midday our cases were full to bursting, so we returned to the camp to lunch. In the afternoon we continued our work, but this time without our native followers, who, when all was said and done, preferred chattering to working, and in more ways than one were in the way.

Leaving the camp, we struck into the forest in a

southeasterly direction, following the course of a tiny stream that evidently had its origin in the mountain range elsewhere described. Game of all sorts abounded ; twice I saw herds of small deer alongside the river bank ; wild swine we continually met with, and once I felt certain the spoor we saw round a big pool was that of an elephant. Indeed, Alie informed me that the natives had often informed her that in their hunting expeditions they had met with these gigantic beasts. This circumstance, perhaps more than anything else, set me wondering where Alie's marvellous island could be located.

By the time the sun declined upon the mountain our boxes were once more full, and we turned our heads campwards, following on our homeward route the course of the same stream we had pursued on our outward journey. It was warm work, and when about half our walk was done we stopped on a little rise to look about us.

Alie seated herself on a fallen tree, and I put down my boxes and took my place beside her. Throughout the afternoon she had been a little quiet, and I must own that my own spirits were none too lively. Enjoyable as our excursion had proved, it was nevertheless a fact that every day was bringing my stay in the island nearer to its close, and, under the circumstances, I could not help feeling that, my duty done, it behoved me to be moving on as soon as possible. And yet the thought of leaving this woman, into whose life I had flashed like a meteor, and whom I had come so desperately to love, was agonising to me.

Alie rolled a small stone into the foaming torrent below us and then turned to me.

"Dr. De Normanville," she began,—and it struck me that she hesitated a good deal over what she had to say,—" when my agent visited you in Hong Kong and induced you to come to our assistance, he promised that, as soon as your work was completed, you should be returned safe and sound to the place whence you started. Your work is completed, and now it only remains for you to say—well, to say when you wish to leave us."

This speech, following on top of what I had been thinking myself, put me in a strange position, and for a minute I did not know how to answer. Then a torrent of words and protestations rose upon my lips, but I pressed them back, and to gain time for reflection asked a question.

"I hope that I have done my work to your satisfaction ? "

"How can you ask such a thing ?" she answered promptly. " You have worked for us as few other men would ever have done. I cannot,"—here her voice trembled a little, and her beautiful eyes filled with tears,—"I cannot ever thank you as I would wish to do."

Either her tear-laden eyes or this expression of her gratitude must have deprived me of my self-control, for when she had finished speaking, my presence of mind completely deserted me, and without more ado I drew closer to her on the tree, and, taking her hand in mine, said, almost without thinking of my words :

" Alie, cannot you see that there can be no question of thanks between *us ?* Cannot you see why I have worked so hard for you ? Cannot you see that I would give my own existence to save for you even the life of the dog you loved ? Have my actions not spoken for themselves ?"

She rose to her feet, but I noticed that she turned her face away and would not look at me. I could feel that she was trembling violently. In spite of this I continued :

"Alie ! You must see that I love you with my whole heart and soul. From the moment I first saw you on your yacht's deck I have been your slave. I know it is madness for a man like me to hope to win such a queen among women as yourself ; but I cannot help it. Send me away from you if you will, but there is one thing beyond your power to do, and that is to take away from me my love."

"Hush, hush ! for pity's sake !"

"No, Alie ; I cannot stop. I have gone too far now to draw back. Day by day I have hidden away in my heart—I have tried to crush down and stifle, this love of mine ; but it will not be hidden, it will not be crushed, it will not be stifled. Now the flood has risen, it has burst its bonds and washed away all thought of prudence. You have learned my secret. Alie, is there no hope at all for me ? I know I am not worthy of you, but I am an honest man, and I love you with my whole heart and soul."

"Dr. De Normanville," she said slowly, turning her tear-stained face towards me, "I am sorry, more sorry than you will ever guess, that you should have told me this. Many men have let me know their love before now, and I was able to tell them without pain to myself that it could not be. Now, you love me, you who have been so true and so brave, and I have to make you see that what you wish can never be possible. Do not think I am insensible of the honour you have done me, for it would honour any woman to be asked to be your wife. Do not think that it does not pain me to hurt you so. But, oh, Dr. De Normanville, cannot you see that I can be no man's wife, much less yours?"

"And why, in Heaven's name, not?"

All this time she had not attempted to withdraw her hand from mine.

"Because, according to your lights, I am not worthy. You have this moment called yourself an honest man. Well, then, judged by your ideas of honesty, I am not an honest woman. Look at your own career; look at the name you have already created for yourself; think of your future; then how can I—a woman, hunted by every nation, a woman on whose head a price is set, who dares not show her face in a civilised country—allow herself to share that name and that future with you. Ask yourself that question, and answer it before you think of making me your wife."

"I can have no future without you!"

"That is no answer to my question. No, Dr. De Normanville, I am sorry, more sorry than you will ever know, that this trouble should have come upon you. But when you have time to reflect, you will see, as clearly as I do, that what you ask is impossible. It can never be!"

"One question before you say it cannot be!" I cried. "I will not insult you by imploring you to tell me the truth. You will do that without my asking. But we will suppose for the moment that you were not the outlaw you declare yourself to be, and I asked you the same question, will you tell me if you would give me the same answer, then?"

"It is unfair of you to put it in that way," she said, toying with a leaf. "But since you *do* ask, I will tell you truthfully. If I were in the position you describe, and you asked me to share your life with you, I would give you this answer, that I would be your wife or the wife of no other man."

"You love me then, Alie?"

My heart seemed to stop beating while I waited for her answer. When it did pass her lips, it was so soft that I could hardly hear it.

"Yes, I do love you."

Before she could prevent me I had taken her in my arms, and rained kisses upon her beautiful face. For a moment she did not resist. Then she withdrew herself, panting, from my arms.

"Let me go," she gasped; "you must not do this. No, no, no! What am I telling you. Oh, why cannot you see that what you wish is impossible?"

"As I live," I cried in return, "it is not impossible, and it never shall be! Since you own yourself that you love me, I will not live without you. I love you as I verily believe man never loved woman before. If I were a poet instead of a prosaic doctor, I should tell you, Alie, that to me your smile is like God's sunshine; I would tell you that the wind only blows to carry to the world the story of my love for you; I would tell you all this and more—yes, a thousand times more. But I am no poet, I am only a man who loves you for your own beautiful self, for your sweetness, your loneliness, your tenderness to those about you. What does fame mean for me ! I want only you. Let me have you for my companion through life, and I will go with you where you wish, stay here with you, if you please, or go away, just as you may decide ; I have but one ambition, and that is to be worthy of you, to help you to do good. All I ask is to be allowed to live the life you live yourself ! "

"And you think that I would let you make this sacrifice for me ? No ! no ! Oh, why cannot you see that it is impossible ? "

Again I attempted to take her in my arms. But this time she eluded me, and with a choking sob fled through the scrub towards the camp. Seeing that it was useless to attempt to reason with her in her present state, I followed more leisurely, reaching the huts just as the gong was sounding for dinner. As soon as my ablutions were performed, I sought the dining hut, but my hostess was not there. I waited, and presently the servant arrived to inform me that she was not well, and would dine in her own apartment.

I was not prepared for this, and my thoughts during my solitary meal, and when I was smoking on the plateau before the huts afterwards, were by no means pleasant. Glad though I was that I had made her aware of my sentiments towards her, I almost began to wish, if she were going to avoid me, that I had deferred my explanation until we had reached the settlement again. But I was destined to see her that night after all.

About ten o'clock, just as I was thinking of retiring to my own hut, I heard a footstep behind my chair, and a moment later Alie, accompanied by her dog, stood before me.

"Dr. De Normanville," she said softly, "I cannot imagine what you must think of me? I have come to tell you that I felt I could not sleep until I had apologised to you."

Her penitence sat so prettily upon her that it was as much as I could do to prevent myself taking her in my arms and telling her so. But I managed somehow to keep myself within bounds, and only said in reply :

"You must not say a word about it. I was equally to blame. Great as is my love for you, I should not have forced it upon you in that unseemly fashion."

"No! No! Don't say that. I want you really to understand my gratitude. That I love you, I have said. Perhaps I ought not to have confessed it. But seeing that I have done so, and have told you exactly what my position in the world is, you must see that it is that very love which keeps me from giving myself to you as I should like to do. I don't make my meaning very clear, but can you understand that ?"

"I think I do," I said. "But it does not alter my position. I love you as I shall never love any other woman. As I told you this afternoon, my whole life is bound up in you. It remains for you to say whether I shall be the happiest or the most miserable of men. Remember, save for my sister, I am alone in the world. Therefore, as she is amply provided for, I have only myself to think of. If you will have me, I will give my life to you to do as you please with."

"This generosity is like yourself. Will you let me make a bargain with you ?"

"What is it ?"

"It is this. First, you shall promise not to speak of this to me again until I give you permission."

"I will promise that. And on your part?"

"I will promise to give you my answer at the end of twelve months. In the meantime, you will go back to England, live your own life, and on the first day of May next year, if you still love me, and are as anxious then to make your sacrifice as you are now, I will meet you again and be your wife as soon as you please. What do you say?"

For a few moments I could answer nothing; then, though I am not theatrically inclined as a general rule, I fell on my knee, and taking her hand kissed it, saying in a voice I hardly recognised as my own:

"My queen and my wife!"

"You are content to abide by that?"

"Since you wish it, I am *more* than content," I answered, my heart overflowing with happiness.

"Then let us say no more on the subject. Good-night! and may God bless you!"

She turned and left me without another word, and when I had seen her disappear into her hut, I too sought my couch, to dream, as I hoped, of the happiness that the future had in store for me.

CHAPTER VII.

AN EXCITING DAY.

But though I went to bed to sleep, and was sufficiently romantic to hope that I should dream of the future I was to spend with Alie, I was destined to be disappointed. My mind was in such a state of excitement that no sort of rest was possible to me. Hour after hour I tossed and tumbled upon my couch, now hovering on the borderland of sleep, now wide awake, listening to the murmur of the stream beyond the camp, and the thousand and one noises of the night. When at last I did doze off, my dreams were not pleasant, and I awoke from them quite unrefreshed. Springing out of bed I went to the door to look out. It was broad daylight, and the sun was in the act of rising. To go back to bed was impossible, so, as breakfast was still some hours ahead, I dressed myself, took a rifle from the stand, and slipping a dozen or so cartridges into the pocket of my shooting coat, procured a few biscuits from the dining-hut, and strolled across the open space into the forest beyond. It was a glorious morning for a hunting excursion, and before I had gone half a mile I had secured a fine deer for the camp's commissariat. Fixing the spot where I had left it, and feeling certain some of the natives would soon be on my trail after hearing the report, I plunged further into the jungle, capturing here and there a beetle, a butterfly, or a bird, as they chanced to fall in my way.

While I walked my brain was busily occupied, but dominating all was the remembrance that Alie—the wonderful, the beautiful, the mysterious Alie—loved me. What cared I for the sort of life she led? What did it matter to me, since I had seen and grasped her real character for myself, what other people might say of her? Had I not observed her courage in moments of extreme peril? had I not witnessed her tenderness by the bedside of dying men and women? had I not noted her devotion to what she considered her duty? Yes, and better than all was the knowledge that she had promised to be my wife if I would wait a year for her. Would I wait? Why, of course I would—ten years, twenty, nay a lifetime, if only I could secure her at the end.

With these thoughts in my mind, I trudged briskly on, keeping both eyes open for any specimens, botanical or otherwise, that might come in my way. Then leaving the little stream, whose course we had followed on the previous day, behind me, I struck out towards the west, and presently forsook the forest, to emerge on to an open plain about a mile long by half that distance wide. To the northward lay a high cane brake, to the south a deep ravine, and on the open between them a large herd of deer was feeding quietly. Remembering that I had been told on the previous day that the cook was short of fresh meat, I resolved to see how many I could bring to book. The only way to stalk them was, of course, to approach them upwind, and in order to do this it was necessary that I should cross a stony ridge which ran parallel with the edge of the ravine mentioned above. As there would not be a vestige of cover between us the chances were a hundred to one that I should reveal my presence to them while passing over the open space and then the herd would give one look and be off like the wind. However, I was going to chance that, so throwing myself down flat upon my stomach, I wriggled myself up the side of the little eminence, pausing now and again to take breath, until I reached the summit, thence made my way out on to the bare face of the hill until, at the end of twenty minutes, I was within a thousand paces of them.

The herd still fed on, though once I saw an old buck raise his head and look round as if he scented danger. But as I remained quiet for a few moments he resumed his feeding, and when he had done so I continued my painful crawl. But the worst part of the business was still to come, for having got up to them against the wind I had now, unless I was content to chance a long shot, to descend the hillock again on to the plain. This was a piece of work which would necessitate wriggling myself down a steep incline, head first, and promised to be a most unpleasant experience.

Once on the flat I lay still to recover my wind, and then taking advantage of every tuft and stone, began to approach my quarry. At the end of three-quarters of an hour's hard work, counting from the time I had first seen them, I was near enough to get a shot, and accordingly I took a cartridge from my pocket and slipped it into the breech of the rifle. As I did so my elbow overturned a large stone, which rolled down into the ravine; instantly half a dozen of the herd lifted their heads, including my old friend the big buck, who on nearer approach, turned out to be a really magnificent animal.

Knowing that if their suspicions were once thoroughly aroused they would not stop until they had put miles between us, I sighted for five hundred yards and fired. The buck leaped into the air and fell on his knees. I thought I had got him, and was going to jump up and run towards him, when I saw that I was counting my chickens before they were hatched. He had certainly fallen, but a second later he was on his feet again and off after the others. I was certain, however, that I had wounded him, and pretty severely, too.

My belief proved to be a correct one, for about a hundred yards further on he fell again, and seeing this I picked up my rifle and ran after him. But even now he was not done for, for after laying still a moment he rose to his feet again and hobbled into the jungle on the other side of the plain, at the same spot where the rest of the herd had disappeared. I followed as swiftly as I could, and, when I had gained the cover, descried him lying upon the ground near the edge of a deep but dry water-course. Needless to say I did not lose very much time in coming up with him, taking the precaution to load my rifle as I went. When I did I was able to appreciate the majesty of my kill.

He must have been about three years old, and when I saw that he was not quite dead, I drew my hunting-knife and knelt down beside him to bestow the *coup de grace.* This done, I wiped my knife on the grass, and was preparing to rise again when I felt a heavy hand laid upon my shoulder. Knowing that there was not a soul within five miles of me, my surprise may be better imagined than described. But it was nothing to the terror that seized me when I looked round to discover who my friend really was.

Standing behind me, and seeming to fill the whole universe, was an enormous orang-outang—the largest I have ever seen or heard of. His wicked eyes gleamed down at me, his teeth protruded ferociously from beneath his bluey gums, while his great hairy arms, more powerful than any coal-heaver's, were opened as if to embrace me. I looked once, and then—how I managed it I shall never be able to tell—wriggled myself out of his clutches like an eel, and, leaving my gun behind me, took to my heels. But before I had proceeded ten yards the great beast was after me, rolling from side to side in his stride like a drunken sailor on a pavement. So close was he behind me that it seemed as if I could almost feel his breath upon the short hair of my poll. One thing is very certain—I ran then as I had never run in my life before, and as I shall probably never run again. Hardly conscious where I was going, knowing only that I must get out of his reach, I fled across the open space with the intention of making for the plain where I had stalked my deer; but the ape headed me off, and would have caught me had I not stopped at a tree and dodged quickly round it. Then back I went in the direction I had just come, making this time for the opposite jungle. But once more he headed me off and drove me back on my tracks. My agony was intolerable, my breath was almost spent, and I had begun to give myself up for lost, when I espied a tree on the further side, with a branch close to the ground. Putting forth a new effort I made for this, dodged round it, and, once on the other side, swung myself into it with, I flatter myself, as much dexterity as the most accomplished gymnast could have shown. In that instant I seemed to live my whole life over again. All the events of my career, even those connected with my earliest childhood, flashed through my brain. But the activity of my thoughts did not detract from the quickness of my legs, and I mounted the tree as fast as I could go. No sailor could have climbed a mast in better style. Then down I crouched amid the branches. Through the leaves I could see my tormentor standing looking stupidly about him, puzzled to know what had become of me. Presently a trembling of the leafy canopy above him must have attracted his attention, for he clutched the lowest bough and began to mount the tree in search of me. Seeing this, I was at a loss to know what to do. To climb higher would only be to cut off all chance of retreat, and would inevitably mean capture or a leap which would, in all human probability, break my neck. In the space of a second I reasoned it all out, and as he approached on one side I descended on the other. Seeing this he descended too, and with such amazing rapidity that, although I had a considerable start, we both landed on the ground at the same instant. Then the old game of catch-who-catch-can commenced. First I dodged this way, then I dodged that, but my dexterity was as useless as it was desperate. He was evidently well accustomed to the sport, and I felt, with despair, that another five minutes would certainly see the end of my career unless something unexpected intervened to prevent it.

Having tried the north, south, and east sides of the plain I now went for the west ; that is to say, towards the dry river bed I have already mentioned. By the time I reached it I was completely done for, and the shock of discovering at least a sixty-foot jump on to the big stones at the bottom did not give me any additional strength. To jump would mean almost certain mutilation, and possibly, if not probably, a long lingering death ; while to remain where I was, and be caught by my horrible pursuer, who had now hemmed me in and had got me at his mercy, meant *certain* death. There was one consolation, however; in those great arms— death, if it would be nothing else, would be swift. I stood on the very edge of the precipice, revolving these two fates in my mind, and every moment my assailant was coming nearer. There was no hope for it now, so I closed my eyes and waited. As I did so, I could hear the thud-thud of his steps drawing closer. I almost felt the arms entwine me. Then a voice I should have recognized in the roar of battle or in the silence of the grave called to me frantically, " Spring to your right ! " As if by instinct I sprang, and, at the very second that I did so, I heard the great loathsome beast go by me. Even at that moment, when life and death trembled in the balance, my curiosity got the upper hand and I opened my eyes and looked.

A wonderful sight it was that I beheld. On the edge of the ravine, swaying to and fro to recover his balance, stood the orang-outang, and at his feet, crouched ready for a spring, was the bulldog Beelzebub, his teeth bared, and his whole body quivering with rage. A second later he leapt into the air, and then a desperate battle

9

ensued. The terrified monkey fought with all the courage he possessed, but the dog had got him firmly by the throat and was holding on with all the dread tenacity of his breed. Added to this, it must be remembered that the orang-outang had to preserve his balance on the edge. Without thinking of my own peril I stood and watched the fight.

Then I heard the same voice, this time steady as of old, order the dog to let go. With his usual obedience he did as he was commanded, and crawled out of reach. The great mass above him stood for a moment bewildered, blood spurting from either side of his throat. Then a rifle cracked, and, with a cry like a soul in torment, the beast fell forward on to the ground, shot through the heart.

I waited for a moment, and then, seeing that he was dead, looked towards the spot by the tree where, a moment before, Alie had stood. She was not there. Then a bit of white skirt caught my eye among the bracken, and, running across, I found her stretched out upon the ground, unconscious.

To fly to a pool close by, to dip my cap into the water, and return with it to her side was only the work of an instant. In three or four minutes I had brought her back to consciousness, and she was able to sit up.

"You are safe?" she gasped, as soon as she could speak. "You are quite sure you are not hurt? I thought that dreadful beast had caught you."

A shudder passed over her as she spoke, and she threw her little hands up and covered her face with them. I assured her as emphatically as I was able that, so far as

I knew, I was without even as much as a scratch, and then we went across the little plain to where the ugly brute lay dead.

It was with a curious feeling that I stood and looked down upon that great mass of inanimate flesh and reflected how near he had been to terminating my own existence. From a contemplation of his ugliness I turned to the dog, who, at his mistress' command, had saved my life. Two ugly red gashes seamed his sides, and these I could only suppose had been made by the talons of the ape.

"Old man," I said to him, as I stooped and patted his ugly head, "you and I will have to be better friends than ever after this. You have saved my life to-day and I am grateful to you." Then turning to his mistress I continued, "Alie, how on earth did you manage to come up just in the nick of time, like that?"

"I heard your first shot," she answered, "and thought I would follow you. Thank Heaven I did, for if I had been five minutes longer on the road I should have been too late. Now we must be getting back to the camp as fast as we can go. Breakfast will be ready, I expect, and at twelve I want to send a messenger back to the settlement with letters."

Accordingly we set off at a good pace on our return, reaching the huts in something under three-quarters of an hour.

As we approached the plateau we saw a man on horseback enter it from the jungle on the other side. He pulled up before the dining-hut, and then I saw that it was my old friend Walworth, covered with dust and showing all the signs of having ridden in great haste. On seeing Alie he dismounted and removed his helmet, waiting respectfully for her to speak.

"Have you bad news, Mr. Walworth," she said, "that you come in such haste?"

"I have a letter for your consideration that is of the utmost importance," he answered; "the junk arrived with it this morning."

I must here explain that communications from the outside world were conveyed by well-chosen messengers once every month to a certain spot in the group of islands, about two degrees west of the settlement. Thence they were brought on to their destination by a swift-sailing junk, the property of the Beautiful White Devil, which had already conveyed and handed over the outward mail in exchange. Thus a regular service was kept up, to the advantage of both parties.

Taking the letter from Walworth's hand she gave him an invitation to breakfast, and then passed with it into her own hut. I took him to mine, and when the gong sounded for the meal we sought the dining saloon together. A moment later Alie joined us, and I gathered from her face that there was something serious toward. Until the meal was finished, however, she said nothing. Then, suggesting that we should bring our cigars outside, so as to be away from any possible eavesdroppers, she intimated that she had something important to tell us. We accordingly rose and followed her into the open air, across the plateau to the glade in the jungle where I had told her of my love the previous day. Throughout the walk she did not speak, and when she turned and bade us be seated, her face was as hard set as when she had sentenced Kwong

Fung to death in her verandah more than two months before.

"Gentlemen," she said, "I have brought you out here in order that I may consult you on a most important matter. Dr. De Normanville, before I begin I may say that I have had an excellent opportunity of studying your character, while you have had an equal chance of studying mine. You know now exactly what my life is, but at the same time I cannot keep from myself a remembrance of the fact that you are only here as a visitor; if you wish therefore to withdraw before you hear any more I will give you free permission to do so. On the other hand, if you will give me your advice, I assure you I shall be most grateful for it. You, Mr. Walworth, have been my trusted and faithful servant for many years past, and I could not have a better. Doctor, I await your decision."

She looked fixedly at me, and I began to see the reason of her speech.

"I beg that you will let me advise you," I answered promptly. "I think you know that you can place implicit trust in me?"

"I am quite sure of that," she answered solemnly, and, as she said it, she took from her pocket the letter she had that morning received.

"This communication," she began, "is from a person in Singapore, whose word I have the very best of all possible reasons for being able to trust. He tells me that my own confidential agent in that place, a man in whom I have hitherto placed the most implicit confidence, whom I have saved from ruin, and worse, who owes his very life to my generosity, contemplates selling me to the English authorities. My correspondent, who holds a high position in the Straits Settlements, informs me that this dastardly traitor has already hinted to the authorities that it is in his power to disclose my long-sought rendezvous. He only stipulates that, seeing the nature of his communication, and the dangerous position in which he stands regarding me, the reward offered shall be doubled. The authorities, of whom my informant is one, have asked him to wait until the arrival of the new English admiral, who is expected in Singapore, *en route* for Hong Kong, early next month. As soon as he arrives this man's evidence will be taken and decisive measures adopted to rid the world of the notorious White Devil."

"The traitor—the scoundrel—he shall pay for this!" came from between Walworth's clenched teeth. I said nothing. But perhaps I was like the owl, and thought the more. At any rate I told myself under my breath that it would be an exceedingly bad day for the man if he ever fell into my hands, and, after a glance at Alie's face, I thought it would be a worse one for him should he fall into hers. She resumed the conversation.

"There is one point I may count in my favour, however," she said; "and that is, he will be hardly likely to reveal the fact that for the last five years he has acted as my agent, and for that reason it will be only possible for him to give his evidence on hearsay."

"He must be prevented from giving it at all," cried Walworth, looking swiftly up at her.

"But how?" she answered.

"A warning would be of no avail, I presume?" I said.

"Not the least," she answered; "even if he took it I should always be in danger of him. In that case I should have to discharge him, and his very life would be a continual menace to me!"

"Is he a married man?"

"No; he is not."

"Has he an extensive business? I mean by that, would his death or departure be the means of bringing misery upon other people?"

"He has no occupation at all, save what I have given him. No. He has idled away his life on the bounty I have paid him for keeping me informed of all that goes on."

"And now he is going to kill the goose that lays the golden eggs? The man must be mad to contemplate such an act of folly."

"There is a method in his madness, though," she answered. "He evidently believes I am on the eve of being captured, and as the reward is a large one, he wishes to secure it before it is snapped up by anybody else."

I thought for a little while and then spoke again.

"You say he is unmarried; in that case he has no wife or children to consider. He has no business—then he cannot bring ruin upon a trusting public. I should say abduct him before he can do any harm. Surely it could be managed with a little ingenuity?"

Alie was silent for a few moments. Then she looked up and her face brightened.

"I believe you have hit on the very idea," she said. "I will think it over, and, if possible, it shall be carried into effect. Yes, I will abduct him, and bring him here. But we must remember that he has always been most suspicious, and he will be doubly so now. For every reason it is impossible for me to go into Singapore and abduct him in my own proper person, so I must do it in disguise."

"No!" I answered promptly; "you must not run such a risk. Supposing he should recognise you?"

"He has never seen me in his life," she replied; then, smiling, she continued, "And you have evidently not yet grasped my talent for disguising myself."

"But somebody must accompany you," said Walworth, who all this time had been turning my scheme over and over in his mind; "and the worst part of it is, he knows me so well that I dare not go."

Long before this I had made up my mind.

"I think, since you have honoured me with your confidence," I said, turning to Alie, "I have a right to ask a favour at your hands."

She looked at me with a little surprise.

"And what is that favour, Dr. De Normanville?" she asked.

"That in whatever you are going to do you will let me help you. No; I am not making this offer without thought, I assure you. It is my greatest wish to be of any service I can to you."

I saw Walworth look at me in rather a peculiar fashion, but whatever he may have thought he kept to himself. Alie paused before replying, then she stretched out her little hand to me.

"I accept your offer in the spirit in which it is made," she said. "I *will* ask you to help me to get this traitor out of the way. Now we must consider the *modus operandi*."

Many and various were the schemes proposed, discussed, and eventually thrown aside. Indeed, it was not until nearly midday that we had decided on one to our liking. Once this was settled, however, we returned to the camp. Orders for starting were immediately given, and, by the time lunch was over, the packs were made up, the loads distributed, the ponies saddled, and we were ready to start upon our return journey to the settlement.

It was a long and tedious ride, and it was far into the night before we arrived at our destination. But late though it was, no one thought of bed. Too much important business had to be transacted before daylight.

On arrival, we repaired instantly to the bungalow on the hill, where a hasty supper was eaten, and an adjournment made from the dining-room to the large chart-room at the rear of the house. In this apartment were stored the latest Admiralty charts of all the seas and harbours in the world, and it was here, as I gathered later, that the Beautiful White Devil concocted the most cunning and audacious of her plans. Arriving in it, she bade us seat ourselves while she gave us the details of the plan she had prepared.

"I have come to the conclusion," she said, "that your scheme is an excellent one, Dr. De Normanville, and I have arranged it all as follows : We will proceed in the yacht to-morrow morning (I have already sent the necessary instructions down to the harbour) to Java. In Batavia we shall meet a young English doctor named De Normanville, who will accompany me to Singapore. I shall remain with a companion in that place for a short time while I do the sights, stopping at the Mandalay

Hotel, where the man resides whom we want to catch. You will gradually make his acquaintance, and, having done so, introduce him to me. All the rest will be plain sailing. Do you think my scheme will do?"

"Admirably, I should say."

"It will be necessary, however, Dr. De Normanville, that you should remember one thing: you must not, for your own sake, be seen about too much with me. You are just to be a casual acquaintance whom I have picked up while travelling between Singapore and Batavia. Do you understand? After your great kindness, I cannot allow you to be implicated in any trouble that may arise from what I may be compelled to do."

"Pray do not fear for my safety," I answered. "I am content to chance that. In for a penny, in for a pound. Believe me, I am throwing my lot in with you with my eyes open. I hope you understand that very thoroughly?"

"I am perfectly sensible, you may be sure, of the debt we are under to you," she answered. "Now we must get to business, for there is much to be done before daylight."

Accordingly we set to work perfecting all the ins and outs of our plan, and when it was completed, and my bags were packed and despatched to the harbour, the stars were paling in the eastern heavens preparatory to dawn.

Walworth had preceded us to the yacht some time before, and nothing remained now but for me to follow with Alie and the bulldog.

A boat was waiting for us at the same jetty on which I had landed on my arrival nearly three months before, and in it we were rowed out to the *Lone Star*, whose outline we could just discern. It was an uncanny hour to embark, and my feelings were quite in keeping with the situation. I was saying good-bye to a place for which I had developed a sincere affection, and I was going out into the world again to do a deed which might end in cutting me off from my profession, my former associates, and even my one remaining relation. These thoughts sat heavily upon me as I mounted the ladder, but when, on reaching the deck, Alie turned and took my hand and gave me a welcome back to the yacht, they were dispelled for good and all.

Side by side we went aft. Steam was up, the anchor was off the ground, and five minutes later, in the fast increasing light, we were moving slowly across the harbour towards what looked to me like impenetrable cliffs. When we got closer to them, however, I saw that one projected further than the other, and that between the two was a long opening, the cliffs on either side being nearly a hundred and fifty feet high. This opening was just wide enough to let a vessel pass through with the exercise of extreme caution.

At the further end of this precipitous canal the width was barely sufficient to let our vessel out, though at that particular point the cliffs on either side were scarcely more than eighty feet high. Here, lying flat against the walls of stone, were two enormous, and very curious, gates, the use of which I could not at all determine.

We passed through and out into the sea. By the time we reached open water daylight had increased to such an extent that, when we were a mile out, objects ashore could be quite plainly distinguished.

"Look astern," said Alie, who stood by my side upon the bridge, "and tell me if you can discover the entrance to the harbour."

I did so, but though I looked, and looked, and even brought a glass to bear upon the cliffs, I could see no break in the line through which a vessel of any size might pass.

"No!" I said at last, "I must confess I cannot see it."

"Now you will understand," she said, smiling at my bewilderment, "the meaning of those great doors. On the seaward side they are painted to resemble the cliffs. Could anyone wish for a better disguise?"

I agreed that no one could. And, indeed, it was most wonderful. A man-of-war might have patrolled that seemingly barren coast for weeks on end and still have been unaware of the harbour that lay concealed behind.

"Now you will want to rest, I know," she said. "I think you will find your old cabin prepared for you."

"And you?"

"I am going below too. Look, the coast is fast disappearing from our sight. There it goes beneath the horizon. Now will you wish our enterprise good luck?"

"Good luck," I said, with a little squeeze of her hand.

"Thank you, and may God bless you," she answered softly, and immediately vanished down the companion-ladder.

CHAPTER VIII.

A QUEER SURPRISE.

Within a week of our leaving the island behind us, as narrated in the previous chapter, we had brought the Madura coast well abeam, and were dodging along it waiting for darkness to fall in order to get into Probolingo Harbour. Here it was arranged I should leave the yacht and travel by the Nederlands-India line of steamers to Batavia. A vessel of this line, so we had discovered, called at Probolingo about the end of each month, and for this reason our arrival was timed for the afternoon of the day of her departure.

Shortly before three o'clock we brought up at the anchorage, about a mile from the shore. It was a lovely afternoon, and I could see that the steamer, which was to carry me on, was already preparing for her departure. The boat was alongside, my traps were safely stowed in her, and nothing remained but to bid Alie good-bye. As soon as this was accomplished I went down the gangway, took my seat in the stern, and we pushed off. Ten minutes later I was on board the steamer *Van Tromp*, had paid my passage-money, secured my berth, and was waiting to see what the next item of the programme would be.

From the deck of the Dutch vessel, as she swept by us under full sail, her course set for Batavia, the *Lone Star* looked as pretty a craft as any man could wish to see. I noticed, however, that during the three months she had been in her own harbour her colour, and indeed her whole appearance, had been entirely changed. When first I had made her acquaintance she was white as the driven snow; now she was a peculiar shade of red. Her bows seemed bluffer than when I had seen her last, indeed from the present shape and construction of her masts and gear it would have been extremely difficult to tell her for the same vessel.

At six o'clock, and in the eye of a glorious sunset, we got up our pressure and steamed out to sea. Of that voyage there is little to tell. The *Van Tromp* was a clumsy old tub of an almost obsolete pattern, and by the time we reached Tanjong Priok, as the seaport of Batavia is called, I had had about enough of her.

Once there, I repacked my bag and stepped on to the wharf, resolved to take the first train to the city. Arriving there I drove direct to the hotel whose name Alie had given me and booked my room.

Batavia is a pretty place, and at the time of our visit was looking its best. So far I had seen nothing of Alie, and I did not like to make inquiries concerning her lest by so doing I might excite suspicion. To while away the time till dinner I lit a cigar, and seating myself in the long verandah that surrounded the house, read my book, keeping a watchful eye on the folk about me all the time.

Shortly before five o'clock, I noticed that the Dutch ladies in my neighbourhood ordered afternoon tea, and partook of it in the verandah. Not to be outdone, I followed their example. But just as I was about to pour myself out a cup an interruption occurred which presently assumed annoying proportions.

The table, on which my Malay boy had placed the tray, stood in the full glare of the afternoon sun, and this being hotter than I liked, I bade him move it nearer to the wall, and to facilitate matters, myself took up the tray on which my cup stood, brimming full. Just as he was putting the table down, however, two strange ladies turned the corner of the verandah and came towards us. The taller, and younger of the two, was a fine dark woman, with a wealth of beautiful brown hair rolled tightly behind her head. She was dressed in a well-fitting travelling dress, wore, what I· believe is called, a sailor hat, and walked with a carriage that would have even attracted attention in the most crowded street in the world. Her companion was an older woman, and, if one might judge by appearances, nearer sixty than fifty, with a fine, aristocratic face, and a considerable quantity of grey hair heaped in little corkscrew curls all over her head.

When they came level with where I stood, I stepped back to let them pass, but in doing so came into collision with the younger lady. How it happened I cannot say, but the result was in every way disastrous; the tray slipped, and would have fallen had I not caught it in time, but the cup of tea was too quick for me, and fell to the ground, splashing the young lady's pretty grey dress beyond hope of remedy in its descent. The cup and saucer were broken into a hundred pieces. For a moment the fair sufferer stood silent, hardly, I suppose, knowing what to say; but when I commenced my apologies and wanted to run to my room for a cloth with which to wipe her dress, she found her voice, and said with a strong American accent—

"You must do nothing of the kind. It was all my fault. I declare I'm downright sorry."

It would have been one of the prettiest voices I had ever heard but for the Yankee twang that spoiled it. I hastened to assure her that I could not let her take the blame upon herself, and once more begged to be allowed to sponge the tea off her dress. This, however, she would not permit me to do.

"It won't hurt," she assured me for the twentieth time, "and if it did, it's an old dress, so don't bother yourself. But now, look here, you've been deprived of your tea, and that's not fair at all. Say, won't you come right along to our verandah and take a cup with us? You're English, I know, and it's real nice to have somebody who speaks our own tongue to talk to. Promise ' Yes ' right away and we'll be off."

There was something so frank about her that, though I didn't at all want to go, I could not resist her. So putting the remnants of the cup and saucer back upon the tray I accepted the invitation and accompanied them round the hotel garden to their own verandah on the other side. As I went I kept my eyes open for any sign of Alie, but though I thought I saw her once I presently found I was mistaken. I could not help wondering what she would think if she met me in this girl's company. However, as I had let myself in for it I had nobody to thank but myself.

When we reached the ladies' quarters we found tea prepared. Before we sat down, however, the

younger lady said, without a shadow of embarrass-
ment—

"I reckon, before we begin, we'd better do a little introducing, don't you? This lady (she pointed to her companion) is my very kind friend Mrs. Beecher, of Boston,
with whom I am travelling; you've probably heard of
Beecher's patent double-action sofa springs, I reckon? I
am Kate Sanderson, of New York, only daughter of million-
aire Sanderson, of Wall Street, whom I guess you've heard
all about too. So you see we're both of the United States
of America, and very much at your service."

"I am very glad to have met you," I answered. "My
name is De Normanville, and I hail from London."

"Not Dr. De Normanville, of Cavendish Square,
surely?"

"Yes, the same. Cavendish Square was my London
address two years ago. But how do you come to know
it?"

"Well, now, if that isn't real extraordinary! I thought
I recognised you directly I set eyes on you. But it's
mighty plain you don't remember me! That's not much
of a compliment any way you look at it. Is it, Mrs.
Beecher?"

The elder declined to commit herself, so Miss Sanderson
once more turned to me.

"Just think now, Dr. De Normanville," she said.
"Look at me well, and try to remember where we have
met before."

I looked and looked, but for the life of me I could not
recall her face, and yet somehow it seemed strangely
familiar to me. All the time I was watching her she sat
gazing at me with an amused smile upon her face, and

10

when she saw that it was useless my cudgelling my brains any more, gave another little silvery laugh, and said—

"Do you remember, just three years ago, being called in to the Langham Hotel to attend a young American lady who had a fish-bone stuck in her throat?"

"I remember the circumstance perfectly," I answered, but that young lady was only one or two and twenty."

"You think then I look older than that? Well! I reckon you are really not very complimentary. But you must remember that that was three years ago, and I was only a girl then. When once we get grown up, and past a certain point, over on our side, we age pretty fast. That's so, I reckon. Well now you know me, don't you? What a day that was, to be sure, wasn't it? Lor! how pap and mammie did go on! Anybody'd have thought I was going to Kingdom Come right away to have heard them. D'you know, I reckon I must have got the marks of that bone in my throat to this day."

"It was a very nasty scratch, if I remember rightly," I answered, glad to have at last discovered who this talkative creature was, and where I had seen her face before.

"Are you remaining very long in Java, Mrs. Beecher?" I asked the elder lady, feeling that so far she had been rather neglected.

"No, I think not," she answered thoughtfully; "we are trying to make up our minds whether to take a British India steamer home from here, or to go up to Singapore and intercept a Peninsular and Oriental there. Miss Sanderson has taken a great fancy to the East, and I must confess I am very loth to leave it."

"You are quite right," I said. "I can fully sympathise

with your feelings. I am sadly reluctant to go back to foggy old England myself, after my trip out here."

" And do you intend going back very soon ?" asked Miss Sanderson, who had been smoothing out her gloves upon her knee.

" Within the next month or so," I answered, with a sigh. " My business in the East is at an end, and I have no excuse for staying longer."

From this point the talk drifted on to general topics, and when tea was finished I seized the first opportunity that presented itself, and, making an excuse, withdrew. Just as I stepped from the verandah, one of the small native *dos-a-dos* carts entered the grounds and drew up near the end of my corridor. Two ladies descended from it, and, having paid the driver, entered their rooms. One was tall, and the other rather shorter. At last I felt convinced Alie had arrived.

As they disappeared the gong warned us to prepare for dinner ; but, heedless of my costume, I seated myself outside my door and waited. Though I remained there for some time, however, they did not emerge again, and at last I was compelled to go in and make myself present-able without having seen them.

At dinner, which was served in the palatial marble dining saloon standing in the centre of the gardens, I discovered to my annoyance that my place was laid at a long table at the further end, exactly opposite those occupied by the American ladies with whom I had taken tea.

From where I sat it was quite impossible for me to see all over the room, and, in consequence, I could not tell whether Alie was present or not. As soon, however, as the meal was over I rose, and, before walking out, looked about me. Some of the residents were still dining, and at the end of the middle table, farthest from me, were, without doubt, the two ladies whom I had seen arrive. At the distance I was from them it was quite impossible to tell who they were, but from the poise of her head and the shape of her beautiful arms and shoulders, I felt convinced that the taller of the two was the woman I loved, and whom I had all the afternoon been so anxiously expecting.

Seeing, however, that it was just possible I might be mistaken, and remembering the instruction Alie had given me to let our meeting appear accidental, I could not walk down the length of the room and accost her, so I betook myself into the marble portico and waited for them to come out. But, as it happened, Miss Sanderson and her friend were the first to emerge, and the voluble young American took me by storm at once. From what she told me I gathered two things, first, that hitherto she had found her evenings dull, and, second, that on this particular occasion there was to be an open-air concert on the King's Plain, distant about a mile from the hotel. She and her friend had intended going, if they could find an escort, and there and then she asked me if I would officiate in that capacity. I did not know what to say. They were women, and I could not be rude; and, moreover as they had evidently set their hearts upon going, and I was not positively certain that Alie had arrived, I felt I had no right to decline the honour of escorting them. Accordingly I assented, and went across the garden to get my hat. Five minutes later they met me at the gates, and we strolled down the road together towards the plain.

There are few prettier places in the world than Batavia, and I have met with few handsomer girls than the distinguished-looking American by my side; but for all that I was not contented with my lot. I wanted to be back in the verandah at the hotel watching for Alic.

Leaving a handsome street behind us we passed on to the plain, where a large crowd of people were promenading to the strains of a military band. At any other time the music would have been inspiriting. but, in the humour I was in, the gayest marches sounded like funeral dirges. For over an hour wo continued to promenade, until I began really to think that I should have to ask my friends to accompany me home or remain where they were without me. But at last the concert came to an end, and we once more turned our faces in the direction of our hotel.

"You have been very quiet this evening," said Miss Sanderson to me as we left the turf and stepped on to the road again.

"I hope my being so has not spoilt your enjoyment," I said, trying to beg the question.

"Oh, dear no!" Then, as if something had suddenly struck her, "Do you expect to see anyone in Batavia? I have noticed that you scan every lady wo pass as if you were on the look-out for an acquaintance."

"I *did* expect to see someone, I must confess," I answered. "You have sharp eyes, Miss Sanderson."

"They have been trained in a sharp school," was her brief reply.

By this time we were within five minutes walk of home, and in the act of crossing one of the numerous bridges that, in Dutch fashion, grace Batavia's streets. We paused for a few moments and leaned over the parapet to look down at the star-spangled water oozing its silent way towards the sea. It was all very quiet, and as far as we could see we had the street to ourselves. Suddenly Miss Sanderson dropped her American accent, and said in quite a different voice—

"Dr. De Normanville, this has gone far enough. Do you know me now?"

It was Alie!

To say that I was taken by surprise would not be to express my condition at all. I was simply overwhelmed with astonishment, and for some seconds could only stand and stare at her in complete amazement. Her disguise was so perfect, her American accent was so real, her acting had been so wonderfully maintained, that I never for an instant suspected the trick she had been playing upon me.

"You! Alie," I cried when at last I found my voice. "Is it possible that Miss Sanderson has been a myth all the time?"

"Not only quite possible, but a fact," she answered, with a laugh. "Yes! I am Alie, and no more Miss Sanderson, of New York, than you are. Do me the justice to remember I warned you I was good at disguising myself. My reason for not revealing my identity to you before was that I wanted thoroughly to test the value of the part I was playing, and since you, who know me so well, did not recognise me, I am inclined to believe nobody else will."

"It is simply marvellous. If you had not declared yourself I should never have known you. And your companion is therefore not Mrs. Beecher, whose husband's patent double-action sofa springs are so justly famous, any more than you are Miss Sanderson?"

" No, both the husband and the sofa springs are creations of my own imagination."

" But the incident you recalled to my memory. The bone in your throat that I extracted at the Langham, how do you account for that ? "

" Easily ! One day in your surgery at the settlement you casually mentioned having extracted a fish bone from a young American lady's throat at that hotel. I thought it unlikely, as it was the only time you ever saw her, that you would remember her name or face, so I assumed that character in order to try the effect of my disguise upon you."

" You are a wonderful actress; you would make your fortune on the stage."

" Do you think so ? What a sensation it would cause in the East. Under the patronage of His Excellency the Governor of Hong Kong, the Admiral and Commander-in-Chief, the Beautiful White Dèvil as Ophelia, or Desdemona shall we say, why, what houses I should draw. But now to business. As we may not have another opportunity, let us see that our plans coincide. By the way, the French boat leaves to-morrow afternoon for Singapore. You have booked your passage, of course ? "

I nodded assent, and she continued—

" You must board her alone. We shall join just before she sails. When we get to Singapore we must drive separately to the Mandalay Hotel, and figure there in the light of casual travelling acquaintances. Before you have been in the place half a day you will probably have been introduced to Mr. Ebbington, the man we want. He will see you talking to me, and by hook or crook you must introduce him to me. Whatever you do, don't forget, however, that my name is Sanderson. Having done this, leave the rest to me. Do you think you thoroughly understand ? "

" Thoroughly."

" That's right. Now let us be getting home. To-morrow we must be early astir."

We continued our walk, and in five minutes had bade each other good-night in the hotel gardens, and separated.

By sundown next day we were on board the Messageries Maritimes Company's boat, steaming out of Tanjong Priok Harbour, bound for Singapore. I joined the steamer some time before her advertised sailing hour, but it was close upon the time of her departure when Alie and her companion made their appearance.

In my capacity of casual acquaintance I raised my hat to them as they came up the gangway, but did not do more. They went below, while I stayed on deck, watching the business of getting under way.

Just as the last sign of the coast line disappeared beneath the waves someone came up and stood beside me. On looking round I discovered that it was Alie !

" So you managed to get on board safely," she said, after the usual polite preliminaries had been gone through. " Our enterprise has now fairly started, and if we have ordinary luck we ought to be able to carry it through successfully."

" Let us hope we *shall* have that luck then," I answered. " But I confess I tremble when I think of the risk you are running in appearing in a place like Singapore, where you have so many enemies."

" Even disguised as Miss Sanderson, the American

heiress? No, you cannot mean it. If you think that, what will you say to another plot I am hatching?"

"Another? Good gracious! and what is this one to be?"

"Listen, and you shall learn. Three years ago, in a certain island of the South Pacific, there was a man—an official holding a high office under Government—who very nearly got into serious trouble. The charge against him was that by his orders two native women had been flogged to death. By some means he managed to disprove it and to escape punishment, but the feeling against him was so bitter that it was thought advisable to transfer him elsewhere. You would have imagined that that lesson would have been enough for him. Not a bit. On the new island he began his reign of tyranny again, and once more a death occurred; this time, however, the victim was a man. The authorities at home were immediately appealed to, with the result that an inquiry was held and his retention on that island was also considered injudicious. He was removed from his high estate. That was all; he had murdered, I repeat it, deliberately murdered three people; in fact, flogged the lives out of two women and one man, and the only sentence passed upon him was that he should be transferred elsewhere. It makes my blood boil to think of it."

"I can quite understand it."

"Yes. That was all, nothing more was done. The man went free. The poor wretches were only natives, you must understand. And who cares about a few natives? No one. You may think I'm exaggerating, but I am not. Now it so happens that I have an agent living on that very island whom I can perfectly trust. He was a witness on the inquiry commission, he saw the flogging in question, and in due course he reported the facts to me. I must also tell you that that man boasted publicly that if he caught me he would—but there, I dare not tell you what he said he would do. Now his friends have used their influence and he has been appointed to a post in one of the treaty ports of China. I hear he is a passenger on the mail boat touching at Singapore next week."

"And what do you intend to do?"

"It is my intention, if possible, to catch him, to punish him as he deserves, and, by so doing, to teach him a lesson he will remember all his life."

CHAPTER IX.

On arrival at Singapore we took rickshaws and drove direct from the wharf to the Mandalay Hotel, a palatial white building of two stories, boasting vivid green shutters on every window, and broad luxurious verandahs on every. floor. I was the first to reach it, and, remembering my position of casual acquaintance, I booked a room for myself, leaving Miss Sanderson and her companion to follow my example when they should arrive.

It was then late in the afternoon, and by the time we had thoroughly settled in night had fallen. and the preliminary dressing gong had sounded for dinner. So far, I had seen nothing of the person of whom we were in search, but I did not doubt that at the evening meal I should become acquainted with his whereabouts, even if I did not actually meet the man himself.

The dining-room at the Mandalay is at the rear of the hotel, and looks out upon a charmingly arranged garden. Immediately upon my entering it a waiter came forward and conducted me to my place at a table near the window. On my left was seated a portly, red-faced gentleman, whom, I discovered later, was an English merchant of considerable standing in the place. The chair on my right was vacant, but before we had dismissed the first course it was taken by a man whom my instinct told me was none other than Mr. Ebbington himself. Why I should have come to this conclusion I cannot explain, but that I did think so, and that I was right in so thinking, I discovered a minute or two later, when a question was addressed to him by an acquaintance on the other side of the table. I continued the course without betraying my excitement, and when my plate was removed, sat back and casually took stock of him.

From Alie's account, and some kind of preconceived notion as to what sort of appearance such a dastardly traitor should present, I had expected to see a small, shifty-eyed, villainous type of man, wearing on his face some token of his guilt. But in place of that I discovered a stout, well set-up, not unhandsome man of about forty years of age. His complexion was somewhat florid ; his eyes were of an uncertain hue, between gray and steely blue ; he had a pronounced nose, and a heavy, almost double, chin. Indeed, had it not been for his hesitating mode of speech, I should have been inclined to put him down for a military man.

During the progress of the meal I found an opportunity of doing him some small service, and on this meagre introduction we fell into a desultory conversation, which embraced Singapore, the latest news from England, and the prospects of a war between China and Japan. When dinner was over I rose and followed him into the verandah, offered him a cheroot, which he accepted, and seated myself in a lounge chair beside him. We had not been smoking five minutes before my sweetheart and her companion passed close to where we sat, *en route* to their rooms. As she came opposite to me, Alie stopped.

"Good-evening, Dr. De Normanville!" she said; "isn't this hotel delightful?"

I rose and uttered an appropriate reply, at the same time noticing that Ebbington was taking thorough stock of her. Then, after another commonplace or two, she bowed and passed on her way. I resumed my seat, and for nearly a minute we smoked in silence. Then my companion, who had evidently been carefully thinking his speech out, said, with that peculiarly diffident utterance which, as I have said, was habitual to him:

"You'll excuse what I am going to say, I hope, but a friend and I were having a little discussion before dinner. The proprietor tells me Miss Sanderson, the American heiress, is staying in the house. I do not wish to be impertinent, but might I ask if the lady to whom you have just been speaking is Miss Sanderson?"

"Yes, she is Miss Sanderson," I replied. "You do not know her, then?"

"Never saw her before in my life," was his reply. "Pieces of good fortune like that don't often occur in Singapore. If they did, few of us would be here very long, I can assure you. But perhaps I am talking in too familiar a strain about your friend? If so, you must forgive me."

"Indeed no!" I answered. "Don't trouble yourself on that score. I travelled up with them from Batavia in the French boat that arrived this afternoon. From what little I have seen of her she seems very pleasant, and, as you may have observed, is evidently inclined to be friendly."

"There is no doubt about the money, I suppose?" he continued. "Since Vesey, of Hong Kong, was so completely taken in by the Beautiful White Devil, we have been a little sceptical on the subject of heiresses down this way."

"On that point, I'm afraid I cannot inform you," I said laughingly. "She seems, however, to travel in very good style, and evidently denies herself nothing. But you spoke of the Beautiful White Devil. I am most interested in what I have heard of that personage. Are you well up in the subject?"

"How should I be?" he answered, as I thought, a little quickly. "Of course I know what every other man in the East knows, but no more. Thank goodness she has never done me the honour of abducting me as she did the Sultan of Surabaya and those other Johnnies. But with regard to Miss Sanderson, I wonder if I should be considered impertinent if I asked you to give me the pleasure of an introduction."

Of course I did not tell him that it was the very thing of all others that I desired to do, but at the same time I could hardly conceal my exultation. I had, however, to keep my delight to myself for fear lest he should suspect; so I relit my cigar, which had gone out, and then said, with as much carelessness as I could assume:

"I don't know altogether whether I'm sufficiently intimate with her to take the liberty of introducing you; but, as I said just now, she seems a jolly sort of girl, and not inclined to be stand-offish, so if ever I get an opportunity I don't mind risking it. Now, I think, if you'll excuse me, I'll say good-night. That wretched old bucket of a steamer rolled so all the way up from Tanjong Priok that I have hardly had a wink of sleep these three nights past."

" Good-night, and thank you very much for your company. Glad to have met you, I'm sure."

I reciprocated, and, having done so, left him and went to my room, where I turned into bed to dream that I had abducted Alie, and could never remember in what part of the world I had hidden her.

Next morning, as soon as breakfast was over, I went down into the town, shopping. When I returned about eleven o'clock I discovered Alie and her chaperone sitting in the verandah, waiting for a double rickshaw which one of the hotel boys had gone out to procure. Ebbington was seated in a chair near by, and evidently seemed to consider this a good opportunity for effecting the introduction he had proposed the night before. I entered into conversation with him for a few moments, and then, crossing the verandah, asked the ladies in which direction they contemplated going.

" Where do you think ? " said Alie, with her best New York accent. " Well, first I guess we're going to look for a dry goods store, and then I reckon we'll just take a *pasear* round the town."

" You should go and see Whampoa's Garden," I said, hoping she would understand what I was driving at. " They tell me it's one of the sights of the place."

" But how do you get there ? " asked Alie, her quick perception telling her my object. " We must know the way, I reckon, before we start, or we'll just get lost, and then you'll have to call out all the town to find us."

" One moment and I'll inquire."

Ebbington, having overheard what had passed between us, as I intended he should do, had risen, and now approached us. I turned to him and said :

"My friends want to find the way to Whampoa's Garden, Mr. Ebbington. Could you direct them? But first, perhaps, I ought to introduce you. Mr. Ebbington—Mrs. Beecher—Miss Sanderson."

They bowed politely to each other, and then Ebbington, having begged the ladies' permission, gave instructions in Malay to the rickshaw coolie, who by this time had drawn up at the steps. Tendering their thanks to him they stepped into their conveyance and were drawn away.

When they had disappeared round the corner, Ebbington crossed the verandah, and sitting down beside me favoured me with his opinions. Even in this short space of time the charm of the heiress seemed to have impressed itself upon him. Though inwardly writhing at the tone he adopted, I had to pretend to be interested. It was a difficult matter, however, and I was more relieved than I can say, when he remembered business elsewhere, and betook himself off to attend to it. So far all had gone well. The bait was fixed, and it would be surprising now if the victim did not walk into the trap so artfully contrived for him.

That evening after dinner I fell into casual conversation with the proprietor of the hotel, and it was not until nearly half an hour later that I managed to escape from him and get into the verandah. When I did, to my surprise, I found the ladies reclining in their chairs listening to the conversation of Mr. Ebbington. He was regaling them with a highly-coloured account of his experiences in the East, and from the attention his remarks were receiving it was evident he was doing ample justice to his subject. I pulled a chair up beside Alie and listened. Within five minutes, however, of my arrival he introduced Mr. Vesey's name, and instantly she stopped him by saying:

"Now, where have I heard that name before? It seems, somehow, to be very familiar to me."

"Perhaps you've heard the story of his abduction by the Beautiful White Devil," said Ebbington, who saw that I was about to speak and was anxious to forestall me.

"No, I guess not," answered Alie. "I reckon I was thinking of Klener W. Vesey, of Wall Street, who operates considerable in pork. But tell me, who is this Beautiful White Devil one hears so much about, anyway?"

There was a pause, but I held my peace and let Ebbington's tongue run riot with him.

"Ah! there you have me at a disadvantage," he began, pluming himself for the big speech I could see was imminent. "Some say she's a European lady of title gone mad on Captain Marryat and Clarke Russell. Others aver that she's not a woman at all, but a man disguised in woman's clothes. But the real truth, I'm inclined to fancy, is that she's the daughter of a drunken old desperado, once an English naval man, who for years made himself a terror in these seas."

When I heard him thus commit himself, I looked across at Alie, half expecting that she would lose control of herself and annihilate him upon the spot. But save a little twitching round the corners of her mouth, she allowed no sign of the wrath that I knew was raging within her breast to escape her. In a voice as steady as when she had inquired the way to Whampoa's Garden that morning, she continued her questions.

11

"I'm really quite interested. And pray what has this, what do you call her, Beautiful White Devil, done to carry on the family reputation?"

Again Ebbington saw his chance, and, like the born yarn-spinner he was, took immediate advantage of it.

"What has she not done would be the best thing to ask. She has abducted the Sultan of Surabaya, the Rajah of Tavoy, Vesey of Hong Kong, and half a dozen Chinese mandarins at least. She has robbed the *Vectis Queen*, the *Ooloomoo*—and that with the Governor of Hong Kong on board; stopped the *Oodnadatta* only three months ago in the Ly-ee-moon Pass, when she went through the bullion-room to the extent of over a million and a half, almost under the cruisers' noses."

"But what mission does she accomplish with this vast wealth when she has accumulated it, do you think, Mr. Ebbington?" said the quiet voice of Mrs. Beecher from the depths of her chair. "Does she do no good with it at all?"

"Good!" that wretched being replied, quite unconscious of the trouble he was heaping up for himself. "Why, she never did a ha'porth of good in her life. No, I'll tell you what she *does* do with it. It is well known that she has a rendezvous somewhere in the Pacific, a tropical island, they say, where scenes are enacted between her cruises that would raise blushes on the cheeks of an Egyptian mummy."

"You are evidently very much prejudiced against her," I answered hotly. "Now *I* have heard some very different stories. And with all due respect to you, Mr. Ebbington——"

But fortunately at this juncture my presence of mind returned to me, and, a servant approaching to take our empty coffee cups, I was able to seize the opportunity and bring my riotous tongue to a halt. When the boy had gone, Alie turned the conversation into another channel, and after that all was plain sailing once more. To add to our enjoyment, about ten o'clock another servant came to inform Mr. Ebbington that a gentleman desired to see him in the smoking-room, and accordingly, bidding us good-night, he went off to interview him. Mrs. Beecher then made an excuse and retired to her room, leaving us alone together.

"Alie," I said reproachfully, "if anything had happened just now you would have had only yourself to blame for it. That man's insolent lying was more than I could stand. In another moment, if that servant had not come in, I believe I should have lost all control of myself, and, ten chances to one, have ruined everything. Why did you do it?"

"Because I wanted to find out how he was in the habit of talking about me. That was why."

"But do you think he was really in earnest? May it not have been only a mask to prevent anyone from suspecting that he is your agent in this place?"

"No. He meant it. Of that there can be no doubt. The man, I can see, for some inscrutable reason hates the real *me* with his whole heart and soul, and the treachery he is preparing now is to be his revenge. Couldn't you hear the change, the grating, in his voice when my name occurred? Ah, Mr. Ebbington, my clever man, you will find that it is a very foolish policy on your part to quarrel with me."

"When do you mean to make the attempt to capture him ? "

"On Friday evening ; that is the day after to-morrow. The new admiral will be here on Saturday morning at latest, and I must anticipate him, for I have learned that Ebbington received a note from the authorities this morning, definitely fixing the hour for the interview at eleven o'clock. He need make no arrangements, however, for he won't be there ! "

"It will be an awful moment for him when he realises who you are. I would not be in his shoes for all the gold of India."

"You would never have acted as he has done," she answered softly, turning her head away.

This was the opportunity for finding out what she intended concerning myself, so I drew a little closer to her.

"Alie," I said, "the time has now come for me to ask you when you wish to say 'good-bye' to me. I have done my professional work for you, and on Friday I shall have assisted you to the very best of my ability in the matter of this wretched fellow. What am I to do then ? Am I to say farewell to you here, or what ?"

Her voice had almost a falter in it as she replied :

"Oh, no ! we will not say 'good-bye' here. Cannot you return with me ? I have been counting so much on that." Here she paused for a moment. "But no ! Perhaps I ought not to ask you—you have your work in life, and, seeing what you have already done for us, I should be the last to keep you from the path of duty."

"If you wish me to come back with you, Alie," I answered quickly, "I will come with a glad heart. I have no duty to consider, and as I have given up my practice, I have no patients to give me any concern. But how shall I get back to England later on ? ”

“ I will arrange that you shall be sent down to Torres Straits, and you can go home via Australia, if that will suit you. Never fear, I will attend to that part of it when it becomes necessary.”

“ Then I will go with you.”

“ I thank you.   Good-night ! ”

I bade her good-night, and she left me to go to her room. As, however, I was in no humour for sleeping myself, I stayed in the verandah, looking down the quaint lamp-lit street, along which only an occasional belated foot passenger, a Sikh policeman or two, and a few tired rickshaw coolies wended their way. I was thinking of the strangeness of my position. When I came to work it out, and to review the whole chain of events dispassionately, it seemed almost incredible. I could hardly believe that George De Normanville the staid medical man, and George De Normanville the lover of the Beautiful White Devil, and assistant in a scheme for abducting one of Singapore's most prominent citizens, were one and the same person. However, I was thoroughly content ; Alie loved me, and I wanted nothing more.

Next morning, after breakfast, I discovered that Miss Sanderson and her companion were setting off for a day's pleasuring, and that Mr. Ebbington was to be their sole conductor and escort. It was noticeable that he had donned a new suit of clothes in honour of the occasion, and I saw that he wore a sprig of japonica in his buttonhole. From his expression I concluded that he was very well satisfied with himself, but whether he would have been quite so confident had he known who his fair friends really were was quite another matter, and one upon which I could only conjecture.

They returned in time for tiffin, and during the meal Ebbington confided to me the fact that the heiress had been most gracious to him. From what he said I gathered that, unless somebody else interfered and spoiled sport, he felt pretty confident of ultimately securing her.

"Take care your friend the Beautiful White Devil, or whatever you call her, doesn't get jealous," I said with a laugh, wishing to get him on to delicate ground in order to see how quickly he would wriggle off it again.

"Don't mention them in the same breath, for goodness' sake," he answered. "Miss Sanderson and that woman—— Why, man alive, they're not to be compared!"

"Ah!" I thought to myself, "if you only knew, my friend, if you only knew!"

"Don't you wish you were in my place?" he said with a smile, as he rose to go.

"No; if you wish me to be candid," I answered, "I cannot say that I do."

He thereupon left me and went out into the verandah. We spent the afternoon with the ladies in the garden, and at their request remained to take tea with them. During this *al fresco* meal, which was presided over by Miss Sanderson herself, my companion stated that it was his desire to arrange something a little out of the common for the ladies' amusement.

" What shall it be ? " he asked, with the magnificence
of an Oriental potentate to whom all things are possible.
" A picnic?   But that is not much fun here.   A dance?
But it's too hot for that.   What would you like ? "

Alic seemed to reflect for a few moments, and then
she said, with an appearance of animation :

" Do you really want to give us a treat, Mr. Ebbington ?   Then I reckon the nicest thing you can possibly
do, on these hot nights, would be to take us for a trip
on the water.   I know Mrs. Beecher thinks so too.
Now, you just get us a launch and trot us round.   I
guess that 'll be real delightful."

She clapped her hands and appeared to be so pleased
with the idea that, whatever he may himself have
thought of it, there was nothing for Ebbington to do but
to assent.

" We'll take some supper," she continued, as if a new
idea had struck her, " and you gentlemen shall bring
your cigars, and we'll spend a delightful evening.   I'm
fonder of the sea than you can think.   But I do just
wish you could see New York Harbour.   You should
see Newport, too, where my papa's got a cottage.   It's
real fine."

After dinner that evening Ebbington reported that he
had engaged a steam launch, and also that he had
ordered the supper.   Thereupon, to encourage him, Miss
Sanderson professed herself to be looking forward to
the trip more than she had ever done to anything else
in her life.

Accordingly next evening, immediately after dinner,
we saw that our charges were carefully wrapped up,
chartered rickshaws, and set off for the harbour.   It

was a lovely night, with a young moon just showing like a silver sickle above the roofs. We were all in the highest spirits, although, I must confess, my own were not unmixed with a slight dash of nervousness as to what the upshot of our excursion would be.

Arriving at the harbour side, we found the launch in waiting. She was a smart, serviceable little craft, manned by two native sailors and an engineer. We descended the wharf steps in single file, and, as I was nearest to her, I stepped on board and gave Alie my hand to assist her to embark. She squeezed it gently, by way of wishing me good luck of our enterprise, sprang aboard, and when we had taken our places aft the order was given and we pushed off.

The harbour was densely crowded with craft of all nationalities and descriptions, and in and out among them we threaded our way, now dodging under the bows of a Messageries Maritime mail boat, now under the stern of a P. and O. steamer, or a Norwegian timber boat, between native praus and dingy ocean tramps, steam launches, and small fry generally, and finally out into the open sea.

Inside the water was as smooth as a mill pond, but when we left the shelter of the high land and passed outside, the complexion of affairs was somewhat altered. But as our party were all good sailors, the tumbling and tossing we endured hardly mattered. For over an hour we steamed up and down, and then, pausing in the shelter of the harbour again, cast about us for a suitable spot to have our supper.

I had noticed all through the evening, and, for the matter of that, throughout the day, that Ebbington's manner towards Alie was every moment growing more unpleasantly familiar. By the time he had completed his first bottle of champagne at supper, it was about as much as I could stand ; indeed, twice he called her by her assumed Christian name, and once he tried to take her hand. Remembering, however, what would follow later, I kept a tight rein upon myself, and did not allow any expression of my feelings to escape me.

"After all, give me American girls," our hero was saying, with an insolent freedom for which I could have kicked him, as he lit his cigar. "There's none of that stand-offishness about them that there is with our English women. You can say more to them without their being offended and wanting to call their fathers in to you."

"You mean, perhaps, that we are more good-natured," said Alie. "I'm afraid, however, we're sometimes un-wise enough to permit people to become familiar on a three days' acquaintance, and that's a very foolish thing."

"Oh, come now, Miss Sanderson," said our host, uncorking another bottle of champagne, filling up Alie's glass, and then helping himself liberally. "I think that's a little severe, isn't it? One thing I know, though, you don't mean it, do you?"

"I am not so certain of that," she replied. "It's just possible that I may be compelled to do so. But let us talk of something else. What a lovely night it is, isn't it? I think this harbour's just delightful by moonlight. Say, Mr. Ebbington, couldn't we come on to-morrow morning for a while, about eleven o'clock. Just to oblige me, don't you think you could man-age it?"

Knowing that eleven was the hour at which he was to see the admiral, I waited to hear what answer he would make. It was easy to see that he was a little nonplussed, for he expressed his sorrow that, through an important business engagement, he would be quite unable to comply with her request, and for some time sat in sulky silence. Just as he was going to speak again, however, we descried a boat pulling across towards us from the wharves on the other side. As it approached the shore Alie signed to me, and, divining her intention, I went down to inquire its errand. The boat having grounded, a native waded ashore, and handed me a large packet and a letter, which I immediately conveyed to Alie. She took it, and then turning to Ebbington, who had been surveying the scene with no small astonishment, said:

"I'm afraid, Mr. Ebbington, this means some business which will necessitate our going back to the hotel at once. Do you mind so very much?"

"Not at all," he answered promptly; then, as if he thought he might turn it to account, continued, "You know that my only ambition is to serve you."

Disregarding this polite speech, which was uttered with a leer that made my fingers itch to be alongside his head, Alie led the way up the plank and on board the launch again. We pushed off from the shore and began to steam ahead. Then Alie nodded to me, and I tapped the engineer on the shoulder and signified that he should stop. He looked surprised, but obeyed. Ebbington, however, did not like this interference on my part, and sprang to his feet.

"Why did you tell that man to stop?" he cried, angrily. "I'll trouble you to remember that I'm——"

"And I'll just trouble you to sit down where you are and hold your tongue, Mr. Ebbington," said Alie, dropping her American accent altogether, and drawing a revolver from beneath her cloak. "The game is over as far as you are concerned, so you may as well submit with as good a grace as possible."

"What does this mean, Miss Sanderson?" he cried excitedly.

"Sit down there, as I tell you," she answered, "and don't make any noise, or you'll get into trouble. I shall answer no questions, but if you attempt to move I promise you I'll shoot you there and then."

He said no more, but sat between us trembling like the arrant coward he was. Alie went forward to the engineer and said something in Malay; then, after a moment's conversation with one of the crew, she returned aft, took the tiller, and steered for the open sea. The little craft fumed and fussed on her way for an hour or so, tossing the foam off either bow, and covering the distance in first-rate style.

Suddenly the look-out, posted forrard, uttered a cry, and next moment we saw ahead of us a green light. It was obscured and revealed three times. This, I knew, was the yacht's signal, and in less than a quarter of an hour we were alongside, had hitched on, and were safely aboard. The launch's crew were then suitably rewarded and sent back to Singapore.

As we reached the deck Ebbington must have read the yacht's name on a life-buoy, and realised into whose hands he had fallen. For a moment he stood rooted to the spot, then he staggered a pace forward, clutched at a stay, and, missing it, fell upon the deck in a dead faint. As I stooped to see what was the matter with him I felt the tremor of the screw. Our errand was accomplished. Singapore was a thing of the past. We were on our way back to the island once more.

CHAPTER X.

RETRIBUTION.

AFTER the exciting events in which I had been a participator that evening, it may not be a matter for surprise that, on going to bed, my night was a troubled one. Hour after hour I tumbled and tossed in my bunk, and with the first sign of day, finding sleep still impossible, dressed and went on deck. It was as lovely a morning as any man could wish to see, with a pale turquoise sky overhead, across which clouds of fleecy whiteness sped with extraordinary rapidity. A fine breeze hummed in the shrouds, and the peculiar motion of the schooner, combined with one glance over the side, was sufficient to convince me that a brisk sea was running. I walked aft, said "Good-morning!" to the officer of the watch, who was the same taciturn individual, with the scar upon his face, I have described earlier in the story, and then, partly from curiosity and partly from force of habit, took a squint at the compass card. Our course was N. N. E. exactly, but as I did not know whether or not this was a bluff of some kind, such a circumstance told me but little. I therefore leaned against the taffrail, looked up at the canvas, bellying out like great balloons above my head, and resigned myself to my thoughts. It had an exhilarating, yet for some reason bewildering, effect upon me, that stretch of canvas standing out so white against the clear blue sky, the chasing clouds, the bright sunshine, the dancing, rolling sea, and the splashing of the water alongside. The schooner was evidently in a playful mood, for one moment she would be aiming her jib-boom at the sun and the next be dipping her nose down into the trough and sending a shower of spray rattling on the fo'c's'le like hail. Not a sail was in sight, though it was evident from the presence of a lookout in the fore-top, and the constant scrutiny of the south-western horizon maintained by the officer of the watch, that one was momentarily expected.

I had seen nothing of Alie since I had said good-night to her the previous evening, nor did I receive an invitation to visit her until breakfast had been over some time. Then Walworth entered my cabin.

"Her ladyship," he said, taking a seat on my locker, "has sent me to say that she would be glad to see you aft, if you could spare a few moments. Before you go, I want to explain the situation to you. The matter on hand, as you may guess, is the case of that scoundrel Ebbington, and, as he will be present, she thinks it best that a little precaution should be observed."

"In what way do you mean?" I answered. "Of course I am ready to do anything she may wish, but I'd like to have my instructions clearly explained to me first."

"Well, I have been commissioned to inform you that she thinks it would be better, in case of accident, that Ebbington should suppose she has abducted you as well as himself. That is to say, instead of being her guest on board the schooner, you are her prisoner. Do you understand?"

"Perfectly! She is afraid lest any harm should

occur to me, when I leave her yacht, by reason of my association with her! It is like her thoughtfulness."

"Shall we go?"

I signified my assent, and we set off.

When we reached Alie's cabin, we found her reclining on a couch at the further end, the bulldog, as usual, at her feet. She held a packet of papers in her hand which, previous to our arrival, it was evident she had been perusing. At the other end, near the companion-ladder, but on the starboard side, between two sailors, stood the prisoner, Ebbington. He looked, as well he might, hopelessly miserable. He opened his eyes in astonishment when he saw me enter. I, however, crossed the cabin with Walworth and stood on the port side without letting him see that I recognised him. Then solemn silence fell upon us all for nearly a minute. While it lasted Alie sat with her chin on her hand staring steadfastly at Ebbington. Under her gaze, he lowered his eyes, and when I noticed that his fingers twined convulsively over and round each other, I could imagine the state of his mind. The fellow was plainly as frightened as it was possible for him to be. Then Alie lifted her head and spoke in a voice as soft as a kitten's purr.

"Mr. Ebbington," she said, "do you know me?"

He did not answer, but I saw the first finger and thumb of his right hand clutch at his trouser leg and hold it tight. That action was more significant than any words. Again she spoke:

"Mr. Ebbington," she said, "my trusted servant, my faithful friend, my honourable agent, I ask you again, do you know me?"

Once more he refused to answer.

"You seem undecided. Well, then, let me trespass upon your time and tell you a little story, which will, perhaps, help you to remember. You may listen, Dr. De Normanville, if you please. You must know, Mr. Ebbington, that once upon a time there was a woman, who, for no fault of her own, found herself at enmity with the world. She had necessarily to be continually moving from place to place, and to be always on her guard against betrayal. The better, therefore, to conduct her business, she engaged a man to reside in a certain place and to supply her, from time to time, with certain important information. The man was poor, she made him rich ; he had nothing, she gave him everything ; he was despised, she made him honoured ; he was in trouble, she saved him, not once, but twice, and made him happy. You, Mr. Ebbington, who are such an honourable man, would think that that man would have been grateful, wouldn't you ? Well, he pretended to be, and perhaps for a little time he really was. But his feelings soon underwent a change towards his benefactress. When he had money he wanted more ; he knew his employer's secret, and at last, as a brilliant finale, he resolved to trade upon it. Then what idea do you think came into that faithful servant's mind ? You will never guess. Why ! neither more nor less than the betrayal of his benefactress to her enemies. And for what reward, think you ? Millions ? A million ? For half a million ? A quarter ? No ! no ! For the miserable sum of five thousand pounds. It seems incredible that a man could be so foolish and so base, doesn't it ? But, nevertheless, it is true. Perhaps he

thought the woman, having escaped so often, must inevitably be caught before long, and, being a business man,
he remembered the old adage that 'a bird in the hand is
worth two in the bush.' At any rate, he went to the
authorities,—this noble, trustworthy, grateful man,—and
like Judas, proffered his perfidy for a price. But he
was bargaining without his host—or hostess. For if he
could be so clever, the woman could be cleverer still.
She was warned in time, and thereupon hatched a
counterplot for his destruction. How well that plot
has succeeded, I don't think I need tell you, Mr. Ebbington. Dr. De Normanville, I am exceedingly sorry that
you should have been drawn into it too. But, under
the circumstances, you will see that it was quite impossible for me to leave you behind to give evidence
against me. You need have no fear, however. If you
will pass your solemn word to me that you will reveal
nothing concerning me or my actions when you go back
to civilisation, I will trust you so far as to give you
your freedom again, and on the first possible opportunity.
Do you think you can let me have that promise?"

I saw the part I was expected to play, and at once fell
in with it. Affecting to take time to consider, I presently
said :

"What can I do? I am in your hands entirely, and
it would be worse than useless for me to resist. I will
give you that promise, of course."

"Very good. Then I will let you go."

She turned from me to Ebbington.

"As for you, sir, I hardly know what punishment is
severe enough for you. Even death seems too good for
such a contemptible creature. Let me tell you that only

12

three months ago I hanged a man for murder—a far less serious offence in my eyes than yours. Why should I spare you? If I were vindictively disposed, I should recollect how you spoke of me the other evening. Do you remember?"

"I did not know to whom I was speaking," the wretched man answered hoarsely.

"That is a very poor excuse," Alie replied, with withering scorn. "Think of the baseness of what you said! However, it shall be counted as an extenuating circumstance that you did not know me. Now——"

But whatever she was about to say was stopped by a hail from the deck. On hearing it Alie immediately rose.

To the men guarding Ebbington she gave an order in their own tongue, and they at once removed their prisoner. Then turning to Walworth, she said:

"The mail boat is evidently in sight. Were your instructions explicit to the men on board her? Do you think they thoroughly understand what work they have to do?"

"Thoroughly," he answered, "I schooled them myself! There will be no bungling, you may rest assured. Matheson is in command, and he has never failed us yet."

"In what capacities did they ship?"

"Matheson as a missionary bound for Shanghai, Calderman as a tourist for Nagasaki, Burns as a tea merchant for Fu-Chow, Alderney as a newspaper correspondent to the East generally, Braham as an American mill owner travelling home via Yokohama and San Francisco, Balder as an Indian civilian on furlough visiting Japan."

" Very good.   And your instructions to them ? "

" Will be rigidly carried out.   As they come up with the yacht, after seeing our signal of distress, Matheson and Balder will make an excuse and get upon the bridge ; once there they will cover the officer of the watch with their revolvers, and do the same for the skipper if he is there, or directly he comes on deck.   They will then compel him to heave to.   Burns by this time will have taken his station at the first saloon companion ladder, Alderney doing the same at the second ; Calderman will be at the engine-room door, and Braham at the fo'c's'le ; then we shall send a boat and take off our man."

" That will do, Mr. Walworth.   You have arranged it admirably, and I am sincerely obliged to you."

A flush of pleasure rose on the man's usually sallow cheek.   He did not answer, however, only bowed and went on deck.   Then Alie turned to me.

"Dr. De Normanville," she said, "I have not yet thanked you for your help in this last adventure ; without your assistance I don't know whether I could possibly have brought it to such a successful issue."

" You must not thank me," I answered.   "Is it possible that you can imagine I would have let that scoundrel betray you?   Alie, you know how much I—— But there, I have given you my promise, so I must not say what I want to do."

She took my hand and looked into my face with a sweet smile that was very different to the one she had worn when she talked to Ebbington.

"Not yet," she said very softly.   "Some day you shall say it as often as you please.   In the meantime we must get to business.   Will you come on deck and see this comedy played out, or would you rather remain down here ? "

"I should like to go on deck with you," I answered, and we accordingly went up the companion ladder together. When we emerged from the hatch, what a change was there ! I looked, and could hardly believe my eyes. Aloft, where only an hour before the two well-stayed masts had reared their graceful heads, now hung a raffle of broken timber and disordered cordage. Forrard of the foremast the port bulwark was completely broken down, or appeared to be, while over the side from it hung another display of broken gear. In spite of the gay awning aft, and the R.C.Y.S. burgee at the gaff end, the *Lone Star* presented the appearance of a complete wreck. But the meaning of it all was what puzzled me. However, I had not very long to wait before I received enlightenment.

Alie had gone aft, and was now leaning against the port bulwark watching, with a glass, the movements of a large steamer fast rising on the horizon. I strolled up just in time to hear her say to Walworth and the officer of the watch, who were both watching it :

"She is steering directly for us. Run up the English ensign to half-mast, Mr. Patterson, and, when you think she's near enough, throw out more urgent signals for assistance."

Her orders were carefully obeyed, and before very long the vessel was near enough for us to distinguish her answering pennant. The wind had completely dropped by this time, and the sea was as smooth as glass.

When the vessel was scarcely more than two miles distant, Alie turned to her chief officer, and said :

"I think she's close enough now. Tell her that we're going to send a boat."

While she was speaking a string of flags had broken out upon the mail boat.

Walworth read them through the glass he held in his hand.

"She wants to know our name."

"Reply, ' Yacht *Sagittarius*, owner Lord Melkard, from Rangoon to Nagasaki.' He is one of the directors of the company, and that will induce them to give us their immediate attention, or I shall be very much surprised."

She was quite right, for no sooner had the message been deciphered than another went up.

Again Walworth reported. This time it ran :

"Send your boat."

"Despatch the boat," said Alie.

Instantly Walworth and the tall man with the scar on his face, whose name I have said was Patterson, went forrard, and within three minutes Alie's own gig was manned and overboard. Walworth, I noticed, was in command of her, so I took up the glass he had left upon the skylight, and brought it to bear upon the mail boat, now less than a mile distant. She presented a handsome picture as she lay there, her great bulk riding upon the smooth water as securely as if it would be possible for her to defy the elements, whatever storm might rage.

With the aid of the strong glass I was using I could plainly distinguish her, and from the scarcity of passengers on her decks it was evident that something unusual was occurring on board. Presently our boat got alongside and the gangway was lowered. A consultation seemed to be going on upon the bridge, and after a few moments a man was seen to ascend and descend the steps leading to it. Five minutes later two men passed down the gangway, and once more our boat put off to us.

When she had overcome about half the distance I chanced to look forrard. To my surprise the raffle, which a few moments before had been disfiguring the side, was gone, and even the bulwark itself had recovered its proper shape and comeliness. Moreover, the tarpaulin which had hitherto covered the centre of the deck was being removed, and by the time the boat had completed three parts of the distance that separated us from the steamer, a funnel had been uncovered and erected. The chief officer came aft.

"Is everything prepared, Mr. Patterson?" inquired Alie.

"Everything, madam," replied the officer, looking at the boat.

"Steam up?"

"It has been for the last five minutes."

"Very well then, pipe all hands to quarters, and stand by to receive the boat when she comes alongside."

As she finished speaking the officer blew a whistle, and immediately the crew, who had hitherto been ordered to remain below, appeared on deck and placed themselves at their respective posts. Against the foremast I noticed a curious mechanical contrivance, the use of which at any other time I should have inquired. Now, however, there was a look upon Alie's face that warned me not to be too inquisitive.

At last the boat came alongside, the gangway was lowered, and a moment later Walworth, accompanied by a big, clumsily built man with a heavy sensual face, small ferretty eyes, a curled moustache, and dark hair, appeared up the side. He seemed to wonder what was required of him, and it was evident that so far he had no idea into whose hands he had fallen. I glanced at Alie, as he appeared on deck, to discover that she was regarding him out of half-closed eyes, just as she had looked at Kwong Fung before she had ordered him off to execution, and at Ebbington in the cabin half an hour before.

"Will you let me say that I am more than pleased to see you, Mr. Barkmansworth?" she said in her silkiest tone as he gained the deck. "It was only last month I heard that you were coming to China to take up your residence among us. It is my desire to offer you a warm welcome to the East, hence this reception in mid-ocean. Mr. Walworth, will you be good enough to bring Mr. Ebbington to me?"

Walworth went below, and presently returned with the prisoner.

"Mr. Ebbington," said Alie, as the man she addressed took his place beside the newly erected funnel, "I have sent for you in order that you may see for yourself how I show my appreciation of those whom the world, to my thinking, does not properly reward. Mr. Barkmansworth, in case you may not know in whose presence you now stand, let me inform you that I am the woman you have so often expressed a desire to meet. I am she whom you boasted in Sydney, a year ago, you would flog when she fell into your hands, as you flogged those unfortunate South Sea Islanders. In other words, Mr. Barkmansworth, I am the Beautiful White Devil."

Though he must have realised his position long before she had finished speaking, the unfortunate man now, for the first time, showed signs of fear. Indeed, it is my opinion he would have fallen to the ground had not Walworth upheld him on one side, the coxswain of the boat which had brought him doing the same upon the other. Alie continued in the same quiet voice :

"Tell me, you sir, have you anything to say why I should not treat you as you deserve? So far you have craftily managed to escape punishment from your own authorities, but you must see that cunning will not avail you here. If you have anything to say, say it quickly, for I cannot keep your boat waiting."

The wretched man took a step forward, and, the eyes of all on board being upon him, tried to carry the matter off with a high hand.

"What business is it of yours what I do ? " he asked.

"It is my business," Alie replied, "because you have threatened what you would do to me when you caught me, and also because no one else will see justice done to you."

"You dare not punish me," he cried. "You shall not ! I warn you I am in high authority, and I'll exterminate you as I would a rat, if you dare to lay a hand upon me."

"So you try to bluster, do you ? " said Alie quietly. "Very good. In that case I need have no scruples at all in carrying out my plan. You flogged those poor women in Yakilavi, and that man at Tuarani, to death.

I will be more merciful. But flogged you shall be.
Men, do your duty ! "

The words were hardly out of her mouth before four
of her crew, who had evidently been instructed in the
parts they were to play, sprang forward, seized him by
his arms and legs, and bore him swiftly from the gangway to the object whose use I had been wondering.
Once there his feet were firmly secured, the upper part
of his body was stripped to the skin, while, at a signal,
a powerful native stepped forward from the crowd,
carrying a cat-o'-nine-tails in his hand.

" Lay on twelve lashes," said Alie sternly.

The man had a broad white back, and the first cut
raised its mark, the second put another alongside it, and
by the time the twelve strokes had been administered
the blood had begun to flow. After the first cut the
wretched culprit no longer attempted to comport himself like a man ; he struggled, whined, and finally
bellowed outright. When the number was completed,
the native paused and looked at Alie. Her face was
turned away, but it was as hard as iron.

" You have so far had six lashes for each of the
women you killed," she said ; " now you will have six
more for the man you butchered, and six more on top
of them to teach you to respect myself and the name of
Woman. Go on ! "

By this time the wretched man's pluck was entirely
gone. He entreated to be let off, offering large sums of
money, to be faithfully paid directly he got ashore, if
she would only abate one lash. He might, however, as
well have appealed to a stone : the second twelve were
duly administered, and he was then cast loose. He fell

in a heap on the deck, and for some time refused to budge ; but, on being promised an additional half-dozen if he did not do as he was ordered, he soon found his feet, and bolted down the gangway into the gig alongside, which immediately set off for the mail steamer.

Half an hour later the boat returned, bringing with her the men whose part it had been to ensure the stoppage of the vessel and the capture of the passenger. Steam was up by this time, and within five minutes of raising the boat to the davits we were under weigh. In an hour we had lost sight of the mail boat, and were making as straight a course as possible back to the settlement.

That evening I received an invitation from Alie to dine with her in her cabin, and, as may be supposed, I accepted it. But as the lady whom I had only known as Mrs. Beecher, and who had been confined to her cabin by ill-health ever since our leaving Singapore, was present, we only conversed on general topics during the progress of the meal. When, however, we sought the deck afterwards alone, and came to our favourite spot at the taffrail, Alie said :

"Up to the present you have seen a good many sides of my character, have you not? I hope, among them, they will not make you think too badly of me."

"Make me think badly of you, Alie?" I cried. "That would be impossible. What *have* I seen? Let me think. First, I have seen you collecting about you and befriending many of the world's unfortunates ; second, I have seen you toiling day and night, without thought of yourself, for the welfare of the lives you loved ; and, last, I have seen you always just and forbearing, a good ruler and a firm friend. Is there anything in any of those circumstances to make me think badly of you? No, no!"

"You are too generous to me, I fear. However, to-day you have seen me in the character of Retribution; you have seen that I can bite as well as bark. I should be sorry if I lost your good esteem. Now, with regard to Mr. Ebbington, I want to consult with you as to the course I should pursue with him."

"I hardly know," I answered. "I have been thinking it over this afternoon. The man is already nearly mad with fear; that flogging this morning was an awful lesson to him."

"I hope it was; but cannot you see the position I am placed in? After all that has passed between us, I cannot let him go out into the world again, and yet I do not want to keep him a perpetual prisoner at the settlement. A man of that kind might do serious mischief even there."

I did not know what to advise, so saying I would think about it, we dismissed the subject for the present. Alie was looking across the sea astern.

"We're in for a spell of bad weather, I fear," she said. "Do you see that bank of cloud away to the northeast? I hope it won't delay our getting back to the settlement. I have been watching it coming up, and I don't like the look of it at all."

We walked along together to the bridge, where she gave the officer of the watch some instructions. This done she turned to me and held out her hand.

"Good-night!" she said; "I am going below now to try and get some sleep in case we are to have trouble later. I have left orders that I am to be called if anything unusual transpires."

"Good-night!" I answered, when I had walked to the companion-ladder with her.

As soon as she had left me I lit another cigar, and, seating myself on the rail, fell to smoking and dreaming of the future. Every hour was bringing the time closer for me to bid the woman I loved good-bye, and to go back to England. After that, for a year, I told myself, I would work hard at my profession, and at the end of the time stipulated, she would arrive to be my wife. What my life was to be after that I could not of course determine, but however it should turn out, I would be prepared for it, and with Alie for my wife how could I fail to be happy? As soon as my cigar was finished, I tossed the stump overboard and retired to my cabin.

On entering it I thought I heard a noise, and as it turned out I was not mistaken. To my surprise the occupant was none other than the prisoner, Ebbington. He seemed a trifle disconcerted at my catching him, and began to apologise profusely for his presence there.

"I came in here to consult you professionally, Dr. De Normanville," he managed to get out at last. "But you were not in, so I thought I'd wait. Can you do anything for me? I am not at all well?"

"Sit down," I said, pointing to the locker, "and tell me how you feel."

There was something in the poor wretch's face that, much as I detested him, touched a chord of pity in my heart. Thus encouraged, he delivered himself of his symptoms, and asked to be treated. Long before he had finished his tale, however, I had convinced myself that there was nothing, save fright, the matter with him. But I heard him out, and then said :

"Now own up, Ebbington. What was the real reason of this visit? For you know very well you're no more ill than I am."

He stared for a moment, and then seeing it would be useless arguing with me, said :

"No, I'm not ill, but I want to ask you a question. What does this woman intend doing with me? It's all very well for her to pretend she abducted you ; I know better. You were in her confidence at Singapore and you're in it now. For Heaven's sake don't play with me—tell me the truth. Is she going to flog me as she flogged that poor devil this morning, or is she going to hang me, as I hear she did Kwong Fung the pirate ? "

"I know no more about what she intends doing with you than you do," I answered ; "and if I did, I'm certain I shouldn't tell you. Look here, Mr. Ebbington, I don't want to hit a man when he's down, but I must own, I think, whatever you do get won't be too much for you. You would have betrayed her, if you could have managed it, without a second thought. Now, if I had been in her place—well, I don't somehow think I should have been as merciful as she has been."

His face instantly became black with fury.

"Wouldn't you ! wouldn't you ? " he hissed ; "spy, traitor, coward ! wouldn't you ? A fig for you and your thoughts."

I laughed ; thereupon he walked up to me, and, with his features convulsed with rage, deliberately spat in my face. I knocked him down, and, having done so, picked him up and threw him outside into the saloon. I then locked my cabin door and went to bed.

I don't suppose, however, I had been asleep more than an hour before I was awakened by a loud hammering at my door. Thinking that the ship must be in danger, I sprang from my bunk and unlocked it as quickly as possible. On looking out I discovered Walworth and the officers' steward standing before me.

"What on earth is the matter?" I asked, I'm afraid a trifle irritably. "What on earth are you making all this row about?"

"Something's very much the matter," Walworth answered, taking my arm and drawing me along the saloon. "Ebbington's taken poison."

"The deuce he has!" I cried. "Let me see him at once."

I was thereupon conducted to his cabin, which was on the port side of the vessel, at the further end of the saloon. I found the patient stretched on his back in his bunk, holding an empty laudanum bottle in his hand.

One moment's examination showed me that life was extinct; he had been dead nearly an hour. In this fashion had Alie's difficulty been solved for her, and, perhaps, all things considered, though it seems rather a cruel thing to say, in the best possible manner for all parties.

"Is there no chance at all of saving him?" asked Walworth, who had been watching me intently during my examination.

"Not one!" I answered. "Ebbington's gone where even the Beautiful White Devil's vengeance won't reach

him.   Poor devil !   Fancy coming into the world for
such a fate as this ! ”

“ Humph !   Frightened out of his senses, I expect.
Well, now, I suppose I must go and tell her ladyship.
I’m sorry, doctor, to have troubled you in vain.”

“ Don’t mention it.   I’m only sorry nothing could be
done.   Good-night ! ”

“ Good-night ! ”

I drew the blanket over the face, and then locking the
door behind me, went back to my own cabin to think it
all out.   One thing became perfectly plain to me when
I examined my medical chest—and that was, Ebbington’s
reason for being in my berth.

CHAPTER XI.

A TYPHOON.

At five o'clock next morning, being unable to bear the closeness of my cabin any longer, I dressed myself and went on deck. To my surprise the schooner was stationary, and wrapped in as dense a fog as ever I remember to have seen. So still was the air that every sail hung limp and motionless, and so thick the fog that, when I emerged from the companion hatch, I could hardly distinguish the bulwarks on either side. It was the intense quiet, however, that was at once the most mysterious and the impressive part of the scene. The steady drip of the moisture on the deck, and now and again the faint lip-lap of a wavelet against the side, the creaking of a block in the rigging above my head, or the subdued tones of a man's voice coming from the forrard of the foremast were all the sounds that I could hear. It was most depressing; so, for the sake of companionship, I fumbled my way over to the starboard bulwark, and, having found it, ran it along to the bridge, where I almost fell into some person's arms. The fog here was so thick that I could not see his face, so I inquired his name.

"Walworth," was the reply, "and from your voice you should be Dr. De Normanville."

"Quite right," I answered. "But what a fog this is, to be sure! How long have we been in it?"

“Very nearly three hours,” he replied. “It’s most unfortunate. By the way, I want to ask a favour of you on her ladyship’s account. We are going to bury that poor beggar Ebbington in half an hour. Will you conduct the service?”

“Did her ladyship tell you to ask me?”

He answered in the affirmative.

“Then if it is her desire of course I will do so,” I replied, “though I must own I do not very much look forward to the task.”

He thanked me and went below to give the necessary instructions. I waited about, and in half an hour the body was brought on deck, neatly sewn up in a hammock, and covered with a plain white ensign by way of a pall. Though we could hardly see each other, or the bier, we took our place at the gangway, and I at once began to read the beautiful service for the burial of the dead at sea. When I arrived at the place where it is instructed that the body shall be cast into the deep, I gave a signal, and the stretcher was tilted, so that the hammock and its grim contents slid off it and fell with a sullen splash into the water alongside. Just as it disappeared a curious thing happened.

The body could hardly have touched the water before the fog was lifted, as though by some giant hand, and the sun shone brilliantly forth. The transition from the obscurity of semi-darkness to bright sunshine was quite dazzling, and set us all blinking like so many owls. Then I saw every face turn suddenly in one direction, and as they did so every mouth went down. Next moment the officer of the watch had bounded to the engine-room telegraph, there was a confused ringing of

13

bells in the bowels of the ship, and before a minute could have elapsed we were under weigh once more.

And what do you think was the reason of all this commotion? Why, there, not half a mile distant from us, full steam up, and ensign streaming in the breeze, lay an enormous English man-of-war. She was evidently on our trail, and, by altering her course only half a point, might have run us down in the fog. It was very evident she had only just become aware that she was so close to her prey, or she would surely have sent a boat and attempted to take us prisoner. As it was, this sudden lifting of the fog must have caused them as much surprise as it did us, for it was a good minute before we heard the shouting of orders and blowing of bo'sun's pipes aboard her. As soon as I had recovered from my astonishment, I fetched a glass from the rack and brought it to bear on her, at the same time convincing myself that we were in for a warm quarter of an hour.

True to our expectations, before we had been steaming a couple of minutes there came a puff of smoke from her port bow, and an instant later a shot flew in front of us and dropped into the water a mile or so on our left side. It was evidently a signal to us to heave to without any nonsense or further waste of time. But as the boom of the gun died away, Alie made her appearance from the after-companion and came over to where I stood.

"Good-morning, Dr. De Normanville!" she said, as calmly as if we were greeting each other in Hyde Park. "You see how anxious your government is to have me in its keeping. Mr. Patterson, full steam ahead!"

The chief officer touched his cap, gave the order, and then resumed his promenade, stopping now and again to examine the man-of-war through his glass.

"They're going to fire another gun, and then if we don't attend to that they will chase us," said Alie, who was also closely scrutinising her great opponent's movements.

She was correct in her prophecy, for as she finished speaking another jet of flame issued from the cruiser's side, followed by a sullen roar. This time the shot passed through our rigging, fortunately, however, without doing any damage, and next moment we could see that she was under weigh. It was going to be a stern chase and, if they didn't hull us before we got out of range, we knew it would be a long one.

Seeing that we did not intend to heave to, as she ordered, our antagonist sent another shot after us, but this time it fell altogether wide of the mark. Alie called the third officer to her side.

"Inquire from the engine room what we're doing, Mr. Gammel!" she said.

The officer asked the necessary question, and the answer came back, "Eighteen."

"Tell them to give her every ounce of steam she is capable of carrying. We must not allow our friend yonder to get us within range again, or one of those chance shots may hull us."

Then turning to me she continued, as if in explanation, "You see, Dr. De Normanville, I have no desire to fall into their hands yet awhile."

I felt as though I would have given anything to have been allowed to say something at this juncture, but I

remembered my compact with her and wisely held my
tongue. If, however, the masculine reader wishes to
realise my feelings at all, let him imagine the woman of
his heart in such imminent danger as mine was then;
let it be properly brought home to him that the only
thing he can do to save her is to look on and speculate
as to what the result may be, and I fancy he will not
enjoy it any more than I did. All my life long shall I
retain the memory of the quarter of an hour I spent by
Alie's side, watching that sinister vessel lumbering after
us like a giant in chase of a dwarf. But fortunately
for his safety, our dwarf could run, and to such good
purpose that by breakfast time we had drawn completely out of range.

During our meal, of which I partook in the officer's
mess, for I did not breakfast with Alie every morning,
I noticed a nervous, and, as I thought, a hopelessly sad
look upon the chief officer's face. Could it be the presence of the man-of-war that occasioned it? I did not
question him, of course; but when he halted at the foot
of the ladder, glanced anxiously at the barometer, and
returned to the deck, I asked Walworth if anything
were the matter.

"Look at the glass for yourself," he said. "Don't
you see that it is dropping in a most alarming fashion?
And if you listen for a moment you will hear how the
wind and sea are rising."

And so they were! There could be no mistake about
that. I picked up my cap, and followed the chief's
example.

What a different scene presented itself when I gained
the deck! When I had left it to go below to breakfast,

the water had been as smooth as a millpond ; now it ran a comparatively high sea, and its anger was momentarily increasing. The *Lone Star* was still steaming through it like a witch, though her pursuer could only just be discerned on the southern horizon. From the heavy and confused water all round me I turned my eyes aloft and examined the sky, across which a quantity of curious-shaped clouds were flying, resembling well-combed horses' manes more than anything else to which I could liken them. Even to my inexperienced eyes they did not present a reassuring appearance, and it was evident that the officer of the watch shared my anxiety, for he was having everything made snug as swiftly as possible.

By ten o'clock the wind had risen to the strength of a more than moderate gale, and the sea in proportion. It was most alarming, and I must confess that, seeing the strength of the wind, I was a little surprised when, about the middle of the morning, Alie appeared on deck. She came aft to where I was standing, and, having looked at the compass card, gazed round her.

"If I'm not mistaken we're in for a typhoon," she shouted, her glorious hair blowing in tangled profusion across her eyes and about. her face. "Our friend, the cruiser, you see, is out of sight. I expect she thinks it's useless endeavouring to chase us across such a sea." Then, turning to Walworth, who was standing near, she cried : "Send Mr. Patterson to me."

Though it was not Patterson's watch on deck he was too anxious about the weather and his ship to go below. Immediately on receiving Alie's message he came aft, and, having touched his sou'wester, waited for her to speak.

"Mr. Patterson, what is your opinion of the weather?" she shouted in his ear, for it was impossible to make yourself heard by any ordinary means. "Don't you think we had better heave to and endeavour to find out how the centre of the storm bears from us?"

"I was just going to do so," Patterson bellowed, in reply. Then, turning to his subordinate, he gave the necessary instructions in a yell that sounded like a fog horn. The yacht's nose was immediately pointed dead to the wind, which at that moment was due N. E., the requisite number of points to the right of it were then taken, and the centre of the approaching hurricane found to be exactly S. S. E. of our position. At this juncture Walworth, who had been acting under instructions, returned from the cuddy and reported the barometer had fallen to 27.45. It might, therefore, be inferred that we were within the storm circle, and, for the same reason, it was apparent that our safety entirely depended upon our being able to avoid the centre of the field. Having decided the direction of the storm, and discovered that we lay in the due line of its advance,—the most dangerous of all,—there was nothing for it but to run with the wind on our starboard quarter.

Never shall I forget the scene presented as our course was changed. Even now, when I shut my eyes, I can see it as clearly before me as if I were standing in the very thick of it again. I can see the heavens, black with angry clouds, frowning down on a confused and angry sea that dashed against our hull with terrific and repeated violence. I can see the waters one moment raising us on high, the next hurling us deep down into some black and horrible abyss. And all the time I can

hear the wind shrieking and yelling through the cordage like the chorus of a million devils.

It was impossible to hear oneself speak, and on the
bridge almost impossible to retain one's balance against
the wind's pressure. And, what was worse, the anger
of the storm was increasing every moment.

I looked from Alie, who, enveloped in oilskins, was
clinging to the starboard railing, then to the chief
officer gazing anxiously aloft, and from both to the
men struggling and straining at the wheel. Now, when
a great wave, seemingly mountains high, dark as green
jade, and topped with hissing foam, would come tearing
towards us, obscuring half the horizon, I would shut my
eyes and wait for it to engulf us. Then I would feel
the noble little vessel meet it, rise on to its crest, and
next moment be sinking again, down, down, down into
the trough. Then once more I would draw breath and
open my eyes, just in time to see another rise and meet
her forrard, to break with a roar upon the fo'c's'le head,
carrying away a dozen feet of bulwark and one of the
boats as if both were built of so much paper.

For nearly five hours the hurricane continued with
the same awful violence, and all that time I remained on
the bridge with Alie, afraid to go below, lest, when the
vessel went to pieces, as I infallibly believed she must,
I should be separated from the woman I loved. It may
be said that I proved myself a coward. I do not deny
it. I will confess that I was more frightened then than,
with the exception of one occasion to be hereafter
narrated, I have ever been in my life. And yet, somehow, I am not without a feeling that, after all, mine
should have been classed as of the magnificent order of

courage ; for, though my heart had absolutely lost all hope, I spared my companions any exhibition of my terror, and nerving myself for the occasion, looked Death in the face with an equable countenance, believing every moment he would snatch me into the hollow of his hand.

Towards the middle of the afternoon the strength of the gale began somewhat to abate, the sea lost its greater fury, and the barometer in a measure recovered its stability. It seemed incredible that the *Lone Star* could have come through it so safely, for, with the exception of one man washed overboard, another who had three of his ribs smashed in by a marauding sea, a portion of the port bulwark and a boat carried away, as above described, and another crashed to atoms on the davits, we had experienced no casualties worth mentioning.

By the time darkness fell, the sea was almost its old calm, placid self again, so quickly do these terrible typhoons spring up and die away. As soon as we were certain all danger was past, the yacht was returned to her course, and we once more proceeded on our way. What had become of our pursuer, or how she had weathered the storm, we could not tell. Up to the time daylight left us nothing was to be seen of her, and we began devoutly to hope we had given her the slip for good and all.

How wonderful and inscrutable is the mighty deep! Next day the weather was as peaceful as ever I had seen it—bright sunshine, gentle breezes, and a sea as smooth as polished silver. After breakfast, the awning, which on account of the storm had been unshipped the day before, was rigged again, and, drawing a deck chair aft, I settled myself down to read beneath its shade. A few minutes later Alie and her companion joined me. I brought them seats, and then, for the first time, I saw the Beautiful White Devil—for I must sometimes call her by her picturesque Chinese cognomen—engaged in needlework. Why I should have found anything extraordinary in such a circumstance I cannot say. Possibly it may have been because I had never imagined that there could be sufficient leisure in her life for such a homely occupation. At any rate, I know that to watch her bent head, with its glorious wealth of hair; to see those beautiful white fingers, unadorned by jewellry of any sort, twisting and twining among her silks, and to make out one little foot peeping beneath her snow-white dress, sent a thrill through me that made me tingle from top to toe.

Suddenly one of the hands engaged upon some work in the fore-rigging uttered a cry in the native. Alie and her companion sprang to their feet ; and, though I did not understand what had happened I followed their example. We ran to the starboard bulwark, but nothing was to be seen there. Not being able to make it out, I asked what had occasioned the alarm.

"One of the hands reports a boat away to starboard," said Alie.

She turned to one of the younger officers, who was standing near, and ordered him aloft to take the boat's bearing. As soon as this was discovered the yacht was put over on a tack that would bring us close up with it, and after that there was nothing for it but to wait patiently for the result.

For some time we could not see anything; then a small black speck made it appearance about two points off our starboard bow and gradually grew plainer.

"Keep her as she goes," said Alie to the man at the wheel, while we strained our eyes towards the tiny dot.

Little by little it became more distinct until we were sufficiently near to make out with a glass that it was a man-of-war's gig pulled by two men and containing three others. Ten minutes later the yacht was hove to, and Patterson clambered on to the rail of the bulwarks.

"Are you strong enough to bring her alongside, do you think?" he bellowed, "or shall we send a boat to tow you?"

The man steering, who was evidently an officer, funnelled his mouth with his hands and shouted back that they thought they could manage it. Then, as if to prove his words, the men who had been rowing, but had now stopped, resumed their monotonous labour. Bit by bit the tiny craft crept over the oily surface towards us until she was close enough for us to see with our naked eyes all that she contained.

As she came alongside, our gangway was lowered, and within an hour from the time of our first sighting her the boat's crew stood upon our deck. In spite of their man-of-war dress, a more miserable, woe-begone appearance could not have been imagined than the party presented. It consisted of one lieutenant, a midshipman, and three able seamen, and out of curiosity I glanced at the cap of the man standing nearest me. It bore the name H. M. S. *Asiatic*. Then I looked round for Alie, only to discover that she had mysteriously disappeared. It was left for Patterson to welcome the poor fellows to the yacht, and this he accordingly did, with a hearty kindness that I should hardly have expected from him.

"Before you tell me anything about yourselves," he said, "let me arrange for the comfort of your men." Then calling a hand to him, he continued, pointing to the three Jacks who stood sheepishly by, "Take these men forrard and tell the cook to give them all they want. You can supply them with hammocks among you and find room somewhere for them to sling them." Then, turning to the officers again, he said, "Will you be so good as to follow me, gentlemen?" and led the way down the companion to the cuddy. Thinking my professional services might possibly be required I followed with Walworth.

On reaching the cabin they were conducted to seats, and food was immediately set before them. They fell upon it like starving men, and for some time only the sound of steady munching and the clatter of knives and forks was to be heard. When they had finished, the midshipman, without warning, burst into a flood of tears, and was led by Walworth to a cabin near by, where, when his torrent had worn itself out, the poor little chap fell fast asleep.

"Now," said Patterson, as soon as the lieutenant had finished his meal, "perhaps you will tell me your story?"

"It won't take long to do that," the officer began. "I am the first lieutenant of Her Majesty's cruiser *Asiatic*. We were sent out from Singapore last Saturday in pursuit of this very yacht, if I mistake not. As you know, we almost picked you up in the fog, but when it lifted, your superior steaming power enabled you to escape us. Then the typhoon caught us, and in looking after ourselves, we lost sight of you altogether. We rode out the storm safely enough, but, just at sun-time yesterday, she struck an uncharted rock and went down within five minutes."

He stopped for a moment and covered his face with his hands.

"This is terrible news!" cried Patterson, while we all gave utterance to expressions of horrified astonishment. "And was yours the only boat that got away?"

"I'm very much afraid so," he replied. "At least I saw no other. Yes, you are right, it is terrible, and Her Majesty has lost a fine vessel and a splendid ship's company in the *Asiatic*."

When the poor fellow had finished his story he was silent for some minutes. Indeed, so were we all. It seemed almost incredible that the great vessel we had admired, and feared, only the day before, should now be lying, with the majority of her crew, deep down at the bottom of the ocean.

"We are fortunate in having been able to pick you up," said Patterson, after a while. "An hour later and we should have changed our course, and have been many miles away."

"In that case we should have been dead men by nightfall," was the reply. "As it was, we lost one man."

"How did it happen?"

"The poor devil went mad, and jumped overboard. Remember, we had no water and nothing to eat, and so you may imagine it was heart-breaking work pulling in that baking sun. The miracle to me is that the boy stood it as well as he did."

"Poor little chap! It must have been a terrible experience for him."

"And what do you intend doing with us?" asked the officer, after a little pause. "For, of course, we're your prisoners."

"That I cannot say," Patterson answered. "It does not lie within my province. However, you'll hear soon enough—never fear. By the way, I suppose you will give me your word that you will not attempt to play us any tricks. You must remember, please, that to all intents and purposes we are at war!"

"I will give you my word. Is that enough?"

"Quite enough. And now that you have done so I make you free of our ward-room and its contents."

All the time Patterson had been speaking I had noticed that the lieutenant, whose name, it transpired later, was Thorden, had been staring at his face as if trying to recall some countenance it reminded him of. Just as we were preparing to go on deck again his memory seemed to come back to him.

"I hope you will excuse what I am going to say, and stop me if I am recalling any unpleasant memories," he blurted out; "but ever since I came aboard I've been wondering where we have met before. Aren't you Gregory, who was commander of the gunboat *Parcifal* in the Egpytian business of 1879?"

Patterson fell back against the wall as if he had been shot. For a moment his face was as white as the paper I am now writing upon, then, with a great effort, he pulled himself together, and answered :

"I have quite forgotten that I had any existence at all in 1879. May I beg that you will not recall the fact to my memory?" Then, as if to change the subject, he continued, "I expect you would like to rest after all your troubles; pray let me conduct you to a cabin."

"Many thanks," said Thorden; and with that they went along the alleyway together, and I returned to the deck to think out what I had heard. It was, of course, no business of mine; but I was interested in Patterson, and could not help speculating as to what the reason could have been that had induced him to abandon a career in which, even so many years ago, he seemed to have attained such exalted rank.

During the afternoon I received an invitation from Alie to dine with her that evening. She stated in the little note she sent me that she had also asked the rescued lieutenant and his midshipman, and I gathered from this that something out of the common was toward.

About an hour before dusk, as I was reading in the officers' mess-room, the lieutenant came out of his cabin and sat down at the table beside me. He looked round to see that we were alone, and then said in a confidential whisper :

"Your position on board this boat, Dr. De Norman-ville, has already been explained to me. I'm sure I sympathise with you ; but, for rather selfish motives, I am glad you are not in league with this extraordinary woman. I have received an invitation to dine in her cabin this evening, and I want you, if you will, to tell me something about her. Do you know enough to satisfy my curiosity ?"

"I'll tell you all I can," I answered frankly. "What is it you want to know?"

"Well, first and foremost," he continued, with a laugh, "since I've received this invitation, what sort of meal is she likely to give us?"

"A very fair one, I should fancy," I replied. "At least, I hope so, as I am invited to be one of the party."

"You are? Well, I am glad of that. And now another question. What is she like? Of course, one has heard all sorts of reports about her beauty and accomplishments, but when one has travelled about the world one soon learns to believe rather less than half of what one hears."

"Ah, yes; it's as well not to be too sanguine, isn't it?" I answered, resolved, if possible, to mislead him, "especially with regard to women. Now, I've no doubt you expect the Beautiful White Devil to be really young and beautiful?"

"And is she not? Well, well! There goes another illusion. Before I came out here I had my own idea of the East—it was to be all state elephants and diamond-studded howdahs, jewelled Rajahs, mysterious pagodas with tingling golden bells and rustling palm trees, lovely houris and Arabian Nights' adventures. But it isn't like that by a long chalk. And so the Beautiful White Devil goes with the rest, does she? But don't tell me that she's old, and, above all, don't tell me she's fat."

"I won't tell you anything about her," I answered, with a laugh; "you must wait and judge for yourself. One caution, however, before you see her: beware how you behave towards her, and if I might venture a hint, make a good toilet. She's very particular, and it's well to humour her. My things are at your disposal, of course."

He thanked me, and I saw no more of him or the midshipman until a few minutes before dinner time, when I met them on deck and accompanied them to Alie's saloon. Having descended the companion-ladder I drew back the curtain for them to enter. Prepared as I was to see him show astonishment, I had no idea the lieutenant would be filled with such amazement as he betrayed when we entered the beautiful cabin I have before described. As good luck had it Alie was not present, and so we were able to look about us undisturbed.

"Why didn't you prepare me for this?" whispered my companion, after he had glanced round the cabin. "I never saw anything like it before, and I've been aboard scores of yachts in my time."

"There is but one Beautiful White Devil," I said, with serio-comic earnestness.

"Curios, china, skins, divans, musical instruments, a grand piano even, and, by Jove, inlaid with tortoiseshell and lapis lazuli! It's wonderful, it's superb! And now I want to see the woman who owns it all."

"Steady," I whispered; "if I mistake not, here she comes."

As I spoke, the curtains at the other end of the cabin were parted by a tiny hand, and Alie, dressed entirely in black, stood before us. The colour of her costume showed off the superb beauty of her complexion and hair, while its making exhibited her matchless figure to perfection. She stood for a moment in the doorway, and then advanced towards us with that wonderful floating grace which always characterized her, giving me her little hand first, and then turning towards her other guests.

To the lieutenant she bowed and said with a smile :

"Sir, you must forgive my not having personally welcomed you to my boat. But, for reasons which would not interest you, I am not always able to do as much as I could wish. However, I hope my officers have taken every care of you."

She shook hands with the handsome little midshipman as she spoke, and while she was doing so I had time to steal a look at the first lieutenant's face. The astonishment I saw depicted there almost caused me to laugh. He had been amazed at the beauty of the cabin ; but that was nothing compared with the admiration he betrayed for the Beautiful White Devil herself. He murmured a confused, but not altogether inappropriate reply to her last speech, and then we sat down to dinner. Her companion, I learnt on inquiry, was suffering from a severe headache, and had elected to dine in her own cabin.

The dinner was in the chef's best style, and its cooking, serving, and variety, combined with the beauty and value of the table decorations, evidently completed the effect upon the officer that the cabin had begun. Alie herself was in excellent spirits, and talked with the wit and cleverness of a woman who has perfected an originally liberal education by continual and varied study of the world and its inhabitants. By the time the meal was ended and we had bade her good-night, the lieutenant was in a maze of enchantment.

We went on deck together, and once there, out of earshot of the cabin, his enthusiasm broke loose. I will spare you, however, a recital of all the extravagant things he said. Let it suffice. that I gathered enough to feel sure that when he got back to Hong Kong he would add to, rather than detract from, the number of stories already in circulation about the too famous Beautiful White Devil. One promise, however, I took care to extract from both officers, and that was, not to mention my name in connection with the yacht on their return to civilisation. I made the excuse that if such a thing got known it might do me serious harm in the practice of my profession, and both men readily gave me their words that they would not breathe a syllable on the subject.

Their stay with us, however, was not to be of as long duration as we had expected, for early next morning we sighted a small brigantine, who, on being hailed, stated that she was bound for Hong Kong. Passages for the officers and their men were soon arranged, and, within an hour of picking her up she had sent a boat, we had bade our naval visitors good-bye, and were standing on our fictitious course again. As soon, however, as they were out of sight the helm was put up and we were making a bee line back to the settlement.

That evening as I was pacing the deck, smoking my cigar and wondering when the time would come for me to say farewell, I heard a light footstep behind me, and next moment Alie came to my side. We paced the deck for a little while, talking commonplaces about the beauty of the night, the speed of her vessel, and the visit of the man-of-war's men ; then she drew me to the stern, and said :

"Do you remember your first night on board this boat, when we discussed the sea and the poets who have written of her?"

"It was the night of the first day I ever saw you," I answered. "Is it likely I should have forgotten it?"

"Some men forget very easily," she answered, looking down at the sparkling water. "But I'll do you the justice to say I don't think you are one of that kind."

"And you are right; I am sure I am not. I think if I were lying dead in my grave, my brain would still remember you."

She looked roguishly up into my face, and said:

"That is rather a big assertion for a medical man to make, is it not?"

"Bother medicine," I cried impatiently. "It reminds me of the outer world. And by the same token, Alie, I want to ask you something unpleasant again."

"And that is?"

"When I am to say good-bye to you?"

"To-morrow," she answered. "To-morrow night, all being well, we shall pick up a trading schooner off a certain island. Her owner is under an obligation to me, and will take you on board and convey you to Thursday Island. Thence you can travel home via Australia and the Canal or Honolulu and America, as you please."

I had expected that the parting was not far distant, but I did not think it would prove as close as this. I told Alie as much.

"It is the only opportunity that may serve," she answered. "And I must not keep you with me too long for your own sake."

Under cover of the darkness I managed to find and take her hand.

"It is only for a year, Alie. You understand that, don't you? At the end of a year you are to be my wife?"

"If you still wish it, yes," she answered, but so softly that I had to strain my ears to catch it. Then with a whispered good-night she slipped from me and went below.

At sundown next evening, surely enough, a small top-sail schooner hove in sight from behind an island, and, seeing us, ran up a signal. It was returned from our gaff, and as soon as I read it I knew that my fate was sealed. Leaving Walworth to see my luggage brought up on deck I went down Alie's companion ladder to bid her farewell. She was seated on the couch at the further end, reading.

"The schooner has just put in an appearance and answered our signals," I began, hardly able to trust my voice to speak. "I have come to say good-bye. For both our sakes we must not let this interview be a long one. Alie, will you tell me for the last time exactly when I am to see you again, and where?"

"On the first day of May next year, all being well, I will be at an address in London, of which I will take care to acquaint you beforehand."

"But since you last spoke of that I have been think-ing it over. Alie, you must not come to England, the risk would be too great?"

"There will be no risk at all, and I shall take every precaution to ensure my own safety. You may rest assured of that," she answered. "But before you go I have a little keepsake for you, something that may serve to remind you of the Beautiful White Devil and the days you have spent with her, when you are far away."

As she spoke she took from the table, beside which she was now standing, a large gold locket. Opening it she let me see that it contained an excellent portrait of herself.

"Oh, Alie," I cried, "how can I thank you? You have given me the one thing of all others that I desired. Now, in my turn, I have a present for you. This ring " (here I drew a ring from my finger) "was my poor dead mother's last gift to me, and I want you to wear it."

I placed it on her finger, and having done so, took her in my arms and kissed her on the lips. This time she offered no resistance.

Then we said good-bye, and I went up on deck. An hour later the *Lone Star* had faded away into the night, and I was aboard the *Pearl Queen* bound for Thursday Island and the Port of London.

When I came to think of it I could hardly believe that it was nearly four months since Walworth had found me out in the Occidental Hotel, Hong Kong, and induced me to become the servant and at the same time the lover of the Beautiful White Devil.

CHAPTER XII.

THE FIRST OF MAY.

ARRIVING in Thursday Island, one of the hottest and quaintest little spots on earth, I was fortunate enough to catch a British India mail boat in the act of starting for Brisbane. I accordingly had my luggage conveyed to her and was soon comfortably installed aboard her. The voyage from Torres Straits, along the Queensland coast, inside the Great Barrier Reef, though it boasts on one hand a rugged and almost continuous line of cliffs marked with such names as Cape Despair and Tribulation, and upon the other twelve hundred miles of treacherous reef, is quite worth undertaking. I explored the different ports of call, and, on reaching Brisbane, caught the train for Adelaide, embarked on board a P. and O. mail boat there, and in less than six weeks from the time of booking my passage was standing in the porch of my own house in Cavendish Square, had rung the bell, and was waiting for the front door to be opened to me.

It was a cold winter's afternoon ; an icy blast tore through the Square and howled round the various corners, so that all the folk whose inclement destinies compelled them to be abroad were hurrying along as if their one desire were to be indoors and by their fires again without loss of time.

Presently my old housekeeper opened the door, and,

though I had telegraphed to her from Naples to expect me, pretended to be so overwhelmed with surprise at seeing me as to be incapable of speech for nearly a minute. I managed to get past her at last, however, and went into what, in the days of my practice, had been my consulting room. The fire was burning brightly, my slippers were toasting before it, my writing table was loaded with books and papers as usual, and a comfortable easy chair was drawn up beside it. Everything was exactly as I had left it fourteen months before, even to the paper knife still resting in a half cut book, and a hastily scrawled memo. upon the blotting pad. There was something almost ironical about this state of stagnation when I thought of the changes that had occurred in my own life since last I had used that knife and written that memorandum. I told the old housekeeper to let me have my dinner at the usual hour, and having done so, asked her the news of the Square. Her reply was not important.

"James [her husband] an' me, sir," she said, " 'ad the rheumatiz at the beginning of the winter, the young postman with the red whiskers 'ave got married to the parlour maid as burnt herself so bad three years back, at number 99, and the little gal with the golden curls across the way fell down the airey and broke her leg two months ago come next Friday."

Such was the chronicle of the most important occurrences in that quiet London Square during my absence.

After dinner I returned to my study, wrote two or three letters, and then drawing my chair up to the fire, sat down to think. Outside the wind howled and the rain dashed against my windows, but my thoughts were very far away from Cavendish Square; they were flying across the seas to an island, where lived a woman whom I had come to love better than all the world. Closing my eyes, I seemed to see the yacht lying in the little harbour under the palm clad hills; I went ashore, threaded my way through the tangled mass of jungle, and passed up the path to the bungalow on the hillside. There I found Alie moving about her rooms with all her old queenly grace; then like a flash the scene changed, and we were back on the yacht's deck in the typhoon. I saw the roaring seas racing down upon us, heard the wind whistling and shrieking through the straining cordage, noticed the broken bulwarks, and by my side, Alie in her oilskins, with her sou-wester drawn tight about her head, clinging to the rail with every atom of her strength. But all that was past and over, and now for twelve months—nay, to be exact, eleven,— I was to be the staid, respectable London householder I had been before I visited the East. After that— but there, what was to happen after that, who could tell?

After a while the termination of my pipe brought my reverie to an end, so I took up a file of papers from the table and fell to scanning the last few numbers. Suddenly a headline caught my eye and rivetted my attention. It was a clipping from a Hong Kong paper, and read as follows :

"THE BEAUTIFUL WHITE DEVIL AGAIN."

"After a silence of something like four months the Beautiful White Devil has again done us the honour of appearing in Eastern waters. On this occasion, however, her polite attentions have been bestowed upon Singapore, from which place she has abducted, with singular cleverness, a young English doctor, whose acquaintance she had made in Batavia, and with him a certain well-known resident by name Ebbington. These two affairs were managed with that dexterity which the Beautiful White Devil has taught us to expect from her, the sequel, however, we have yet to learn. Surely, and we say it for the fiftieth occasion, it is time some definite steps were taken by Government to bring about the capture of a woman who, while being a picturesque and daring enough subject for a novel, has been a continual menace and danger to the commerce of the East for a greater number of years than the editorial chair cares to reckon."

I cut the paragraph out and, having placed it in my pocket-book, turned to the next issue published a week later. Here I found another quarter column devoted to her exploits. This one was also from the Hong Kong paper and ran as follows :

"THE BEAUTIFUL WHITE DEVIL'S LATEST AND
GREATEST EXPLOIT.

"Last week we described what may be considered two of the cleverest and most daring exploits in the whole of the Beautiful White Devil's extraordinary career. We refer to the abduction of an English doctor, travelling in the East in order to study Asiatic diseases, and a well-known figure in Singapore society, Mr. Arthur James Ebbington, whose bay pony, Cupid, it will be remembered, won the Straits Settlement's Cup last year. The whereabouts of these two gentlemen have not yet, so we learn, been discovered, but to compensate for that we have to chronicle another, and perhaps more serious, act of violence on the part of this notorious character. The facts of the case are as follows :

"On Saturday morning last the mail steamer *Bramah* left Singapore for Hong Kong, having on board a number of distinguished passengers, including the new admiral of the China Station, Sir Dominic Denby, his flag lieutenant, Mr. Hoskin, and a prominent new government official for Hong Kong, Mr. Barkmansworth. There were also among the passengers six gentlemen of unassuming appearance, who, as far as could be judged, seemed to be total strangers to each other. The names they booked under were, as we find by a perusal of the shipping company's books, Matherson, Calderman, Burns, Alderney, Braham, and Balder.

"The first described himself as a missionary, the second was presumably a tourist, the third a tea merchant, the fourth an English newspaper correspondent, the fifth an American mill owner, and the sixth an Indian civilian on furlough. On Sunday morning early, the officer of the watch sighted a sail some few points off the starboard bow. From all appearances it was a large schooner yacht, flying a distress signal. On nearer approach it was seen that she had suffered considerable damage, her topmasts appearing to have been carried completely away.

"On inquiring her name it was elicited that she was the schooner yacht *Sagittarius*, belonging to the Royal Cowes Yacht Squadron, and owned by Lord Melkard, the well-known Home Rule Peer, who was supposed, at the time, to be cruising in these waters. Suspicion being thus entirely diverted, Captain Barryman brought his steamer as close as was prudent and signalled to the yacht to send a boat, which request was immediately complied with. Meanwhile, however, the attention of the officers on the bridge being rivetted on the yacht, two of the men before enumerated, Matherson the missionary, and Balder the Indian civilian, contrary to rules, made their way on to the bridge and implored the captain and chief officer to stand by the smaller vessel, which they declared to be sinking. Then without warning, on receiving a signal from below, these two, to all appearances eminently peaceable gentlemen, drew revolvers from their pockets and covered the astonished officers. The remaining members of the gang by this time had posted themselves at the entrances to the first and second saloons, the engine-room, and the fo'c's'le, and refused to allow anyone to come on to or to leave the deck.

" When the boat came alongside Mr. Barkmansworth, the official before described, who had just had his bath and was completing his toilet in his cabin, was called up from below and ordered to descend into her. After some argument, and a considerable amount of threatening, he complied with the request and was pulled over to the yacht. Once there, he has seized, stripped to the skin, dragged up to a triangle, and remorselessly flogged. He was then sent bleeding and almost unconscious back to the steamer, where he was immediately placed under the doctor's care. On the return of the boat alongside, the six desperadoes, who had all the time been mounting guard, as before described, entered it and were conveyed to the yacht, which immediately steamed off in a southwesterly direction.

"That this last insult to the Powers-that-Be will have the result of inducing them to take more effective action against this notorious woman is too much to expect. But with a reckless confidence somewhat unusual to us, we are now pinning our faith 'on the newly arrived naval authority, the more so as he was himself a witness of the whole disgraceful affair. We can only point out one fact, and that is, that unless this woman be soon brought to justice, travelling by mail boat in Eastern waters will be a thing of the past. When steamers are stopped, and well known and respected government officials publicly flogged in mid-ocean, it is evident that affairs are coming to too atrocious a pass altogether."

Putting this criticism into my pocket-book with the other, I took a glimpse at my locket and went to bed.

Next morning, immediately after breakfast, I donned the orthodox top hat and frock coat and set off to walk to South Kensington to call upon my sister Janet—who, by the way, was a widow, her husband having died of malarial fever when with his regiment on the west coast of Africa.

I found her in the morning-room in the act of writing a note of welcome to me. She greeted me with all her old sisterly affection, and when she had done so, made me sit down before the fire and tell her all my adventures.

"We have heard the most wonderful tales about you,"

she said, with a smile. "How you were captured by a sort of female Captain Kidd of fabulous beauty, who carried you off to an island in the Pacific, where you were made to dig sufficient gold to pay your ransom."

"Indeed?"

"It has been recopied into all sorts of papers," she continued. "But I've no doubt it was a mass of mere fabrication. Own the truth now, wasn't it?"

"Every bit," I answered candidly. "I have been very much annoyed by those stupid newspaper paragraphs. It is just like the rabid craving of the age for sensationalism. But before I go any further, Janet, I want to tell you something. I am going to be married."

"You! George! Why, you always used to say you had made up your mind never to do anything so foolish."

"So I did; but you see I have changed my mind."

"So it would appear. And now, who is she? Tell me where you met her and all about her."

This was what I dreaded, but it had to be met and faced.

"Well, in the first place, her name is Alie. She is twenty-seven years of age and an orphan. Her father was a captain in the English navy, but is now dead. She is very sweet, very accomplished, and very beautiful; and I feel sure, Janet, if only for my sake, you will offer her a hearty welcome when she comes home."

"You know me well enough to be sure of that, don't you, dear old George? And is anything settled yet? How soon does she come home? and when are you going to be married?"

"To your first question I can only answer, as soon

after the first of May as possible. On the first Alie will arrive in England. Now will you wish me happiness, Janet?"

"With all my heart and soul. But I am dying to know more; tell me where you met her, and indeed all about your adventures; remember, you have been away a whole year."

I told her as much as I thought prudent without revealing Alie's identity, and when my story was ended, we sat chatting on till lunch time.

When I left the house in the afternoon, I knew I had insured a kind reception for Alie when she should arrive in England.

Now I must skip the greater part of a year and come to the middle of the last week in April, just three days, in fact, before I knew I might expect my darling. It would be impossible for me to tell you how I spent the time. I don't think I know myself. I was in such a fever of impatience that each minute seemed an hour, each hour a day, and each day a year. And the nearer the time came the greater became my impatience. I even scanned the shipping lists with feverish earnestness, though I knew they could not possibly tell me anything I wanted to know.

At last the evening of the 30th of April arrived, a warm spring night with the promise of a lovely morrow. I kept myself busily occupied after dinner, and went to bed counting the hours till morning should appear. But try how I would I could not sleep—the memory of the joy that awaited me on the morrow kept me wide awake, devising plans for Alie's happiness. Slowly the hours went by. I heard one, two, three, four, and five o'clock strike, and still sleep would not come to me. At last I could stand it no longer, so I rose, dressed myself, and went out into the silent Square. Then I set myself for a walk, taking care, however, to return home in time to receive my letters from the postman. They were three in number, two from friends, the third a circular, but not one from Alie. The disappointment was almost more than I could bear. But I put it behind me, and resolved to wait for the next delivery, which would take place about an hour after breakfast. Again the postman came round the Square—but this time he had nothing at all to deliver when he reached my door. Once more I was disappointed.

The morning rolled slowly on and lunch time came and went without any communication. The early afternoon delivery brought me no news, and by tea time I had almost lost hope. Could Alie have forgotten her promise or had she met with an accident which prevented her from coming? The latter thought redoubled my anxiety.

But I had her own assertion that she would be in England on the first of May and I had never known her fail to keep her word. Just as that thought passed through my brain there was a ring at the bell, and a few seconds later my man brought up a telegram on a salver. With fingers trembling with eagerness I tore the envelope open and read the following message :

Arrived this morning. Bundaberg House, Surbiton. Come quickly. ALIE.

That little slip of paper transformed my dismal world into a second heaven. There and then I ran out of the room, gave the telegraph boy in the porch half a crown for his trouble, seized my hat and stick, hailed a hansom, and bade the cabman drive me with all possible speed to Waterloo. The man was a smart whip, and as he possessed a good horse we covered the ground in grand style. When we reached the station I paid him off, purchased my ticket, and ran on to the platform just in time to catch the 6.15 express. Punctually at five and twenty minutes to seven I left the train again at Surbiton, and proceeding into the station yard called another cab.

"Do you know Bundaberg House?" I asked the man, as I took my place in the vehicle.

He shook his head and called to one of his mates.

"Where's Bundaberg House, Bill?"

"Out on the Portsmouth Road nearly to Thames Ditton," was the reply. "That big house with the long brick wall next to Tiller's."

"I know now, sir!" said the man, climbing on to his box.

"Very well, then! An extra shilling if you hurry up," I cried, and away he went.

At the end of a short drive we pulled up before a pair of massive iron gates. A passer by threw them open for us and we drove in, passed round a shrubbery, and pulled up at the front door. I paid the cabman off and then, having watched him drive down and through the gates again, rang the bell. Next moment the door opened and a trim maid servant, without inquiring my name, invited me to enter. The front door opened on to a nicely built and furnished hall and from it I passed into a handsome drawing-room. It was empty but, before I had time to look round, the folding doors on the other side were thrown back and Alie entered the room.

I must leave you to imagine our greeting. I can only say that it sends a tremor through me to this day to remember it. I know that while I held Alie, who seemed more beautiful than ever, in my arms she whispered :

"You are still of the same mind, George ? "

"Doesn't this look as if I am, darling ? " I whispered. "Yes, I love you more fondly than ever, and I have come to-night to claim the fulfilment of your promise."

" You have been very patient, George ! "

"It was because I loved and believed in you, Alie !" I replied. "But come, darling, I want my answer."

"And you shall have it," she said softly. " There it is ! "

As she spoke she raised her beautiful white hand and pointed to the ring I had given her, saying as she did so, " It has never left my finger since you placed it there ! "

"My best of girls," I cried, raising the little hand to my lips and kissing it fondly, " I am the very happiest man in the world. And now I must hear all your doings; tell me how you got home ! "

" There is little to tell," she answered. " I followed your route via Thursday Island, Brisbane, Sydney, and Melbourne. I stayed in the latter place for nearly a month, and while there advertised for a companion. The result was Mrs. Barker, a nice, amiable little person, whom you will shortly see. When we reached Naples I happened to see an advertisement concerning this

15

furnished house in an English paper, telegraphed about it, received an answer in Paris, engaged it, and arrived here this morning."

"And how did you leave the settlement? And, by the way, where is Mr. 'Beelzebub'?"

"The settlement was very well when I came away. They were busy building the new Communal Hall I used to talk to you about. And poor old Bel is left at the bungalow. I was afraid he might excite remark and possibly draw suspicion upon me."

"Alie, do you think you are safe in London?" I cried in alarm, all my old fears rushing back upon me at the mention of that one word *suspicion*. "What ever should I do if any one suspected you?"

"You need have no fear on that score, dear," my intrepid sweetheart answered, "there is no one in England who could possibly recognize me, and the only people in the whole world who could do so are Vesey of Hong Kong, the Sultan of Surabaya, the Rajah of Tavoy, Barkmansworth, and that lieutenant and midshipman. The first is dead; the second never leaves his own territory, the third is in bad odour with the English Government just at present and little likely to come home. Barkmansworth is, I presume, still in Hong Kong, and the lieutenant and his junior are with their ship in the China Sea."

"All the same, I shall not be satisfied until we are safely out of Europe again, Alie."

"You say *we*, then you mean to come away with me, George?"

"Of course, with whom else should I go? Hark! somebody is coming!"

"It is Mrs. Barker, my duenna. Now we must be matter of fact folk once more."

As she spoke, Mrs. Barker, a dapper little lady with silver gray hair and a very pleasant expression, entered the room.

"Let me introduce Dr. De Normanville to you," said Alie, rising from her chair and going forward to meet her. "Dr. De Normanville, Mrs. Barker."

I bowed and Mrs. Barker did the same, then we went in to dinner. What happened during that very pleasant meal, how Mrs. Barker found occasion to require something from her bedroom afterwards, and so left us alone in the drawing-room together, I need not relate ; suffice it that when I got home about twelve o'clock I was the happiest, and, at the same time, the most nervous, man in England.

Next morning I called for Janet and, willy nilly, carried her off there and then to call on Alie. We found her walking in her garden, which led down to the river, and I must be excused if I say that, proud as I was of my darling, I was infinitely prouder as I noticed the look of astonishment and admiration that came into Janet's face when she was introduced to her. Alie's radiant beauty and charming manners were irresistible, and before they had been together half an hour the two women were on the best of terms. It was Alie's earnest desire that we should remain to luncheon, and she herself walked to the railway station with us when we at last took our departure.

"Now, what do you think of my sweetheart?" I asked, as we steamed out of the station.

"I think that she is a very beautiful and charming

girl," was my sister's immediate reply, " and, if I know anything of my sex, she is as good as she's beautiful."

This pleased me, as you may be sure, and when Janet went on to tell me that she had invited Alie and Mrs. Barker to spend a few days with her, and that the visit would commence the following afternoon, my opinion of my sister's kindness became even more exaggerated than before.

And so that week went by, and another after it, till Alie had thoroughly settled down among us and nearly all the preparations for our wedding were complete. By that time, you may be sure, she had won golden opinions on every side. On each occasion that I saw Janet she was more and more profuse in her praises of her, until I had really to tell her that unless she moderated them a little I should soon become insufferably conceited about my good fortune.

One morning, when I was beginning to think of getting up, the following note was brought to me with my shaving water. It was from my sister, and had evidently been written the previous evening :

SOUTH KENSINGTON, MONDAY EVENING.

DEAR OLD GEORGE :

I have succeeded in inducing Alie and Mrs. Barker to prolong their visit to me until Saturday. On Wednesday evening we hope to witness the new play at Drury Lane. Alie, you know, has never seen a spectacular melodrama. We shall of course want a gentleman to escort us. Would you care for the position, or must we look elsewhere ? On that occasion we dine at 6.30, and, unless I hear from you to the contrary, I shall lay a place for you.

In haste.

Your affectionate sister,

JANET.

Need it be said that I accepted? or that on Wednesday evening I was proud of my charges as they took their seats in the box Janet had been at some pains to secure?

The house was packed from pit to gallery, and I noticed that more than one glass was levelled at the beautiful girl who took her place at Janet's side in the front of the box. Alie herself, however, seemed quite unconscious of the admiration she excited, and throughout the piece kept her eyes fixed upon the stage with never failing earnestness. What the play was I have not the very vaguest recollection.

In the middle of the first act I noticed that three gentlemen entered the box opposite us, and from the vociferous nature of their applause, gathered that they had evidently been dining, not wisely, but too well. After a while their glasses were so continually brought to bear on our box that I began to feel myself, foolishly enough, becoming excessively annoyed. The face of one of them struck me as familiar, and during the next interval, seeing that they had left their box, I made an excuse and went out to endeavour to discover who he was and where I had seen his face before. For a little while I was unsuccessful in my search, then, just as the next act was commencing, I turned a corner and almost ran into their arms. The man whose face I had been puzzling about was furthest from me, but I knew him instantly. *It was Barkmansworth!* My heart seemed to stand still with terror, and when I recovered my wits he was gone.

What was I to do? I dared not tell Alie before my sister and Mrs. Barker, and yet I knew, if Barkmansworth had recognised her, not an instant must be lost in getting her out of harm's way. For a moment I stood in the vestibule feeling more sick and giddy than I have ever felt before or since, and all the time trying vainly to think how to act. Then, when I took my seat again and saw that the occupants of the box opposite had left, I resolved to put off all consideration of the matter for that evening and to call and tell Alie first thing in the morning. Oh, that little bit of indecision! How fatal were its consequences!

When I had conveyed my fair charges home I made a severe headache an excuse, and bidding them good-night, set off on foot for my own abode. But my brain was too full of anxiety to entertain any idea of bed, so, turning off from the direct route, I wandered down to the Green Park and on to the Embankment, thence through Lincoln's Inn Fields to Oxford Street, and so round to Cavendish Square. By the time I let myself into my house it was nearly three o'clock and a beautiful morning. Passing along the hall, I went into my consulting room and lit the gas. A letter lay upon the table, addressed in my sister's handwriting, and marked "Immediate." With a sickening fear in my heart, I tore it open and read :

DEAR GEORGE :
  Come to me at once, without an instant's delay. Alie has been arrested.
Your frantic sister,
JANET.

The blow had fallen! My little shirking of an unpleasant duty had ruined the woman I loved. Oh, how bitterly I reproached myself for my delay in reporting my discovery. But if I had hesitated then, I did not do so now. A second or two later I had let myself out again and was off, as fast as I could go, on my way back to South Kensington.

REMANDED.

NEVER shall I forget the misery of that walk back from Cavendish Square to South Kensington ; I seemed to be tramping for ever, and all the time the words " Alie has been arrested ! " " Alie has been arrested ! " were singing and drumming in my ears with relentless reitera-tion. When I reached the house the sun was above the roof tops and I was wearied almost to the point of drop-ping. I rang the bell, and the peal had not died away before poor, heavy-eyed Janet had opened the door to me. Without a word she led me into her morning-room, the room where I had first told her of my love for Alie, and, having made me sit down, would not let me speak until I had partaken of some refreshment. I filled my glass, but pushed my plate away from me ; I could drink, but I was far too miserable to eat.

"Janet," I cried, "for Heaven's sake tell me, as quickly as you can, all that has happened ! "

"My poor George," she said ; "as I told you in my note, Alie has been arrested. You had not left the house more than a quarter of an hour before two men called and asked to be allowed to see me on most impor-tant business. They were shown in here and, when we were alone, requested permission to see Alie. I went to fetch her and brought her down with me. Then one of the men advanced towards her with a paper in his hand

and said 'Alic Dunbar, in the Queen's name I arrest you on a charge of piracy upon the High Seas.' Oh! it was horrible, and I can see it all now!"

"And what did my poor girl say?"

"Nothing! She was just as calm and collected as she always is. She simply took the paper from the man's hand and looked at it, after which she said: 'There must be some mistake; however, you are only doing your duty, I suppose. Where do you wish to take me?' 'To Scotland Yard first, madam,' the man said, 'then on to Bow Street.' Hearing that, Alic turned to me, and putting her arms round my neck, said: 'You will soften this blow as much as you can for George, won't you, Janet?' and then announced that as soon as she had changed her dress, and procured her hat and cloak, she would be ready to accompany them. These changes in her costume she was permitted to make, and, when they were accomplished, we set off, but not before I had written that note to you. We expected you would follow us at once, and be able to arrange the matter of bail."

"I did not get your letter until after three o'clock. I was in such a strange state of mind last night that I went for a long walk after leaving you. Janet, it is all my fault. Did you notice those men in the box opposite us at Drury Lane? If so, you may have observed that they continually stared at Alic through their glasses?"

"I *did* notice them, and very ill-bred fellows I thought them. I think Alic must have thought so too! But what have they to do with this matter?"

"Why, the man at the back of the box was none other than the person mentioned in that last newspaper paragraph about the Beautiful White Devil. He was the man, Barkmansworth, in fact, whom the Beautiful White Devil took from the mail boat and flogged in mid-ocean."

"But what has this to do with Alie?"

"Why, simply that,—no there can be no shirking it now, it must come out, and I know it is perfectly safe for me to tell you,—simply, Janet, because Alie *is* the Beautiful White Devil."

"Oh, George, my dear old brother; is this terrible thing true?"

"Perfectly true, Janet!"

"And you, of all men, were going to marry the Beautiful White Devil?"

"Don't say 'were,' say 'are'! Janet, it is only half-past five now. An hour and a half must elapse before I can do any good at the police station. If you will listen I will tell you the story of Alie's singular life, and how I became mixed up with her. Then, remembering what you have seen of her yourself, you will be able to judge what sort of woman the Beautiful White Devil really is!"

Thereupon I set to work and told her all my adventures. I described Alie's father's treatment by his government; his setting up a kingdom for himself in the Pacific; the events which followed his death and Alie's accession to the throne; the feud between herself and the Eastern Governments; her acts of justice and retribution; the outbreak of small-pox in her settlement, and her sending for me; what I saw on the island, and how I first came to love her. It was a long story, and by the time I had finished it was nearly seven o'clock. Then I looked at Janet, and found big tears standing in her eyes.

"What do you think of the Beautiful White Devil now?" I asked.

"I think that, come what may, George, we must save her."

"Of course we must, and now I'm going off to see her. May I give her any message from you?"

"Give her my fondest love, and tell her that, come what may, she shall be saved."

"It will cheer her to know that, in spite of what has happened, you believe in her. Good-bye!"

"Good-bye, my poor George."

I left the house, and hurrying down to Gloucester Road, took the underground train for the Temple, walking thence to Bow Street. On entering the police station I asked to see the officer in charge. To this grim official I stated the nature of my business, and begged to be permitted an interview with his prisoner. This he granted with a very civil grace; the jailer was accordingly called and I was led down a long corridor.

"Seeing that she is a lady," that official said, as he unlocked a door on the right, "we have given her a somewhat better room than we usually allow our prisoners. I have orders to permit you a quarter of an hour together."

He opened the door and I went in. With a little cry of joy, Alie, who had been sitting on a sofa at the further end, sprang to her feet and ran towards me, crying as she did so:

"Oh, George, dear, I knew you would come to me as soon as you could."

I took her in my arms and kissed her again and again ; her dear eyes were flooded with tears when I released her, but she brushed them away and tried to look brave for my sake. Then I led her back to the sofa and sat down beside her.

"Alie," I said softly, "this is all my fault. I saw Barkmansworth at Drury Lane last night and ought to have warned you. I intended to have done so this morning, but it was too late."

"Hush !" she answered, "you must not blame your-self. I, too, recognised him last night and should have spoken to you about it to-day. It is too late *now*, as you say."

"Can nothing be done, Alie ?"

"I cannot say yet. I have been too much upset since my arrival here to think. But you must find me a lawyer at once, George, who will defend me at the preliminary examination, and if it looks as if the case will go against me you must find some means by which I can escape."

"Escape ? Alie, you do not realise how impossible that is."

"Nothing is impossible when one has brains enough to devise a plot and sufficient money to work it out."

"If I could only feel as you do about it. But have you any scheme to suggest ?"

"Not yet, but I shall devote my whole attention to it and it will go hard with me if I cannot hit on some-thing. Would you have the courage to dare very much for my sake, George ?"

"I would dare anything under the sun for you, Alie, and though you asked me such a question, I do not think you feel any doubt as to what answer I would give."

"I had no doubt. Do not think that. And now, George, tell me what your sister says, now that she knows who I am?"

"Janet is more your friend than ever. I told her your story this morning, and she bade me give you her love and tell you we would save you yet."

Again the tears rose in Alie's eyes.

"What will the East say when it hears that the Beautiful White Devil is caught at last?"

"I don't know, and I don't care. One thing I'm certain of, however, and that is that I should like to have five minutes with Mr. Barkmansworth alone. I think then he'd know that——"

But what I was going to say was interrupted by the entrance of the officer who had brought me to the room.

"Time's up, I'm sorry to say, sir."

I rose immediately and turned to say good-bye! Being a good-hearted fellow, the man left us alone together for another moment, and during that time I was able to whisper an assurance to my sweetheart that no stone should be left unturned to secure her release. Then bidding her be of good cheer, I passed out, feeling as if the bolts clanging behind me were closing on my heart.

It was well after eight o'clock before I left Bow Street and turned homewards; the shops, in most cases, had their shutters down, but though I looked for a newspaper board, it was some time before I sighted one. Then for the first time I saw the headline I had been dreading:

" Sensational Arrest of the Notorious Beautiful White Devil."

I stopped and bought a paper and then continued my journey, pausing at a telegraph office to send a wire to my old chum, Brandwon, in which I asked him, as he valued our friendship, to come to me without a moment's delay. When I got home I changed my clothes—had a cold bath, which restored me somewhat, and then ordered breakfast, which I felt I could not touch, and while it was preparing, sat down to read the account of the arrest. It was but a short report and published the barest details.

Nine o'clock had just struck when a cab drew up at the door and Brandwon jumped out. I opened the front door to him myself, and, as I did so, felt as if we were one step at least on the road to Alie's release.

"Look here, my friend," he said, as I led him across the hall to my dining-room. "This is all very well, you know, but what in the name of fortune makes you send for me at this unearthly hour. Have you poisoned a patient and find yourself in need of me to square matters, or have you been jilted and hope to bring an action for the damage done to your broken heart? Out with it. But forgive my chaff if it's anything more serious."

He must have seen by my face that something was very wrong, for his jocular manner suddenly left him and he sat down all seriousness.

"There is something very much the matter, Brandwon," I said ; " read that ! "

I handed him the morning paper and pointed to the paragraph detailing the arrest. He read it through and then, seating himself at the breakfast table, poured himself out a cup of coffee and buttered a piece of toast, before he spoke. When he did so, he said solemnly, " I think I understand. You are interested in this lady and want me to undertake her defence—is that so ? "

" That is exactly what I want. I was at my wit's end to know what to do, when suddenly it flashed through my brain, ' Send for Edward Brandwon.' I sent that wire accordingly, and here you are. If there is any man living who can save the woman I love, you are he."

" I'll do my best, you may be sure, for your sake, old boy. Now, where is she ? "

" At Bow Street. She is to be brought before the court this morning at twelve o'clock."

He took out his watch and looked at it.

" Well, I've none too much time. I'll go down and have an interview with her at once. Keep up your heart, old chap, we'll do our best and nobody can do more ! "

I wrung his hand, and then, hailing a cab, he jumped into it and set off for the police station.

Long before twelve o'clock I was in the court, waiting for the examination to come on. The news of the case must have gone abroad, for the hall was densely packed with people anxious to catch a glimpse of the famous Beautiful White Devil, whose exploits were almost as well known in England as in the East. Every rank of life seemed to be represented and, when the magistrate took his seat on the bench, I noticed that the chairs on either side of him were occupied by two illustrious personages whose dignity should have prevented them from giving such an exhibition of idle curiosity. Seeing the rush there was to stare at my poor unfortunate sweetheart, I could have found it in my heart to hit out like a madman at those round me.

Precisely at twelve o'clock the door on the right hand side of the court opened and Alie stepped into the hall and ascended the iron dock. She walked with her usual queenly step, held her head high, and when she reached her place, looked proudly round the dingy hall. Such was the effect of her wonderful beauty upon those present, that, despite the efforts of the officers of the court to prevent it, a loud buzz of admiration came from the spectators. She was dressed entirely in black, a colour which, as I have said before, displayed her white skin and beautiful hair to the very best advantage. Having taken her place, she bowed politely to the presiding magistrate, who returned her salute, and then the examination commenced. The first proceeding was for the police to make a statement of their case to the court. It was then shown that, although a warrant had long been out for her arrest, the Beautiful White Devil had evaded justice for many years. Indeed, it was only for the reason that information had been supplied to the London police within the last few days, that they had become aware that the Beautiful White Devil had left the East and arrived in England. Inquiries were instantly made, and on the strength of them the prisoner now in the dock had been arrested. They, the police, did not propose to call witnesses at this preliminary hearing, but would merely ask that the information should be read over, the evidence of arrest given, and then a remand granted in order that the arrival of an officer from Singapore might be awaited and further inquiries made.

At this point Brandwon rose to his feet, and, adopting a quiet, sober attitude of respectful remonstrance, begged to be allowed to place before the court what he considered and would unhesitatingly call a deliberate and cruel injustice. He pointed out the small likelihood there was of the charge being true, he dilated upon the facts of Alie's arrival from Australia, of her quiet, lady-like demeanour, spoke of her impending marriage with a gentleman, a personal friend of his own, well known and universally respected in London, and brought his remarks to a close by declaring it a monstrous thing that, in this nineteenth century and in this land of which we pretend to be so proud, it should be within the power of a public body like the police, without a tittle of evidence at their back to bear their case out, to bring so shameful a charge against an innocent girl, who might possibly have to suffer from the effects of it all her life. He would not ask the court to consent to a remand ; on the contrary, he would ask His Worship to dismiss the case altogether, and, at the same time, to issue a stinging and well-merited rebuke to the police for their officiousness and quite uncalled-for action in the matter.

Clever and impressive as his harangue was, it, however, failed utterly in its purpose. The magistrate had evidently carefully considered the case beforehand and determined upon his course of action. The decision given, therefore, was "remanded for a week. Bail refused."

I saw Alie bow gravely to the court, the policeman

16

open the door of the dock, and a moment later, feeling quite sick and giddy, I was in the throng leaving the court. By the time I reached the street my darling was on her way to Holloway.

That afternoon, at three o'clock, Janet and I drove out to the prison, and, having shown our authorities, were instantly conducted to the room in which prisoners are permitted to interview their friends.

What the two women I loved best in the world said to each other during that interview I cannot remember. I only know that Janet kissed Alie and cried over her, and that Alie received it all with that gentle graciousness which was so wonderfully becoming to her. When we had discussed the events which had led up to the arrest, I asked Alie if she were quite comfortable.

"Perfectly," she answered. "My cell is by no means an unpleasant one. I have some books and writing materials, and I have arranged to have my meals brought in to me from a restaurant outside."

"What did you think of Brandwon's speech this morning?" I then asked her.

"I thought it very clever and impressive," she answered, "but I was not surprised when it proved of no avail. No! There is very little chance as far as I can see. In a month the officer from Singapore will be in London, and, unless something happens to prevent it, I shall be sent out East to stand my trial."

"Something must prevent it," whispered Janet.

"But what? You cannot escape so easily in England, I find," she answered. "These stone walls are very strong and the discipline is so perfect."

"But tell me, Alie," I broke in, "what Brandwon

thinks of your chance. You have of course told him everything?"

"He says my only hope is their not being able to prove identity. Barkmansworth's evidence unsupported will not go for very much, he thinks, and, Ebbington and Vesey being dead, there only remain the two native princes, and the man-of-war's men who by chance may not be called. I fear it is a hopeless business, however."

"No! No! You must not think that. Be sure we will find a way to get you off. Trust us." Then dropping my voice, "And if we can't do it legally we'll do it illegally."

"You must run no risk for my sake, George; I could not allow that."

"If only Walworth were here. His wit would hit on something."

"Walworth unfortunately is ten thousand miles away. So it is no use thinking of him. But see, here is the warder—your time is up. Good-bye, dear Janet. I pray that you may find it in your heart to forgive me for having brought this trouble upon you."

But Janet, who by this time had learned to love this fascinating girl with all her heart, would listen to no such talk. When the door opened, like the kind sister she was, she went out first, thus permitting us an opportunity of saying farewell alone. When I joined her again I had a little note in my waistcoat pocket that seemed somehow to make me a happier man than I had been for hours past.

From the prison I drove Janet to her own house and then went back to Cavendish Square.

When I had dismissed the cabman I let myself in and

proceeded to my consulting room. Opening the door, I walked in, only to come to a sudden halt before a man sitting in my own armchair. He was small and queerly built, wore a long coat that reached nearly to his heels, had gray hair, a ferociously curled moustache, and a short, closely cropped white beard. The effect, when he looked at me over the edge of the paper he was perusing, was most comical. For a moment I stood bewildered, but I was destined to be even more so when he rose and came toward me, holding out his hand, and saying :

"Bon jour, Monsieur!" Then in broken English, "Pray, do you not remember your very old friend ?"

I thought and thought, but for the life of me could not recollect ever having seen his face before. I was about to speak when he stopped me, and changing his voice said in excellent English :

"No! I can see you don't." Then pulling off his wig : "Well! Do you now ?"

It was Walworth!

CHAPTER XIV.

Directly I realised who my guest was, I rushed forward and seized his hand with a show of delight greater than, I believe, I have ever felt at meeting a man before or since. If I had been given the pick of all men in the world at that particular juncture in my life's history, I believe I should have declared for *him*.

"We had no idea that you were in England," I said when the first excitement had somewhat subsided. "Both Alie and I thought you were ten thousand miles away. You have heard the awful news, I suppose."

"How could I help it when every board in the streets sets it forth, and all the paper boys are bellowing the latest news of the capture of the Beautiful White Devil. But I want to know the real facts."

"You shall know everything directly. But first tell me what has brought you home in this providential manner?"

"I came because I heard that Barkmansworth was coming. I received a warning from Hong Kong that he had applied for leave, and I knew that if he found out her ladyship was in England he would lose no opportunity of revenging himself for that affair outside Singapore. But he got away before me, and my welcome to London yesterday was the news of her lady-ship's arrest. You did not see me at the preliminary examination this morning, I suppose?"

"No! I certainly did not. And I thought I scanned every face."

"And yet I was standing beside you all the time!"

"Good gracious, how do you mean?"

"Pray tell me who stood next to you? Wasn't it a medium sized military-looking man in a much worn frock coat with a velvet collar."

"Now I come to think of it, it was!"

"Well, I was that man. I'm beginning to think my disguises are artistic after all."

"But *why* all this disguise? What are you afraid of in London."

"I am afraid of our friend Barkmansworth, if you want to know. I was the man who took him off the mail boat, remember, and my face must be unpleasantly familiar to him. If he saw me, I should be arrested within an hour, and whatever happens, seeing the work that lies before us, that must not!"

"Do you think you can be of use to her ladyship in her defence then?"

"It must never come to a defence. It would be fatal to allow her to be sent to Hong Kong. They would convict her at once. No! There is nothing for it but for us to plan some means of escape for her, and yet, when one thinks how perfect English police arrangements are, that seems wellnigh impossible. However, done it must be, by hook or crook, and we must set about it at once."

"But how? Have you any idea in your head?"

"Not at present, but it will be strange if I don't hit upon one before very long. If only her ladyship could help us!"

"Wait one moment. Perhaps she can. When I left her this afternoon she gave me a note, which I was not to open until I got home. Let us see what it says."

I took it out of my waistcoat pocket, opened it, and read it aloud. It certainly contained the germs of an idea and ran as follows:

"I have been thinking over what we spoke of this morning and it seems to me that, if I am to escape at all, the attempt must be made during the time I am being conveyed from Bow Street to Holloway in the prison van. The question is whether sufficient temptation could be put before the driver and the guard to induce them to assist me. Will you think this out?"

When I had finished reading, I asked Walworth for his opinion. But for nearly five minutes he allowed no sign to escape him to show that he had heard my question, only laid himself back in his chair, looked up at the ceiling, and meanwhile slowly tore my newspaper into rags. When he had finished his work of destruction, he sat up straight and slapped his hand on his knee.

"Her ladyship is always right. I believe I *do* see a way now!"

"What is it?" I asked, in almost breathless excitement.

"You must not ask me just yet. I'll go away and make a few inquiries first. To-night at nine o'clock I'll come back here, and we'll go into the matter thoroughly.   For the present then, good-bye, and keep up your heart.   Have no fear, we'll rescue her yet."

There was something so strong and confident about the man that this assurance roused and braced me like a tonic.   I stopped him, however, before he could reach the door.

"One word first, Walworth.   Do you know the position in which I stand towards Alie ? "

"I know that you were to have been married within the next three weeks, if that's what you mean ?" he answered.   "And so you shall be yet if I can bring it about.   Dr. De Normanville, you have got a woman for whom we all would die.   This is your chance to show yourself worthy of her, and, if you will allow me to say so, I think you will.   I am your faithful servant as well as hers, remember that.   Now I must go ! "

" Good luck go with you ! "

I let him out by the front door, and then went back to my room to try and discover what the idea could be that he had got into his fertile brain?   I felt I would have given anything to have known something a little more definite.   However, as I *didn't* know, there was nothing for it but to exercise my patience until nine o'clock should arrive.

It may be guessed how anxiously I watched the hands of the clock upon my mantelpiece.   At last, however, they drew round to the appointed hour and I prepared myself for Walworth's arrival.   But, though I saw no sign of him, I had not very long to wait for a visitor.   The last stroke of nine had hardly died away before my ear caught a ring at the bell and a moment later a "Mr. Samuel Baker" was ushered into the room. As he entered, I took stock of him, half fearing he might be some sort of police officer in-disguise. He was a stout, rather pompous man of middle height, with fluffy whiskers, clean shaven chin and upper lip, and from his dress might have been a linen draper or small tradesman from some cathedral town. Having warmly shaken hands with me he put his top hat down on a chair, seated himself on another, mapped his forehead with a red bandanna handkerchief, took off and carefully wiped his spectacles, returned them to his nose, and then said quietly. "What do you think of this for a make-up, Dr. De Normanville?"

"Walworth," I cried, in utter amazement. "You don't really mean to say it's you. I was just beginning to wonder how I should manage to rid myself of Mr. Samuel Baker before you should arrive. You are certainly a genius at concealing your identity, if ever there was one."

"I have had to do it so often," he replied, "that I have reduced it to a science."

"Have you anything to report?"

"A good deal," he answered. "But before I begin, may I light a cheroot? I see from the ash trays you smoke in here!"

"Smoke as much as you please," I replied. "May I also offer you some refreshment. Perhaps you haven't dined? If so, I can tell them to bring you up something!"

"No, thank you," he answered; "I have dined, and excellently. Now let us get to business without any further waste of time."

"With all the good will in the world," I said, seating myself again. "Go on. Tell me all."

"Well! in the first place, you must understand that when I left here this afternoon I went for a walk to think out my plan. To begin with, I saw quite clearly that any attempt to rescue her ladyship from either Bow Street police station itself or Holloway Gaol would only be a farce, and by proving a failure would end by completely spoiling the whole thing. I settled it, therefore, that the only time when it could be done, with any hope of success, would be on the journey *from* the court *to* the prison. In other words, during the time she is in the van. But how that is to be managed is more difficult to see. To bribe the officials, as her ladyship suggests, would be altogether too hazardous a proceeding, even if it were possible, nor is it to be imagined that we could secure the van for ourselves."

"It seems a very difficult matter."

"Difficult, certainly, but by no means as hopeless as you would be inclined to suppose. No! I have an idea in my head that looks promising, and you must assist me in carrying it out."

"You have every reason to know that you may count upon my doing that," I answered. "Who would so gladly assist as I ?"

"Of course I understand that, but I have to warn you that this will mean, either way you look at it, social extinction for you. If it fails and we are caught, you are done for as far as your reputation here is concerned. If we are not caught, well, I suppose you will fly with her, and in that case you will certainly never see England again."

" Do you suppose I shall allow my own social position to weigh with me, if by risking it I can save her ? "

" No, I don't think you will. But now let me detail my scheme as I have thought it out. In the first place I have ascertained that the van leaves the prison at a definite hour every day. It drives down, takes the prisoners up, and drives back again. This being so, it is certain, as I have said before, that it must be stopped on its way *from* the prison *to* the court, and in such a way that it cannot go on again for at least half an hour. In the meantime another van must drive down equipped in every way like the real one. This one will take up the prisoner and drive off. Once out of sight of the station it will drive into the yard of an empty house, a conveyance will then be in waiting in the other street, her ladyship passes through the house, gets into that and drives off to a railway station ; there a Pullman must be in readiness to take her to the seaside, whence a yacht will convey her to some place where we can have the *Lone Star* to meet her. I shall cable to Patterson to set off and be in readiness to pick us up directly we have decided where that place shall be."

" But how will you cable to him without exciting suspicion ? "

" You need have no fear on that score ; we have a means of communicating of our own, which I would explain now only it would be waste of time. What do you think of my scheme ? "

" It sounds all right, but is it workable ? "

" I really think so ! However, we will discuss it, item by item, and try and arrive at a conclusion that way. To begin with, money must be considered no object. If even £10,000 is necessary to its success, £10,000 will be spent. In the first place, we must find a competent coachbuilder at once. If he has a van on hand, which is hardly likely, we'll purchase it! If not, well, then he must put on all his hands and make one, even if he has to work day and night to do it."

"But how will you explain the purpose for which we want it?"

"I have thought of that, and, when I left you, I sent the following telegram : "

Here he produced a duplicate form from his pocket and read it aloud :

"To the Lessee Olympic Theatre, Manchester:

"What dates this month? Reply terms, Stragaus, West Strand Telegraph Office.

"Maximillien Stragaus."

"But who on earth is Maximillien Stragaus, and what has the Royal Olympic Theatre, Manchester, to do with our scheme ? "

"Everything. In the first place you must realise the fact that I am Maximillien Stragaus, the world-renowned theatrical *entrepreneur*, and that you are his secretary, Fairlight Longsman. Having received a reply from Manchester, I decide to open there with my wonderful and intensely exciting prison drama, 'Saved by a Woman's Pluck,' on the third Saturday in June. Here is the preliminary announcement. I had it struck off this afternoon."

He took from the small bag he had brought into the room with him a large theatrical poster, covered

with printing of all colours of the rainbow. It read as
follows :

ROYAL OLYMPIC THEATRE,
MANCHESTER.

Lessee, ... Mr. William Carrickford.

For Ten Nights Only,
Commencing Saturday, June 20th.

Mr. Maximillien Stragaus' World-renowned Standard Company,
in the intensely exciting Prison Drama,

"SAVED BY A WOMAN'S PLUCK."

Detectives—Police—Bloodhounds—Real Horses and Real
Prison Vans.

Sole Manager and Proprietor, Mr. Maximillien Stragaus.
Secretary, ... Mr. Fairlight Longsman.

"There! what do you think of that for a poster?"

"Very startling," I answered. "But I must reiterate
my former remark, that I do not understand in the very
least degree what it has to do with us."

"Why, look here, it means that to-morrow morning
we go to that coachbuilder I was speaking of and give
him an order for a prison van. Incidentally we will
show him this poster, and state that, owing to change
of dates, we must have the van delivered this day week.
Don't you see? If we hadn't something to show, he
might suspect; this poster, however, will set his mind
completely at rest, and, at the same time, be an excuse
for haste. Now, do you understand?"

"I do, and I must say I admire your wonderful
resource. What next?"

"Well, the next thing will be to obtain two police

uniforms and two trustworthy men, one to drive the van the other to act as guard. That, however, will be easily managed. The next item will be rather more difficult!"

"What is that?"

"Why, to find a sure and certain means of stopping the real van on its way down to the court."

"We couldn't waylay the driver and keep him talking, I suppose?"

"We could try it, of course; but it wouldn't be sure enough. He might be a conscientious man, you see, and not like to stop, or he might stop and afterwards whip up to make up lost time. No! we must hit on something that will absolutely prevent him from going on for at least half an hour, and yet something that will not excite suspicion. I think I see a way to do it, but it will require the most minute and careful working out to insure its success. To begin with, I shall have to find a first-class man for the job, and possibly I shall have to cable to America for him."

"What is your idea?"

"To arrange a collision. To have a runaway, and crash into the horses."

"Would that do, do you think?"

"If I can find the right man and the right sort of horses."

"I don't like it. To quote your own words, it doesn't sound sure enough."

"We shall have to do it if we can't hit out a better way. Then we must discover a house somewhere in a handy neighbourhood; it must have a yard at the back, opening into an obscure street. The yard must have high gates and be in such a position that it cannot be overlooked by the neighbours. Then the day before the business comes off we must find an invalid carriage, engage a Pullman car for Portsmouth, and hire a yacht for a voyage to the Cape.”

“It will mean simply superhuman labour, if it is all to be accomplished in a fortnight.”

“It will, but I don’t think either of us is afraid of work. Aren’t we fighting for what is more precious to her than her life? Yes! We’ll do it between us. Don’t you doubt that. Now I must be off again; I’ve a lot to do before I can get to bed to-night. By the way, will it be convenient for you if I call here at half-past five to-morrow morning? We must be at the coach-builder’s by seven o’clock.”

“Come at three if you like, you will find me quite ready.”

“Then good-night.”

He went away and I to bed. At five o’clock I woke, had a bath, dressed, and went down stairs. Punctually, almost to the minute, a slightly Jewish, black-ringletted man, wearing a profusion of diamonds, put in an appearance, bag in hand. Though I should never have recognised him as Walworth I felt certain it was he, so I let him in and we went into my study together.

“Now,” said my friend, for it was Walworth, as I suspected, “I don’t know what you’ll say to it, but it’s absolutely necessary for the success of our scheme that you should assume some disguise. As you are known to be the affianced husband of her ladyship, the police will be certain to have their eyes on you.”

“Do with me as you like,” I replied; “I am in your hands entirely.”

"Then, with your permission, we will set to work at once. I have taken the liberty of bringing a few things with me. You have an old-fashioned frock coat, I presume."

"A very old-fashioned one," I answered, with a laugh.

"Then put it on, also a pair of light check trousers, if you have them."

I went to my room and did as he desired. When I returned to the study he had arranged a number of articles upon the table—crepe hair, spectacles, a curiously low cut collar, and a soft felt hat with a dented crown. He gazed at me with approval, and then said :

"The effect will be excellent, I feel sure. Sit down here."

I did as commanded and he immediately set to work. As he was occupied behind me I could not of course see what he was doing, but after a while he took off my own collar, put on the low one he had brought with him, cut up some crepe hair and gummed it to my face, with what I believe is technically termed "spirit gum," trimmed its exuberances with a pair of scissors, and finally combed my moustache over it. This accomplished, he placed the spectacles upon my nose and the soft felt hat rather rakishly upon my head, patted me on the shoulder, and said :

"Look at yourself in the glass."

I rose and went over to the fire-place. But, though I looked in the mirror above the chimney piece, I did not recognise myself. My moustache was waxed to a point and stood out above a close-cropped chestnut beard, while over my coat collar hung a profusion of curls of a corresponding colour. Indeed, my whole appearance suggested a man whose aim in life it was to copy, as nearly as possible, the accepted portrait of the Bard of Avon.

"It is wonderful," I said. "Nobody would ever recognise me. I feel a theatrical agent all over."

"Remember you are Fairlight Longsman, the author of several farces, and my secretary. Whatever you do, don't forget that. Now we must be going. Come along."

We left the house unnoticed, and, having hailed a hansom, were driven to the carriage builder's yard at Vauxhall. Walworth had evidently written preparing him for our visit, for, early as it was, we found him waiting to receive us.

"Zir," began Mr. Maximillien Stragaus, in broken English, as soon as he had descended from the cab. "Is it you dot are Mr. Ebridge?"

"That is my name, sir," said the coachbuilder. "And you are Mr. Stragaus, I presume."

"Dot is my name. Dis shentleman is my secretary, Mr. Fairlide Longsman. Now, you know, an' so we can our business begin to dalk!"

"Perhaps you will be good enough, gentlemen, to step into my office first. We shall be more private there?"

We followed him into the room he mentioned, and took possession of the chairs he offered us.

"Now, Mr. Stragaus, in what way can I be of service to you?" he asked, seating himself as he spoke at his desk.

"Zir! My segratary sprechens the Anglaish better nor me, he vill dell you."

17

I felt that it behoved me to do my best, so leaning forward in a confidential manner, I said :

"My employer, as doubtless you are very well aware, Mr. Ebridge, is one of the largest theatrical *entrepreneurs* in England. His dealings are gigantic. And it is the business connected with one of those enormous productions that brings us here. In the first place, you must know that, on the third Saturday in this present month, he has arranged to produce the entirely new and original drama, "Saved by a Woman's Pluck," at the Royal Olympic Theatre, Manchester. By the way, have you the preliminary poster with you, Mr. Stragaus?"

In answer Mr. Stragaus produced from his bag the placard before described and spread it upon the table, at the same time looking at the coachbuilder as if to demand his opinion on such a fine display of colour.

"You will observe, Mr. Ebridge," I continued, when the other had read it, "that the whole production will be on a scale of unparalleled splendour,—police, bloodhounds, live horses, and one large prison van, all on the stage,—it will be one of the greatest successes of the century. But we want your assistance."

"You mean, of course, that you want me to make you a van!"

"Exactly!"

"Just a makeshift affair for the stage, I presume?"

"Oh, dear, no! That is not Mr. Stragaus' way of doing business at all. If he has a fire engine on the stage, as he had in his last production, it must be a real engine, with every detail complete and in proper working order. In the same way then, when he orders a police van, he wants it made in every particular just as you would make it for Her Majesty's Government. There must be no difference at all in any one respect, neither the painting, lettering, nor the internal fittings."

"It will cost you a lot of money, Mr. Stragaus," said the builder.

"Dot is no madder at all to me," replied Mr. Stragaus pompously ; "I vill 'ave de ding berfect or nod at all. Vot is more, I must 'ave it at once."

"Mr. Stragaus, I may point out to you, Mr. Ebridge," I continued, "is in a very great hurry. There has been a slight pushing forward of dates, and in order to insure a success he is willing to pay you handsomely if you will complete the work in a short space of time."

"How long can you give me, sir ? "

"A week exactly. Not a day longer ! "

"Impossible. It cannot be done ! "

"Den ve must go elsewhere, mine vriend," said Mr. Stragaus. "Dot is all. If you will underdake to do de vork and to 'and me over de van gomplete on next Duesday evening at twelve o'glock, I vill pay you dwice de sum you ask me now."

The man looked up in surprise at this extraordinary offer, and asked to be excused for a moment while he consulted with his foreman. While he was absent, Walworth whispered :

"I think he'll do it. And if we can arrange it that way we shall be able to get it safely up to the yard of the house unobserved."

Here the coachbuilder returned.

"My foreman tells me he thinks it can be done, sir. But you must see that it will mean night and day work for us all. And the charge will have to be on a corresponding scale."

"Dot is nodings to me. You do de work, and I vill pay der money. You agree? Den it is arranged I shall send my men for der van 'ere on Duesday night at twelve o'glock, and you will 'ave it gomplete! Den we can zend it on by rail vorst ding in der mornin'. But, mind you dis, if it is not done den, I vill not pay you von farding, you agree?"

"I agree. I have given you my promise, Mr. Stragaus, and whatever happens, it shall be completed by that time!"

"Dot is goot. You might, too, 'ave a tarbaulin to cover it mit, so that de publick shall not see it ven ve take it away. Now, zir, I vish you goot morning. You vill be paid for de van ven my men dake delivery."

"Thank you, sir! Good-morning, gentlemen."

When we were once more in the cab, and on our way back to town, Walworth discarded his German accent and resumed his natural tongue.

"So far so good. That bit of business is satisfactorily accomplished."

"You did not say anything to him about observing secrecy."

"It wasn't necessary. That poster, which you will notice I have left upon his table, will account for everything."

"But supposing the police get to hear of it, and it rouses their suspicions?"

"Well, let them get to hear of it. If they suspect, they will call on Ebridge and make inquiries. He will then describe us and show the poster. They may then possibly telegraph to the Olympic, Manchester, and learn that Mr. Stragaus *has* booked a season there for his new play. That will put them off the scent completely."

" And what are we to do now ? "

" Well, now, you had better come to breakfast with me, I think, at my lodgings. You can there resume your own everyday appearance. During the morning I am going to meet two men I have in my mind for the policemen ; after that I shall visit a tailor's shop and order the uniforms as arranged. In the afternoon I'm going to hunt for a house."

" Can I do anything else to help you ? "

" Not just at present. Unless you can find me a trustworthy lady who will consent to masquerade for a little while as a hospital nurse ? "

" There I think I *can* help you. My sister Janet, I'm sure, would gladly do so. I'll call upon her this afternoon and see."

I did so, and of course secured Janet's immediate promise of co-operation.

CHAPTER XV.

ON looking back upon that dreadful fortnight, I almost wonder how I managed to live through it. Indeed, had it not been for Walworth's indomitable energy and the corresponding spirit it provoked in me, I sometimes doubt if I should have come through it in possession of my senses. The anxiety and the constant dread of failure were the worst parts of it, and the last haunted me, day and night, without cessation.

Every day popular excitement, fanned by the newspapers, was growing greater in London. As more became known of the Beautiful White Devil's extraordinary career, the interest taken by the public in the case increased, until it was generally admitted that at the final examination it would be wellnigh impossible to gain admittance to the court. As, however, my duty on that occasion would lie elsewhere, I did not trouble myself very much about that.

At last the Wednesday preceding the fatal Thursday dawned. This was the last day permitted us in which to perfect our arrangements. I had been warned by Walworth that he would call upon me late in the evening to make his final report, and at his particular request I arranged that my sister Janet should be present. I wrote her a note to that effect, and at eight o'clock precisely she drove up to the door. When we were alone in my room together, I said :

"Janet, it is Walworth's wish that you should be present at our interview. Have you made up your mind definitely? Remember, there is yet time for you to draw back if you wish to do so."

She drew herself up proudly and looked me in the face.

"There will be no drawing back as far as I am concerned," she said. "No! if you and Alie leave England and will take me, I will go with you gladly. Why should I not? I have no one left now to consider, and without you both my life would be too lonely."

"Janet, dear ; what can I say to you?" I answered. "But there, you know how I feel about your generosity, don't you?"

"I do! So let's say no more about it."

Just then there was a ring at the bell, and a few moments later my man ushered in a decrepid old gentlemen of about seventy years of age, who, immediately the door had closed behind him, straightened his back, allowed his cheeks to fill again, and declared himself to be the ever-cautious Walworth. He bowed to Janet, shook hands with me, and then said :

"I couldn't call in the capacity of either Mr. Maximillien Stragaus or my old friend Samuel Baker again, you see! So I adopted this disguise. By the way. it may surprise you to learn that every one who enters or leaves this house is watched and followed. If you go to the window you will see a man leaning against the lamp post on the other side of the street. He is a police agent. But let us proceed to business."

"With all my heart," I said. "I'm sick with longing to know how our preparations are proceeding!"

"Nothing could be more satisfactory," he answered. "The case, as you well know, will not be called on till the afternoon. The instant it *is* over the man I cabled to America for, and in whom I have the most perfect trust, will drive a pair of vicious horses, purchased yesterday, out of a livery stable yard in the direction in which the van will travel. When he sees it ahead of him he will act in such a manner as to lead people to suppose him to be drunk; he will also begin to lash his animals, who will certainly run away. He is one of the finest whips living, and will drive those horses crash into the team of the van, and by so doing will, we sincerely trust, cause such damage as will delay their arrival for at least half an hour. In the meantime our own van will be in readiness, and the instant the case is over will drive into the yard, and after the necessary preliminaries, all of which I have personally worked out and arranged, the prisoner will be put into it, the door locked, and the van will then drive off to us. We shall be awaiting its arrival; you, madam, in your nurse's dress, and you, Dr. De Normanville, as I shall prepare you to act the part of a middle-aged naval man whose one hobby in life is yachting. Arriving at the house we shall carry the patient, wrapped up to the eyes, to an invalid carriage in the front street, and drive off to the station, there to catch the afternoon express for Portsmouth. I have secured a Pullman car; the house is also engaged, and has been partly furnished in order to deceive the neighbours: I have settled that the invalid carriage shall be at the door earlier than it will be wanted, and the yacht, which I have chartered for six months, will be in readiness to get under weigh the instant we're aboard!"

"And what will become of the van and horses?"

"The horses will be taken away from the yard within an hour of our departure. The van can remain there as long as it pleases. We will hope by the time they find it we shall be far away from England."

"And does Alie understand your arrangements?" asked Janet.

"Perfectly. I called at the gaol this morning, disguised as a solicitor's clerk, saw her, and told her all. You need have no fear for her, she will play her part to perfection."

"Then everything is settled, I suppose, and there is nothing for us to do but to wait patiently for to-morrow?"

"Nothing but that! Now, with your permission, I will be going. I don't suppose I shall see you again till we meet at the house."

"Good-bye, and God bless you, Walworth, for all you have done."

After he had left us Janet and I sat talking late into the night, and when we separated at her bedroom door, it was with a heartfelt wish that "good luck" might attend us on the morrow.

Next morning the long hours seemed as if they would never pass. All my personal arrangements had been made some days before, and my luggage sent off to the yacht at Portsmouth, labelled "Captain R. Wakemen," so there was absolutely nothing at all for me to do to kill the time till we were due at the house. At twelve o'clock, sharp to the minute, Janet and I had lunch, and at half-past, set off in different directions, taking particular care to see that we were not followed.

We reached the house almost simultaneously and were received at the door by an irreproachable maid-servant, who did not seem in the least surprised to see us. Walworth we found in a room at the back, this time irreproachably got up as an old family butler. My sister was already dressed in her nurse's apparel, and very sweet and womanly she looked in it. In the passage, outside the one room which had been made habitable, was a curious sort of stretcher, the use of which I could not determine.

"That is the bed place upon which we shall carry your poor invalid wife out to the carriage," said Walworth. "You see it is quite ready for use."

"I see. And when am I to make my toilette? I have brought the clothes you mentioned with me, in this parcel."

"That's right. I was half afraid you might bring a hand-bag, which would have had to be left behind and would very possibly have been recognised. Now I think you had better come into the other room and let me make you up at once."

I followed him, and when I emerged again a quarter of an hour later, I might very well have stood for a portrait of a representative middle-aged English naval man on the retired list. My hair was iron gray, as also were my close cropped beard and moustache ; the very cut of my clothes and the fashion of my neck cloth seemed to set forth my calling as plain as any words could speak. In this get-up I had not the least fear that any one would recognise me. By this time it was nearly two o'clock, and the case was to commence at half-past.

"Is everything prepared?" I asked Walworth, for about the hundredth time, as we adjourned to the sitting-room.

"Everything," he answered, with the same patient equanimity. "Come into the yard and see them harness the horses."

I followed him out into the back regions, where we found two stalwart policemen busily occupied attaching a couple of horses to an enormous Black Maria. They touched their hats to me with as little concern as if the business they were engaged to carry out was one of the very smallest importance. Somehow their stolidity did not seem reassuring to me, and I accordingly called Walworth on one side.

"Are you perfectly sure you can trust these men?" I asked anxiously.

"Absolutely," he answered. "I know them of old, and I can tell you we are extremely lucky to get them. Besides, they know that if they get the prisoner safely away they will each receive a thousand pounds. If they don't they get nothing. Don't be afraid. You may depend implicitly on them. Now come inside. I have had the telephone put in the house on purpose for this moment, and we must watch it."

We returned to the sitting-room and waited. The minutes seemed long as hours, and so horrible was the suspense that I began to conjure up all sorts of calamities. Perhaps I may be laughed at for owning myself such a coward, but let the pluckiest man living try the ordeal I was then passing through, and see if he would be braver. No! I was in a condition of complete terror, and I'll own it!

Suddenly, with a noise that echoed down the empty corridor and braced us to action like a trumpet call, the telephone bell rang out. Both Walworth and I jumped to our feet at the same instant and appropriated the ear trumpets. Then a tiny voice inside the instrument said mysteriously:

"The case is adjourned and the crowd is dispersing."

With a step as steady and a voice as firm as if he were ordering his carriage for an airing in the Park, Walworth went to the back door, I following close at his heels. He gave a signal and then crossed the yard to the gates, which he began to open.

"Are you ready?" he cried to the men.

"Quite ready," the taller of the pair answered, climbing on the box.

"Papers and everything handy?"

"Aye, aye, sir," said the guard on the seat at the back.

"Very well then, go ahead, and good luck go with you!"

The gates were thrown open and the van rolled out into the half-deserted street.

"Now come with me," cried Walworth, "and see if the carriage is at the other door."

We went inside, passed through the house, and out to the front. Yes! The peculiar-shaped hospital car, with the door opening at the end to admit the stretcher, was already pacing up and down. By this time I could do nothing, my teeth were chattering in my head with simple terror.

"Come, come," said Walworth, observing my condition, "you mustn't let yourself go like this. Let me give you a drop of spirit."

He took a flask from his pocket and poured me out half a tumbler of whiskey. I drank it off neat and, I am prepared to assert, did not taste it any more than if it had been so much water. He offered a little to Janet, who sat in the corner in a listening attitude, and when she refused it, screwed on the top again and replaced it in his pocket.

Again we sat in dumb, almost terrified expectancy. Times out of number I thought I heard the van roll into the yard, and sprang to my feet, only to find that it was some cart passing in the street. Its non-arrival in the time we had given it found me almost too frightened to think coherently. I conjured up all sorts of catastrophes in my mind. I saw the horses fall, the driver tumble from his box, I saw our policemen suspected and the plot found out. Then suddenly in the middle of it all I heard the roll of wheels, they came closer and closer, then they stopped, the gates were thrown open, and a second or two later the van rolled into the yard. Before I could have counted ten the guard was down from his perch, the gates were closed again, the door of the van was opened, and Alie ran down the steps. Then, forgetting those about us, I rushed out and took her in my arms. But Walworth would have no delay.

"Come inside quickly," he said. "There is not a second to lose! They may be after us already!"

We followed him into the house, and then for the first time I saw that Alie had dressed herself in the van for the part she had to play. Throwing herself down upon the stretcher, she pulled the coverlet across her, donned a wig with corkscrew curls, drew a veil over her face, and announced herself ready. Janet picked up her reticule, smelling salts, shawls, fans, etc. ; the maid brought an armful of rugs ; I took one end of the stretcher, Walworth the other, and so we went down the steps to the carriage. Then the invalid was hoisted in, Janet and I stepped in and seated ourselves beside her, Walworth sprang onto the box beside the coachman, and away we went for Waterloo as fast as our spirited horse could trot.

Not a word was spoken all the way, and in less than ten minutes we had rattled up the causeway and were disembarking our precious load upon the platform. As the porters came crowding around us, I thought this a fitting opportunity for assuming the rôle I had elected to play. So calling upon two of them to take up " Mrs. Wakeman " and be very careful not to shake her, I led the way toward the Pullman which had been specially reserved for us. Walworth, in his capacity of family servant, had mounted guard at the door, and, when we were inside, went off to his own carriage. A minute later the guard waved his flag, the whistle sounded, and the train steamed slowly out of the station. So far we were safe. But oh ! what an awful risk we had run.

Fortunately the train by which we were travelling was an express, and did not stop anywhere until it reached Eastleigh ; so that as soon as we were under weigh Alie could remove her wig and bedclothes, and sit upright.

" Alie," I whispered, taking her hand and looking

into her beautiful eyes, "can you believe that, so far, you are safe?"

"Hardly," she said. "But we must not relax any of our precautions. By this time the police will have learned the truth, and I shouldn't be at all surprised if the train is searched at Eastleigh. They're certain to telegraph in every direction to stop us."

"But surely they won't suspect *us?*"

"I hope not, but we must not make too sure." Here she crossed the carriage and took my sister's hand. "Janet, what could George have been thinking of to allow you to run this risk? Why did you do it?"

In reply Janet patted her hand, and looked affectionately into her face.

"If you really want to know the reason, it was because we both love you."

"You are too good to me," Alie answered, her dear eyes swimming with tears, "far too good."

"Hush, you must not say that. Let us be thankful that our venture has prospered as it has done."

Mile after mile sped by, and soon we had passed Winchester and were drawing close to Eastleigh. Then Alie resumed her wig and veil, and, having done so, laid herself down once more upon her couch. Closer and closer we came, till presently we entered the station itself, and, with a great rattle and roar of brakes, drew up at the platform. Then ensued the usual scurrying of passengers, the "by your leave" of porters with trucks of luggage, after that the gradual subsidence of bustle, and in three minutes all was ready for proceeding upon our way once more. But just as the guard was about to give his signal the station master stayed his hand.

Next moment an inspector of police, accompanied by a sergeant and two or three constables appeared upon the scene and began slowly to inspect the various carriages. I leaned out of the window and watched them, outwardly calm, but inwardly trembling. Every moment they were drawing nearer to our carriage. I looked behind me. Janet was seated by Alie's side slowly fanning her. From them I turned and glanced down the platform again. The police were already at the next carriage and in a minute would be at my door. What should I do? What should I say? But I dared not think. I felt I must leave it all to chance. A moment later the inspector arrived, and was about to turn the handle.

"Excuse me," I said, pretending to mistake his meaning, "but this carriage is engaged! I think you will find room in the next compartment."

"I'm not looking for a seat," the officer replied, civilly enough, "I'm looking for an escaped criminal."

"Hush! Hush! My good sir, not so loud for mercy's sake," I whispered, as if in an ecstacy of fear. "I have my wife inside dangerously ill. She must not be frightened."

"I beg your pardon, sir," he answered. "I'm sorry I spoke so loud!" Then, as I moved aside to admit him: "Don't trouble, sir, I don't think I need come in, thank you!"

"I'm glad of that," I replied. "And pray who is this escapee you are looking for?"

"The woman there has been such a talk about lately, 'The Beautiful White Devil.' She managed to effect an escape on the way to Holloway Goal this afternoon.

But I am keeping the train. I must get on! Good afternoon and thank you, sir!"

"Good afternoon."

I sat down with an inarticulate expression of my gratitude to Heaven, and, a minute or so later, the train continued its journey, not to stop again until we were in Portsmouth town.

When we arrived at the docks, Walworth and I carried Alie down the steps to the wharf, and as soon as this was accomplished my faithful friend went off in search of the launch which, it had been arranged, should meet and take us out to the yacht, then lying in the harbour. When he had discovered it, we lifted our precious burden on board, and steamed out to where our craft lay. Ten minutes later we had Alie aboard and safely in her own cabin, and were proceeding down the Solent under a full head of steam. *Our rescue was accomplished.*

The yacht was a large one, of perhaps three hundred tons; she was also a good sea boat, and, what was better still, a fast one. By nightfall we had left the Isle of Wight behind us, and brought Swanage almost abeam. Then we stood further out into the Channel and in the gathering darkness lost sight of land altogether. At seven o'clock we dined together in the saloon—the skipper, an old shellback whom Walworth had picked up, sitting down with us. At first he seemed a little surprised at Alie's sudden convalescence, but when I informed him that it was nothing but nerves, he accepted the explanation and said no more.

After the meal was over we left the rather stuffy cabin and went on deck. It was a glorious night. In

18

the west a young moon was dropping on to the horizon, the sea was as smooth as a mill pond, and the air just cool enough to make exercise pleasant. Leaving Walworth and Janet to fight the battle of our escape over and over again on the port side of the deck, we paced the starboard, only to find ourselves aft at our favourite spot, the taffrail.

"George, dear," said Alie softly, when we had been standing there a few moments. "What a lot has happened since we last stood like this, looking out across the sea."

"Yes, darling ; a great deal has indeed occurred to us both," I answered. Then, after a little pause, "Alie, do you know if you had not escaped to-day I should never have been able to forgive myself, for remember it was I who was the means of bringing you home."

"You must not say that !"

"But I must say it ; it is true."

"Then I will forgive you on one condition ! Will you make a bargain with me ?"

"What is it ?"

"That—that——" Here a little fit of modesty overcame her. "That we put into Madeira and you marry me there."

"Alie, darling, do you mean it ?" I cried, delighted beyond all measure at the proposal.

"Of course I mean it."

"But would it be safe, think you ?"

"Perfectly ! They will never dream of looking for us there. You must allow the skipper to understand that it is a runaway match. That will remove his scruples, and make it all plain sailing."

"And you will really be my wife then, Alie?"

"Have I not already been bold enough to ask you to marry me?"

"Then, please God, we will put into Madeira and do as you suggest!"

And that's how it was settled!

CHAPTER XVI.

I AM drawing near the end of my long story now, and, when two more circumstances connected with our flight have been reported, I shall be able to lay down my pen and feel that the story of the one and only romance of my life has been written.

The first of the two circumstances to be recorded is my marriage. On July 18th, seven days exactly after saying good-bye to England, we reached Madeira. Previously to sighting the island, Walworth, in a conversation with the captain, had allowed him to suppose that Alie was a great heiress, and that ours was a runaway match. His nautical spirit of romance was stirred, and he found early occasion to inform me that he would do everything in his power to further the ends we had in view.

As soon, therefore, as we were at anchor in harbour, and the necessary formalities had been complied with, I went ashore, hunted up the proper authorities, and obtained a special license. A parson was the next person required, and when I had discovered him in the little vicarage next door to his church, on the outskirts of the town, our wedding was arranged for the following day at ten o'clock.

Accordingly next morning after breakfast a boat was manned, and Alie, Janet, Walworth, the captain, and myself went ashore. To avert suspicion we separated on landing, but met again at the church door half an hour later. It was a lovely morning, a heavy dew lay upon the grass, and when the sun came out and smiled upon us, the world looked as if it were decked with diamonds in honour of our wedding.

While we were waiting in the little porch and the clerk was opening the doors, Walworth went off and hunted up the parson. Five minutes afterwards they returned together, and then, before the bare little altar, with the sun streaming in through the open door, George de Normanville and Alie Dunbar were made man and wife. The register was then signed and witnessed, and having feed the clergyman and tipped the clerk, we all went back to the town again. It had all been most satisfactorily managed, and I had not the slightest doubt but that the half-imbecile old clergyman had forgotten our names almost before he had discarded his surplice in the vestry.

An hour later we were back on board the yacht, which had by this time replenished her supply of coal; steam was immediately got up, and by three o'clock we were safely out of sight of land once more. Now we had nothing to be afraid of save being stopped and overhauled by a man-of-war. But that was most unlikely, and even in the event of one heaving in sight and desiring to stop us, I had no doubt in my own mind that we possessed sufficiently quick heels to enable us to escape it.

But I am reminded that I have said nothing yet as to the joy and happiness which was mine in at last having Alie for my wife. I have also omitted, most criminally, to give you a full account of the wedding breakfast, which was held with becoming ceremony in the saloon of the yacht, as soon as we had got safely on our way once more. The captain's attempt at speech-making has not been reported, nor have I told you what a singular ass I made of myself, and how I nearly broke down when I rose to reply to the toast of our healths. No! an account of those things, however interesting to those who actually took part in them, could be of little or no concern to any-one else. So for that reason, if for no other, I will be prudent and hold my tongue.

Of the rest of the voyage to the Mascarenhas, there is little to chronicle, save, perhaps, that we sighted Table Mountain in due course, rounded the Cape of Good Hope safely—though we had some choppy, nasty weather in doing so,—and passing into the Indian Ocean, eventually arrived off the island of Reunion an hour before daybreak.

I was on deck before it was light, waiting eagerly for the first signs of day. Not a breath of wind was stirring and as we were only under the scantiest sail our progress was hardly discernible. Then little by little dawn broke upon us, a clear, pearl-gray light, in which the world appeared so silent and mysterious a place that one almost feared to breathe in it. While I was watching, I heard someone come across the deck behind me, and next moment a little hand stole into mine. It was Alie, my wife.

"Can you discern any sign of the schooner?" she asked.

Before answering I looked round the horizon, but there was not a sign of any sail at all. To port showed up the dim outline of the island, with a few small fishing boats coming out to meet the rising sun, but in every other direction, there was nothing but grey sea softly heaving.

"No, darling," I answered, "I can see nothing of her.

But we must not be too impatient.   There is plenty of time for her to put in an appearance yet."

Five minutes later Walworth came up the companion ladder and joined us.   Alie turned to him.

" I hope Captain Patterson thoroughly understood your instructions, Mr. Walworth ? " she said.

" I wired to him to be here a week ago," Walworth answered; " he was to expect us to-day, but, in case of our non-arrival, to continue cruising about in these waters until the end of the month."

" Then we need have no fear," she replied confidently; " we shall sight him before very long, I feel sure."

We then fell to pacing the deck together, talking of the future and all it promised for us.

Half an hour later the lookout whom the captain had sent into the fore crosstrees to report anything he might see, sang out, " Sail ho ! "

" How does she bear ? " cried the skipper from the deck.

" Dead ahead, sir ! " was the man's reply

" What does she look like ? "

" A big topsail schooner, painted white."

" The *Lone Star* for certain, then," said Alie, taking my hand again.

As she spoke, the breakfast bell sounded and we went below to our meal.   When we returned to the deck the distance between the two boats had diminished considerably, and we could make out the schooner quite distinctly. She was little more than five miles away now, and there could be no possible doubt about her identity.   Then, as we watched, she went slowly about and next moment we saw a string of signals break out at her masthead.

Walworth took up a glass from the deck chair and

reported that she was anxious to know our name and where we hailed from.

" Shall I answer ? " he inquired.

" By all means," Alie replied; " did you bring the signals with you ? "

" I have them in my berth," he answered, and dived below, to reappear a moment later with a bundle of bunting under his arms.

Having asked the skipper's permission, he bent them on to the halliards and ran them up to the gaff end. They streamed out upon the breeze, and as he watched them Walworth cried to Alie, with the first and only sign of excitement I have ever known him show:

" That will let them know that you are safe aboard ! "

" Do you wish me to bring the yacht as close alongside as I can ? " asked our skipper, who had been made aware of our intention to say good-bye to him immediately we sighted the *Lone Star*.

" If you will be so kind," I answered.

The necessary manœuvre was thereupon executed, and presently the two yachts lay less than half a mile apart.

" What a lovely craft that is," said Janet, who had just come on deck and was watching her with increasing admiration.

" That is the *Lone Star*," said Alie, putting her arm round Janet's waist in her usual affectionate manner. " The boat which is to carry us to our home, dear Janet ! May you be as happy on board as I have been."

" I think," I said, taking the opportunity of a pause in their conversation to make a practical suggestion, " if you ladies will allow me to say such a thing, it would be as well if we facilitated our transhipping by getting our luggage ready. If I mistake not, Patterson is piping a couple of boats away even now!"

I was right, for as we looked the boats were descending from the port davits.

"George is ever practical, is he not, Alie?" said Janet in a teasing tone. "I fear there is not much romance in his constitution!"

"I am not quite so sure of that," said Alie, with a roguish glance at me, "and, all things considered, I think I may claim to be a very good judge."

"If I am to get the worst of it in this fashion," retorted Janet, with a great pretence of anger, "I shall go below and look after my luggage."

"Let us all go," said Alie, and down we accordingly went.

By the time the necessary work was accomplished and the crew had conveyed our luggage to the deck, the boats from the *Lone Star* were alongside. They were in charge of Gammel, the third officer, who, when he came aboard, raised his hat respectfully to Alie; in return she shook him warmly by the hand and expressed the joy it was to her to see the *Lone Star* again. The luggage was then conveyed down the gangway and put aboard one boat, which immediately set off for the schooner. At Alie's desire I then called the captain aft.

"Captain Brown," I said, "before we leave the yacht I should very much like with your permission to say a few words to your crew."

My request was granted, and the hands were immediately summoned aft. Then, having descended to the cabin for something I wanted, I prepared to make a little speech.

"Captain Brown," I said, "officers and crew of this

yacht, before we leave you to join yonder craft I wish, in my wife's name and my own, to thank you for the manner in which you have performed your respective duties. A pleasanter time than we have had aboard this yacht during the past six weeks no one could desire, and now that we are leaving you I desire to hand you some little souvenirs of our acquaintance. Accordingly I am presenting to your captain a sum of money which will allow each man of you five pounds when he arrives in England, and to the captain and his chief officer these two gold chronometers, which I hope will remind them of our short but intimate acquaintance."

When I had finished and had made the presentations, the captain, on behalf of the ship's company, replied, and then, amid hearty cheers, we descended the gangway, took our places in the boat, and set off for the *Lone Star*.

When we came alongside we discovered the whole ship's company drawn up to receive us. Patterson was at the gangway, and, to my surprise, welcomed us with more emotion than I had previously thought his character capable of exhibiting. I did not know until afterwards that he had become aware by cable of the dangerous situation from which we had rescued his leader.

As soon as we were safely on board, the boats were hoisted to the davits, sail was made, and after an exchange of salutations between the two yachts we separated, each proceeding on our different ways.

Of the voyage across the Indian Ocean there is little or nothing to be told; for the greater part of the distance fine weather accompanied us. We sat on deck or in the saloon, read, related our experiences, "fought our battles o'er again," and watched the ever-changing ocean.

It was our intention not to risk the China Sea, but to pass up through the Straits of Lombok and Macassar to the settlement.

Just before sunset one evening, the dim outlines of the coast of Bali, with Agung Peak towering aloft, was sighted ahead, then Lombok Peak, on the island of the same name, came into view, and before darkness fell we were in the Straits themselves, choosing the eastern channel between Penida Island and the Cape of Banko as the safer of the two. Hereabouts the tides run very strong, and between us and the land there was such a show of phosphorescent water that night as I never remember to have seen elsewhere. We entered the straits at eight o'clock and were clear of them again by eleven.

All next day we were occupied crossing the Java Sea, the water still as smooth as glass, and the sun glaring down fiercely upon us. Naturally we were all most keen to arrive at the settlement and truly rejoiced next day when Patterson informed us that by the evening of the day following we should be within easy reach of it.

The next night passed, and sun-time (mid-day) once more came round. The heat was still intense, the brass work was too hot to touch, and the pitch fairly bubbled in the seams. All the morning we panted in our deck chairs, and only left them to go below to lunch. One thing was remarkable; now that we were almost within touch of safety, Alie had grown strangely nervous, so much so that I felt compelled to remonstrate with her.

" I cannot tell you why I am so frightened," she answered, " but do you remember that night on which we first met when we watched the moon rise and talked of the sea ? "

"Of course, I remember it perfectly," I replied, "but why do you allude to it now?"

"Because I have that same feeling to-night about my fate being mixed up with the sea. I told you I should die at sea, and I have a strange foreboding that, successful as this escape has proved so far, it will yet end in disaster."

"My darling," I cried. "You must not talk like that. What on earth has put such a notion into your head. No, no, my wife; having brought us safely through so much, our luck will not desert us now."

But she was still unconvinced, and no argument on the part of Janet or myself could raise her spirits. Wonderful is the instinct of danger in the human mind; for in a measure what Alie prophesied actually did come true, as will be seen.

Next morning, just after daylight, I was awakened by a loud thumping at my cabin door.

"Who is there?" I cried,

"Walworth! We want you on deck at once."

Pyjama clad though I was, I thrust my feet into slippers and ran up the companion ladder. I found Patterson there anxiously awaiting me.

"What is the matter?" I asked breathlessly. "Why did you send for me?"

"If you want my reason," he said, pointing over our starboard side, "look there."

I looked, and to my horror saw ahead of us, command-the whole strait, two enormous men-of-war. They were within six miles of us, and were evidently making preparations for stopping us.

"What's to be done?" I cried. "Another quarter of an hour and they'll blow us into atoms if we don't heave-to."

" Will you inform your wife, and then, perhaps, we had better hold a council of war," answered Patterson.

Without another word I went below and told Alie. In the presence of this definite danger she was a new woman.

" I will dress and come on deck at once," she said.

I went off to my own cabin and, hastily clothed myself; having done so I returned to the deck to find Patterson looking through his glass at something astern.

" We're nicely caught," he said on becoming aware of my presence. " There's another of them behind us."

I took the glass and looked for myself; what he reported was quite correct. We were caught like rats in a trap. Just as I returned the glass to him Alie appeared and joined our group.

" This is bad news, gentlemen," she said quite calmly. " I suppose there can be no doubt they *are* after us. What have you to suggest?"

" It is difficult to say," answered Patterson. " Two things, however, are quite certain."

" What are they?"

" The first is that unless we are prepared to run the schooner ashore, we must go backwards or forwards. There is no middle course. In either case the result will be the same."

" Have you sent word to the engine-room to get up steam?"

" We have had a full pressure this hour past."

Alie turned to me.

" What do you advise, my husband?"

" There is nothing else for it," I answered, " but to run the gauntlet of them. We must try and get through."

" Very good, then—run it shall be! Are you satisfied, Mr. Patterson?"

"Quite. I agree with Dr. De Normanville it is our only chance."

"Then let us get as close to them as we can, and directly their signals go up, race for it! We shall probably be hit, but we musn't mind that."

The wind was blowing from the most favourable quarter, and every moment was bringing us nearer to our enemies. So far they had made no sign, but it was evident now that they were drawing closer to each other.

When we were within easy range the second officer reported that the larger of the two cruisers was signalling.

"What does she say?" asked Patterson.

The officer put up his glass again and, having looked, studied the Admiralty book lying upon the hatchway.

"Heave-to and let me examine you."

"Very kind, indeed," said Alie. "But we're not to be caught in that way. No, no! my friend, if you want us you will have to use sterner measures than that."

Patterson gave an order and presently a stream of bunting was flying from our own gaff end.

"What are you saying?" I asked when the signals had unrolled and caught the wind.

"I'm asking him why he wants to stop us?" answered Patterson.

All this time we were creeping up between them. Once more a signal broke out, and again the officer reported. This time it ran, "Heave-to and I'll send a boat." But this was equally unregarded.

For ten minutes there was no change save that we had now come up level with them. Then down fluttered the string of flags, and at the same instant a flash of fire came from the nearest vessel followed by a cloud of white smoke.

Almost at the same instant a sharp report reached our ears.

"A blank cartridge to show that they mean business," I answered.

"Hadn't we better go ahead?" Alie remarked.

"I think so," said Patterson, and rang the telegraph. The needle flew round to "Full steam ahead," and off we went.

"Give her every ounce she can carry," shouted Patterson down the speaking tube, and the engineers proved fully equal to the occasion. Before very long the whole fabric of the vessel trembled under the pressure. She quivered like a frightened stag, and cut through the green water at a furious pace. Then, seeing our ruse, the cruiser fired. But, either intentionally or because they had not accurately guaged our distance, the ball went wide.

"We're in for it now," said Alie; "this looks as if it will be the most exciting flight in the *Lone Star's* history.

"If only we could give them one in return," I said longingly. "However, we can't stop for that. So go on, little barkie!" I cried enthusiastically, patting the bulwark with my hand, as if to encourage her, "you know how much depends upon you."

As if she were really aware of it, the gallant little craft dashed on—throwing off the foam in two great waves from her cutwater, and sending the spray in clouds above her bows. The pace was terrific, and it seemed already to have dawned upon the cruisers that if they wanted to catch us they must be quick about it. By this time we had run between them, and therefore they had to turn round before they could pursue us, which meant a start for us that was of the utmost importance in our race for freedom.

Before they attempted to turn, however, both decided on letting us know their tempers, and two guns crashed out almost simultaneously. Again the ball from the bigger of the two fell wide, but that from her consort was more scientifically aimed, and our foretop mast came down with a crash.

"That's the first blood drawn," I said to Alie, as the crew sprang aloft to clear away the raffle. "I wonder what the next will be."

"If we can continue this pace we shall soon be out of range," she answered.

"But can we continue it?" I asked. "The strain must be enormous. Do you feel how every timber is quivering under it?"

As I spoke Alie turned and I saw that Janet had come on deck. With a white face she looked at the two vessels behind us and asked what their presence meant.

"It means," said Alie, going to her and assuming possession of her hand, "that England is determined to try and have the Beautiful White Devil after all."

"But she shan't," said Janet loyally, "not if I have to keep her off with my own hands."

"Bravo, my sister," I cried enthusiastically, "that's the sort of spirit we boast aboard this boat. Never fear, we'll slip them yet; won't we, Alie?"

The girl answered me with a smile that went to my heart, so brave and yet so sad was it.

By this time the men-of-war had turned and were in full pursuit of us; but we had the advantage of a start and were momentarily increasing our lead. Again one ship fired, but as we were all steaming too fast for correct aiming, the ball did no damage. After that they saved their powder, and concentrated all their energies on the task of catching us. All the morning we steamed on, and by three o'clock were a good ten miles ahead.

"If we can only keep this pace up till dusk I think we may manage to give them the slip after all," said Alie, going to the taffrail and looking behind her at the pursuing ships.

Their commanders seemed to realise this too, for they once more began to try long shots at us. But though two fell very close, no harm was done.

About half-past three Patterson left the bridge and came down to where we were sitting aft. He held a chart in his hand, and when he came up with us he knelt down and pinned it to the deck.

"May I draw your attention to this chart?" he said, as soon as his preparations were complete. "You will remember that the first time we were ever chased, it was in this very place! Well, on that occasion we managed to escape by taking this channel between these two reefs. Our pursuer, as doubtless you have not forgotten, drew too much water and could not follow us. Now, if you are willing to chance it, we might try the same plan again."

"What do you think?" asked Alie, turning to me. "It is a desperate risk to run, but then we must remember that we are in a desperate position."

I knelt down upon the deck and carefully examined the chart. It showed a long, straggling reef shaped something like a wriggling snake with an opening in the middle, just wide enough, if the measurements were to be depended upon, to permit our vessel to pass through. One

19

fact was self-evident, and that was that if we did get through we should be saved.

"I am for chancing it," I said, after I had given the matter proper consideration.

"Then we will follow your advice," said Alie. "We will try the passage."

"Very good," Patterson answered quietly, and, having rolled up the chart, returned to the bridge.

After that for nearly half-an-hour we raced on at full speed, the warships coming after us as fast as their steaming capabilities would permit.

Then our pace began somewhat to abate, and looking ahead I could distinguish in the gathering dusk what looked like an unbroken line of breakers stretching away for miles to port and starboard, from far out in the open sea almost to the ragged coast line on our left. Our course had long since been altered and now we were steering directly for the troubled water. The pace was still terrific, but we were slowing down perceptibly.

"We are close to the opening now," said Alie, leading the way up onto the bridge. "If we make a mistake and touch, we shall go to pieces in five minutes. Let us therefore keep together, husband mine."

We stood to windward of the binnacle and watched what was about to happen. The breakers were scarcely half a mile ahead, the warships perhaps six miles astern.

Then two men crawled into the chains and set the leads going—the second officer was sent forrard to reconnoitre and Patterson, dismissing the steersman, took the wheel himself. The third officer was stationed at the telegraph.

Suddenly Patterson drew himself up, spun the spokes

with a preliminary twist to see that all was in working order, and then turned to his subordinate at the telegraph.

"Stop her!" he cried.

The bell tinkled in the engine-room and answered on the bridge. The throbbing of the propeller ceased as if by magic, and next moment we were only moving forward by our own impetus. Almost before one could think, we were among the breakers, but still going forward. I glanced at Patterson out of the corner of my eye. He was standing as erect and passionless as a marble statue, looking straight before him. On both sides the breakers dashed and roared—the spray rising into our faces and falling upon the decks like rain. There was a slight grinding noise for a second or two, and then Patterson gave a shout :

"Full steam ahead!"

The bell answered like magic and instantly the schooner shot forward. *Next moment we were through the reef in smooth water, and safe.*

Looking behind us we could see that the cruisers had stopped and turned, they knew too well what the result would be if they attempted to follow us.

An hour later a large island hid us from sight of the reef and our pursuers. But still, in the gathering gloom, we steamed ahead as fast as our propellers could drive us.

At seven o'clock the gong sounded for dinner, and after a last look round we went below to it. When we remembered how hopeless it had appeared at the beginning, it was difficult to believe that we had emerged so safely from our awkward scrape.

During the meal I could hardly eat for looking at Alie and thinking of all the events which had occurred since first I sat at that table with her. She must have been thinking something of the same kind, for at the end of dinner, just as we were about to go on deck, she bade the steward charge our glasses and proposed this toast:

"I drink to the *Lone Star* and those who have saved us to-day."

We drank the toast with enthusiasm and set our glasses down again. But just as we did so, there was a loud crash, a trembling of the entire vessel, a curious pause, and then another awful crash.

"We have struck something!" I cried, springing to my feet. Then, as if by instinct, I said, "Run to your cabins and get your shawls!"

They did so, and, by the time they emerged again, the hubbub was deafening; the sound of rending and tearing could only be described as awful. Then there was sudden and complete silence which was almost worse than the noise. We ran on deck and made our way as fast as we could to the bridge.

"What has happened?" I cried to Patterson, who was issuing orders as fast as his tongue could utter them.

"We have struck a rock that is not on my chart," he said. "And I have reversed the engines to pull her off."

I could see that we were going astern - but even a child could have told by the way the schooner moved that it was a hopeless case with her.

Even while he was speaking she was sinking perceptibly.

"There is no hope," he said at last, "we must leave her."

All the hands by this time were at their stations, and the boats were lowered with exquisite care and precision. Fortunately they had been that very day uncovered and equipped, in case of accident, so that there was no possible cause for delay.

Keeping Alic and Janet by my side I descended to the boat allotted to us and we took our seats in the stern. By the time we had pulled to a distance of about a hundred yards, the deck of the yacht was level with the water. Five minutes later the gallant but ill-fated *Lone Star* tipped up on end, gave a sullen plunge, and disappeared beneath the waves to be no more seen by mortal man. I slipped my arm round Alic's waist and drew her closer to my side. She was trembling violently.

"Be brave, dear love," I whispered. "For all our sakes, be brave."

She turned her head in the direction where the poor yacht had disappeared and said, almost under her breath :

" Good-bye, *Lone Star*, good-bye."

Then she stooped forward and buried her face in her hands.

To divert her thoughts, I turned to the boat nearest us, which was commanded by Patterson, and asked what he thought we had better do.

"Sail up the coast as fast as we can," he answered. " My boat will take the lead, the rest had better follow in single file. If this wind holds we shall fetch the settlement, or be somewhere thereabouts, by daybreak."

The wind *did* hold and we *did* make the settlement by the time he specified. Then passing behind the great doors which, as I have said before, concealed the entrance to the canal so cleverly that even from the close distance of a mile I had not been able to detect where the imitation began and the real cliff ended, we pulled inside. Then, to cheer us, standing before them all, I unbared my head, and cried, perhaps a trifle theatrically :

"Gentlemen! the queen has come back to her own again!"

As the cheers that greeted my announcement died away we left the canal and entered the little landlocked harbour.

L'ENVOI.

Three years have passed since the wreck of the schooner *Lone Star*, and to-day is the third anniversary of our return to the settlement. It is a lovely morning, and I am sitting in the verandah of our bungalow on the hill-side, pen in hand, waiting for a step whose music grows every day more welcome to my ears. My patience is rewarded when a woman, to whose beauty Time has but added, turns the corner, closely followed by an enormous white bull-dog, and comes towards me. When she reaches me she sets down the rosy toddling infant she carries in her arms, and, taking a seat beside me, says:

"What news had you by the mail this morning, my husband?"

"Nothing of very much moment, Alie," I answer. "The negotiations in England are still proceeding, and Brandwon confidently hopes, in view of certain considerations, that he will be able to carry out his plans and win a free pardon for a certain beautiful lady of my acquaintance."

"Then it is all as satisfactory as we could wish?" she says. "I am thankful for that! And now I have some news for you!"

"Are you going to tell me that I am the happiest husband in the world? or that that boy, playing with old Bel yonder, whom we both worship a good deal more than is good for him, is being spoiled by the entire population of the settlement?"

"Neither of those things! No, it has to do with your sister Janet."

"Ah! then I can guess. She is so enraptured with the settlement that she is willing to prolong her stay indefinitely."

"How did you guess?"

"Have I not eyes, my wife? You don't mean to tell me that you think you alone have seen the outrageous court Walworth has been paying her these six months past?"

"You have no objection, I hope?"

"Not the very slightest. She is a good woman, if ever there was one, and he is certainly a man after my own heart. If they marry and are destined to be as happy as we are, then they'll be lucky people; that's all I can say, my wife."

"Can you truthfully affirm that you have never regretted giving up so much for me?"

"Regretted! How can you ask me such a question? No, my darling; rest assured, if there is one thing for which I am grateful to Providence it is——"

Here I placed my arm round her neck and drew her lovely head down to me.

"What is it?" she whispered.

"That I was permitted to be the husband of the Beautiful White Devil."

THE END.

APPLETONS' TOWN AND COUNTRY LIBRARY.

PUBLISHED SEMIMONTHLY.

1. *The Steel Hammer.* By LOUIS ULBACH.
2. *Eve.* A Novel. By S. BARING-GOULD.
3. *For Fifteen Years.* A Sequel to The Steel Hammer. By LOUIS ULBACH.
4. *A Counsel of Perfection.* A Novel. By LUCAS MALET.
5. *The Deemster.* A Romance. By HALL CAINE.
5½. *The Bondman.* (New edition.) By HALL CAINE.
6. *A Virginia Inheritance.* By EDMUND PENDLETON.
7. *Ninette:* An Idyll of Provence. By the author of Véra.
8. *"The Right Honourable."* By JUSTIN McCARTHY and Mrs. CAMPBELL-PRAED.
9. *The Silence of Dean Maitland.* By MAXWELL GRAY.
10. *Mrs. Lorimer:* A Study in Black and White. By LUCAS MALET.
11. *The Elect Lady.* By GEORGE MACDONALD.
12. *The Mystery of the "Ocean Star."* By W. CLARK RUSSELL.
13. *Aristocracy.* A Novel.
14. *A Recoiling Vengeance.* By FRANK BARRETT. With Illustrations.
15. *The Secret of Fontaine-la-Croix.* By MARGARET FIELD.
16. *The Master of Rathkelly.* By HAWLEY SMART.
17. *Donovan:* A Modern Englishman. By EDNA LYALL.
18. *This Mortal Coil.* By GRANT ALLEN.
19. *A Fair Emigrant.* By ROSA MULHOLLAND.
20. *The Apostate.* By ERNEST DAUDET.
21. *Raleigh Westgate;* or, Epimenides in Maine. By HELEN KENDRICK JOHNSON.
22. *Arius the Libyan.* A Romance of the Primitive Church.
23. *Constance,* and *Calbot's Rival.* By JULIAN HAWTHORNE.
24. *We Two.* By EDNA LYALL.
25. *A Dreamer of Dreams.* By the author of Thoth.
26. *The Ladies' Gallery.* By JUSTIN McCARTHY and Mrs. CAMPBELL-PRAED.
27. *The Reproach of Annesley.* By MAXWELL GRAY.
28. *Near to Happiness.*
29. *In the Wire Grass.* By LOUIS PENDLETON.
30. *Lace.* A Berlin Romance. By PAUL LINDAU.
30½. *The Black Poodle.* By F. ANSTEY.
31. *American Coin.* A Novel. By the author of Aristocracy.
32. *Won by Waiting.* By EDNA LYALL.
33. *The Story of Helen Davenant.* By VIOLET FANE.
34. *The Light of Her Countenance.* By H. H. BOYESEN.
35. *Mistress Beatrice Cope.* My M. E. LE CLERC.
36. *The Knight-Errant.* By EDNA LYALL.
37. *In the Golden Days.* By EDNA LYALL.
38. *Giraldi;* or, The Curse of Love. By ROSS GEORGE DERING.
39. *A Hardy Norseman.* By EDNA LYALL.
40. *The Romance of Jenny Harlowe,* and *Sketches of Maritime Life.* By W. CLARK RUSSELL.
41. *Passion's Slave.* By RICHARD ASHE-KING.
42. *The Awakening of Mary Fenwick.* By BEATRICE WHITBY.
43. *Countess Loreley.* Translated from the German of RUDOLF MENGER.
44. *Blind Love.* By WILKIE COLLINS.
45. *The Dean's Daughter.* By SOPHIE F. F. VEITCH.
46. *Countess Irene.* A Romance of Austrian Life. By J. FOGERTY.
47. *Robert Browning's Principal Shorter Poems.*
48. *Frozen Hearts.* By G. WEBB APPLETON.
49. *Djambek the Georgian.* By A. G. VON SUTTNER.
50. *The Craze of Christian Engelhart.* By HENRY FAULKNER DARNELL.
51. *Lal.* By WILLIAM A. HAMMOND, M. D.
52. *Aline.* A Novel. By HENRY GRÉVILLE.
53. *Joost Avelingh.* A Dutch Story. By MAARTEN MAARTENS.
54. *Katy of Catoctin.* By GEORGE ALFRED TOWNSEND.
55. *Throckmorton.* A Novel. By MOLLY ELLIOT SEAWELL.
56. *Expatriation.* By the author of Aristocracy.
57. *Geoffrey Hampstead.* By T. S. JARVIS.

58. *Dmitri.* A Romance of Old Russia. By F. W. Bain, M. A.
59. *Part of the Property.* By Beatrice Whitby.
60. *Bismarck in Private Life.* By a Fellow-Student.
61. *In Low Relief.* By Morley Roberts.
62. *The Canadians of Old.* A Historical Romance. By Philippe Gaspé.
63. *A Squire of Low Degree.* By Lily A. Long.
64. *A Fluttered Dovecote.* By George Manville Fenn.
65. *The Nugents of Carriconna.* An Irish Story. By Tighe Hopkins.
66. *A Sensitive Plant.* By E. and D. Gerard.
67. *Doña Luz.* By Juan Valera. Translated by Mrs. Mary J. Serrano.
68. *Pepita Ximenez.* By Juan Valera. Translated by Mrs. Mary J. Serrano.
69. *The Primes and their Neighbors.* By Richard Malcolm Johnston.
70. *The Iron Game.* By Henry F. Keenan.
71. *Stories of Old New Spain.* By Thomas A. Janvier.
72. *The Maid of Honor.* By Hon. Lewis Wingfield.
73. *In the Heart of the Storm.* By Maxwell Gray.
74. *Consequences.* By Egerton Castle.
75. *The Three Miss Kings.* By Ada Cambridge.
76. *A Matter of Skill.* By Beatrice Whitby.
77. *Maid Marian, and Other Stories.* By Molly Elliot Seawell.
78. *One Woman's Way.* By Edmund Pendleton.
79. *A Merciful Divorce.* By F. W. Maude.
80. *Stephen Ellicott's Daughter.* By Mrs. J. H. Needell.
81. *One Reason Why.* By Beatrice Whitby.
82. *The Tragedy of Ida Noble.* By W. Clark Russell.
83. *The Johnstown Stage, and other Stories.* By Robert H. Fletcher.
84. *A Widower Indeed.* By Rhoda Broughton and Elizabeth Bisland.
85. *The Flight of a Shadow.* By George MacDonald.
86. *Love or Money.* By Katharine Lee.
87. *Not All in Vain.* By Ada Cambridge.
88. *It Happened Yesterday.* By Frederick Marshall.
89. *My Guardian.* By Ada Cambridge.
90. *The Story of Philip Methuen.* By Mrs. J. H. Needell.
91. *Amethyst :* The Story of a Beauty. By Christabel R. Coleridge.
92. *Don Braulio.* By Juan Valera. Translated by Clara Bell.
93. *The Chronicles of Mr. Bill Williams.* By Richard Malcolm Johnston.
94. *A Queen of Curds and Cream.* By Dorothea Gerard.
95. *" La Bella " and Others.* By Egerton Castle.
96. *" December Roses."* By Mrs. Campbell Praed.
97. *Jean de Kerdren.* By Jeanne Schultz.
98. *Etelka's Vow.* By Dorothea Gerard.
99. *Cross Currents.* By Mary A. Dickens.
100. *His Life's Magnet.* By Theodora Elmslie.
101. *Passing the Love of Women.* By Mrs. J. H. Needell.
102. *In Old St. Stephen's.* By Jeanie Drake.
103. *The Berkeleys and their Neighbors.* By Molly Elliot Seawell.
104. *Mona Maclean, Medical Student.* By Graham Travers.
105. *Mrs. Bligh.* By Rhoda Broughton.
106. *A Stumble on the Threshold.* By James Payn.
107. *Hanging Moss.* By Paul Lindau.
108. *A Comedy of Elopement.* By Christian Reid.
109. *In the Suntime of her Youth.* By Beatrice Whitby.
110. *Stories in Black and White.* By Thomas Hardy and Others.
110½. *An Englishman in Paris.* Notes and Recollections.
111. *Commander Mendoza.* By Juan Valera.
112. *Dr. Paull's Theory.* By Mrs. A. M. Diehl.
113. *Children of Destiny.* By Molly Elliot Seawell.
114. *A Little Minx.* By Ada Cambridge.
115. *Capt'n Davy's Honeymoon.* By Hall Caine.
116. *The Voice of a Flower.* By E. Gerard.
117. *Singularly Deluded.* By Sarah Grand.
118. *Suspected.* By Louisa Stratenus.
119. *Lucia, Hugh, and Another.* By Mrs. J. H. Needell.
120. *The Tutor's Secret.* By Victor Cherbuliez.

121. *From the Five Rivers.* By Mrs. F. A. STEEL.
122. *An Innocent Impostor, and Other Stories.* By MAXWELL GRAY.
123. *Ideala.* By SARAH GRAND.
124. *A Comedy of Masks.* By ERNEST DOWSON and ARTHUR MOORE.
125. *Relics.* By FRANCES MACNAB.
126. *Dodo: A Detail of the Day.* By E. F. BENSON.
127. *A Woman of Forty.* By ESMÈ STUART.
128. *Diana Tempest.* By MARY CHOLMONDELEY.
129. *The Recipe for Diamonds.* By C. J. CUTCLIFFE HYNE.
130. *Christina Chard.* By Mrs. CAMPBELL-PRAED.
131. *A Gray Eye or So.* By FRANK FRANKFORT MOORE.
132. *Earlscourt.* By ALEXANDER ALLARDYCE.
133. *A Marriage Ceremony.* By ADA CAMBRIDGE.
134. *A Ward in Chancery.* By Mrs. ALEXANDER.
135. *Lot 13.* By DOROTHEA GERARD.
136. *Our Manifold Nature.* By SARAH GRAND.
137. *A Costly Freak.* By MAXWELL GRAY.
138. *A Beginner.* By RHODA BROUGHTON.
139. *A Yellow Aster.* By Mrs. MANNINGTON CAFFYN ("IOTA").
140. *The Rubicon.* By E. F. BENSON.
141. *The Trespasser.* By GILBERT PARKER.
142. *The Rich Miss Riddell.* By DOROTHEA GERARD.
143. *Mary Fenwick's Daughter.* By BEATRICE WHITBY.
144. *Red Diamonds.* By JUSTIN McCARTHY.
145. *A Daughter of Music.* By G. COLMORE.
146. *Outlaw and Lawmaker.* By Mrs. CAMPBELL-PRAED.
147. *Dr. Janet of Harley Street.* By ARABELLA KENEALY.
148. *George Mandeville's Husband.* By C. E. RAIMOND.
149. *Vashti and Esther.*
150. *Timar's Two Worlds.* By M. JOKAI.
151. *A Victim of Good Luck.* By W. E. NORRIS.
152. *The Trail of the Sword.* By GILBERT PARKER.
153. *A Mild Barbarian.* By EDGAR FAWCETT.
154. *The God in the Car.* By ANTHONY HOPE.
155. *Children of Circumstance.* By Mrs. M. CAFFYN.
156. *At the Gate of Samaria.* By WILLIAM J. LOCKE.
157. *The Justification of Andrew Lebrun.* By FRANK BARRETT.
158. *Dust and Laurels.* By MARY L. PENDERED.
159. *The Good Ship Mohock.* By W. CLARK RUSSELL.
160. *Noémi.* By S. BARING-GOULD.
161. *The Honour of Savelli.* By S. LEVETT YEATS.
162. *Kitty's Engagement.* By FLORENCE WARDEN.
163. *The Mermaid.* By L. DOUGALL.
164. *An Arranged Marriage.* By DOROTHEA GERARD.
165. *Eve's Ransom.* By GEORGE GISSING.
166. *The Marriage of Esther.* By GUY BOOTHBY.
167. *Fidelis.* By ADA CAMBRIDGE.
168. *Into the Highways and Hedges.* By F. F. MONTRÉSOR.
169. *The Vengeance of James Vansittart.* By Mrs. J. H. NEEDELL.
170. *A Study in Prejudices.* By GEORGE PASTON.
171. *The Mistress of Quest.* By ADELINE SERGEANT.
172. *In the Year of Jubilee.* By GEORGE GISSING.
173. *In Old New England.* By HEZEKIAH BUTTERWORTH.
174. *Mrs. Musgrave—and Her Husband.* By R. MARSH.
175. *Not Counting the Cost.* By TASMA.
176. *Out of Due Season.* By ADELINE SERGEANT.
177. *Scylla or Charybdis?* By RHODA BROUGHTON.
178. *In Defiance of the King.* By C. C. HOTCHKISS.
179. *A Bid for Fortune.* By GUY BOOTHBY.
180. *The King of Andaman.* By J. MACLAREN COBBAN.
181. *Mrs. Tregaskiss.* By Mrs. CAMPBELL-PRAED.
182. *The Desire of the Moth.* By CAPEL VANE.
183. *A Self-Denying Ordinance.* By M. HAMILTON.
184. *Successors to the Title.* By Mrs. L. B. WALFORD.

APPLETONS' TOWN AND COUNTRY LIBRARY.—(*Continued.*)

185. *The Lost Stradivarius.* By J. MEADE FALKNER.
186. *The Wrong Man.* By DOROTHEA GERARD.
187. *In the Day of Adversity.* By J. BLOUNDELLE-BURTON.
188. *Mistress Dorothy Marvin.* By J. C. SNAITH.
189. *A Flash of Summer.* By Mrs. W. K. CLIFFORD.
190. *The Dancer in Yellow.* By W. E. NORRIS.
191. *The Chronicles of Martin Hewitt.* By ARTHUR MORRISON.
192. *A Winning Hazard.* By Mrs. ALEXANDER.
193. *The Picture of Las Cruces.* By CHRISTIAN REID.
194. *The Madonna of a Day.* By L. DOUGALL.
195. *The Riddle Ring.* By JUSTIN McCARTHY.
196. *A Humble Enterprise.* By ADA CAMBRIDGE.
197. *Dr. Nikola.* By GUY BOOTHBY.
198. *An Outcast of the Islands.* By JOSEPH CONRAD.
199. *The King's Revenge.* By CLAUDE BRAY.
200. *Denounced.* By J. BLOUNDELLE-BURTON.
201. *A Court Intrigue.* By BASIL THOMPSON.
202. *The Idol-Maker.* By ADELINE SERGEANT.
203. *The Intriguers.* By JOHN D. BARRY.
204. *Master Ardick, Buccaneer.* By F. H. COSTELLO.
205. *With Fortune Made.* By VICTOR CHERBULIEZ.
206. *Fellow Travellers.* By GRAHAM TRAVERS.
207. *McLeod of the Camerons.* By M. HAMILTON.
208. *The Career of Candida.* By GEORGE PASTON.
209. *Arrested.* By ESMÈ STUART.
210. *Tatterley.* By T. GALLON.
211. *A Pinchbeck Goddess.* By Mrs. J. M. FLEMING (Alice M. Kipling).
212. *Perfection City.* By Mrs. ORPEN.
213. *A Spotless Reputation.* By DOROTHEA GERARD.
214. *A Galahad of the Creeks.* By S. LEVETT YEATS.
215. *Marietta's Marriage.* By W. E. NORRIS.

Each, 12mo, paper cover, 50 cents; cloth, $1.00.

GEORG EBERS'S ROMANCES.

Each, 16mo, paper, 40 cents per volume; cloth, 75 cents.
Sets of 24 volumes, cloth, in box, $18.00.

In the Blue Pike. A Romance of German Life in the early Sixteenth Century. Translated by MARY J. SAFFORD. 1 volume.
In the Fire of the Forge. A Romance of Old Nuremberg. Translated by MARY J. SAFFORD. 2 volumes.
Cleopatra. Translated by MARY J. SAFFORD. 2 volumes.
A Thorny Path. (PER ASPERA.) Translated by CLARA BELL. 2 volumes.
An Egyptian Princess. Translated by ELEANOR GROVE. 2 volumes.
Uarda. Translated by CLARA BELL. 2 volumes.
Homo Sum. Translated by CLARA BELL. 1 volume.
The Sisters. Translated by CLARA BELL. 1 volume.
A Question. Translated by MARY J. SAFFORD. 1 volume.
The Emperor. Translated by CLARA BELL. 2 volumes.
The Burgomaster's Wife. Translated by MARY J. SAFFORD. 1 volume.
A Word, only a Word. Translated by MARY J. SAFFORD. 1 volume.
Serapis. Translated by CLARA BELL. 1 volume.
The Bride of the Nile. Translated by CLARA BELL. 2 volumes.
Margery. (GRED.) Translated by CLARA BELL. 2 volumes.
Joshua. Translated by MARY J. SAFFORD. 1 volume.
The Elixir, and Other Tales. Translated by Mrs. EDWARD H. BELL. With Portrait of the Author. 1 volume.

For sale by all booksellers; or sent by mail on receipt of price by the publishers,

D. APPLETON & CO., 72 Fifth Avenue, New York.

D. APPLETON & CO.'S PUBLICATIONS.

THE STATEMENT OF STELLA MABERLY. By F. ANSTEY, author of "Vice Versa," "The Giant's Robe," etc. 16mo. Cloth, special binding, $1.25.

"Most admirably done. . . . We read fascinated, and fully believing every word we read. . . . The book has deeply interested us, and even thrilled us more than once."—*London Daily Chronicle.*

"A wildly fantastic story, thrilling and impressive. . . . Has an air of vivid reality, . . . of bold conception and vigorous treatment. . . . A very noteworthy novelette."—*London Times.*

MARCH HARES. By HAROLD FREDERIC, author of "The Damnation of Theron Ware," "In the Valley," etc. 16mo. Cloth, special binding, $1.25.

"One of the most cheerful novels we have chanced upon for many a day. It has much of the rapidity and vigor of a smartly written farce, with a pervading freshness a smartly written farce rarely possesses. . . . A book decidedly worth reading."—*London Saturday Review.*

"A striking and original story, . . . effective, pleasing, and very capable."—*London Literary World.*

GREEN GATES. An Analysis of Foolishness. By Mrs. K. M. C. MEREDITH (Johanna Staats), author of "Drumsticks," etc. 16mo. Cloth, $1.25.

"Crisp and delightful. . . . Fascinating, not so much for what it suggests as for its manner, and the cleverly outlined people who walk through its pages."—*Chicago Times-Herald.*

"An original strain, bright and vivacious, and strong enough in its foolishness and its unexpected tragedy to prove its sterling worth."—*Boston Herald.*

AN IMAGINATIVE MAN. By ROBERT S. HICHENS, author of "The Folly of Eustace," "The Green Carnation," etc. 12mo. Cloth, $1.25.

"A study in character. . . . Just as entertaining as though it were the conventional story of love and marriage. The clever hand of the author of 'The Green Carnation' is easily detected in the caustic wit and pointed epigram."—*Jeannette L. Gilder, in the New York World.*

CORRUPTION. By PERCY WHITE, author of "Mr. Bailey-Martin," etc. 12mo. Cloth, $1.25.

"A drama of biting intensity. A tragedy of inflexible purpose and relentless result."—*Pall Mall Gazette.*

A HARD WOMAN. A Story in Scenes. By VIOLET HUNT. 12mo. Cloth, $1.25.

"A good story, bright, keen, and dramatic. . . . It is out of the ordinary, and will give you a new sensation."—*New York Herald.*

New York: D. APPLETON & CO., 72 Fifth Avenue.

D. APPLETON & CO.'S PUBLICATIONS.

GILBERT PARKER'S BEST BOOKS.

THE SEATS OF THE MIGHTY. Being the Memoirs of Captain ROBERT MORAY, sometime an Officer in the Virginia Regiment, and afterwards of Amherst's Regiment. 12mo. Cloth, illustrated, $1.50.

"Another historical romance of the vividness and intensity of 'The Seats of the Mighty' has never come from the pen of an American. Mr. Parker's latest work may, without hesitation, be set down as the best he has done. From the first chapter to the last word interest in the book never wanes; one finds it difficult to interrupt the narrative with breathing space. It whirls with excitement and strange adventure. . . . All of the scenes do homage to the genius of Mr. Parker, and make 'The Seats of the Mighty' one of the books of the year."—*Chicago Record.*

"Mr. Gilbert Parker is to be congratulated on the excellence of his latest story, 'The Seats of the Mighty,' and his readers are to be congratulated on the direction which his talents have taken therein. . . . It is so good that we do not stop to think of its literature, and the personality of Doltaire is a masterpiece of creative art."—*New York Mail and Express.*

THE TRAIL OF THE SWORD. A Novel. 12mo. Paper, 50 cents; cloth, $1.00.

"Mr. Parker here adds to a reputation already wide, and anew demonstrates his power of pictorial portrayal and of strong dramatic situation and climax."—*Philadelphia Bulletin.*

"The tale holds the reader's interest from first to last, for it is full of fire and spirit, abounding in incident, and marked by good character drawing."—*Pittsburg Times.*

THE TRESPASSER. 12mo. Paper, 50 cents; cloth, $1.00.

"Interest, pith, force, and charm—Mr. Parker's new story possesses all these qualities. . . . Almost bare of synthetical decoration, his paragraphs are stirring because they are real. We read at times—as we have read the great masters of romance —breathlessly."—*The Critic.*

"Gilbert Parker writes a strong novel, but thus far this is his masterpiece. . . . It is one of the great novels of the year."—*Boston Advertiser.*

THE TRANSLATION OF A SAVAGE. 16mo. Flexible cloth, 75 cents.

"A book which no one will be satisfied to put down until the end has been matter of certainty and assurance."—*The Nation.*

"A story of remarkable interest, originality, and ingenuity of construction."— *Boston Home Journal.*

"The perusal of this romance will repay those who care for new and original types of character, and who are susceptible to the fascination of a fresh and vigorous style." —*London Daily News.*

New York: D. APPLETON & CO., 72 Fifth Avenue.

D. APPLETON AND COMPANY'S PUBLICATIONS.

BY S. R. CROCKETT.

Uniform edition. Each, 12mo, cloth, $1.50.

*L*ADS' LOVE. Illustrated.

In this fresh and charming story, which in some respects recalls "The Lilac Sunbonnet," Mr. Crockett returns to Galloway and pictures the humor and pathos of the life which he knows so well.

*C*LEG KELLY, ARAB OF THE CITY. His *Progress and Adventures.* Illustrated.

"A masterpiece which Mark Twain himself has never rivaled. . . . If there ever was an ideal character in fiction it is this heroic ragamuffin."—*London Daily Chronicle.*

"In no one of his books does Mr. Crockett give us a brighter or more graphic picture of contemporary Scotch life than in 'Cleg Kelly.' . . . It is one of the great books."—*Boston Daily Advertiser.*

"One of the most successful of Mr. Crockett's works."—*Brooklyn Eagle.*

*B*OG-MYRTLE AND PEAT. Third edition.

"Here are idyls, epics, dramas of human life, written in words that thrill and burn. . . . Each is a poem that has an immortal flavor. They are fragments of the author's early dreams, too bright, too gorgeous, too full of the blood of rubies and the life of diamonds to be caught and held palpitating in expression's grasp."—*Boston Courier.*

"Hardly a sketch among them all that will not afford pleasure to the reader for its genial humor, artistic local coloring, and admirable portrayal of character."—*Boston Home Journal.*

"One dips into the book anywhere and reads on and on, fascinated by the writer's charm of manner."—*Minneapolis Tribune.*

*T*HE LILAC SUNBONNET. Eighth edition.

"A love story pure and simple, one of the old-fashioned, wholesome, sunshiny kind, with a pure-minded, sound-hearted hero, and a heroine who is merely a good and beautiful woman ; and if any other love story half so sweet has been written this year, it has escaped our notice."—*New York Times.*

"The general conception of the story, the motive of which is the growth of love between the young chief and heroine, is delineated with a sweetness and a freshness, a naturalness and a certainty, which places 'The Lilac Sunbonnet' among the best stories of the time."—*New York Mail and Express.*

"In its own line this little love story can hardly be excelled. It is a pastoral, an idyl—the story of love and courtship and marriage of a fine young man and a lovely girl—no more. But it is told in so thoroughly delightful a manner, with such playful humor, such delicate fancy, such true and sympathetic feeling, that nothing more could be desired."—*Boston Traveller.*

NEW YORK: D. APPLETON AND COMPANY.

D. APPLETON AND COMPANY'S PUBLICATIONS.

STEPHEN CRANE'S BOOKS.

THE THIRD VIOLET. 12mo. Cloth, $1.00.

Mr. Crane's new novel is a fresh and delightful study of artist life in the city and the country. The theme is worked out with the author's characteristic originality and force, and with much natural humor. In subject the book is altogether different from any of its predecessors, and the author's marked success proves his breadth and the versatility of his great talent.

THE LITTLE REGIMENT, and Other Episodes of the American Civil War. 12mo. Cloth, $1.00.

"In 'The Little Regiment' we have again studies of the volunteers waiting impatiently to fight and fighting, and the impression of the contest as a private soldier hears, sees, and feels it, is really wonderful. The reader has no privileges. He must, it seems, take his place in the ranks, and stand in the mud, wade in the river, fight, yell, swear, and sweat with the men. He has some sort of feeling, when it is all over, that he has been doing just these things. This sort of writing needs no praise. It will make its way to the hearts of men without praise."—*New York Times.*

"Told with a *verve* that brings a whiff of burning powder to one's nostrils. . . . In some way he blazons the scene before our eyes, and makes us feel the very impetus of bloody war."—*Chicago Evening Post.*

MAGGIE: A GIRL OF THE STREETS. 12mo. Cloth, 75 cents.

"By writing 'Maggie' Mr. Crane has made for himself a permanent place in literature. . . . Zola himself scarcely has surpassed its tremendous portrayal of throbbing, breathing, moving life."—*New York Mail and Express.*

"Mr. Crane's story should be read for the fidelity with which it portrays a life that is potent on this island, along with the best of us. It is a powerful portrayal, and, if somber and repellent, none the less true, none the less freighted with appeal to those who are able to assist in righting wrongs."—*New York Times.*

THE RED BADGE OF COURAGE. An Episode of the American Civil War. 12mo. Cloth, $1.00.

"Never before have we had the seamy side of glorious war so well depicted. . . . The action of the story throughout is splendid, and all aglow with color, movement, and vim. The style is as keen and bright as a sword-blade, and a Kipling has done nothing better in this line."—*Chicago Evening Post.*

"There is nothing in American fiction to compare with it. . . . Mr. Crane has added to American literature something that has never been done before, and that is, in its own peculiar way, inimitable."—*Boston Beacon.*

"A truer and completer picture of war than either Tolstoy or Zola."—*London New Review.*

NEW YORK: D. APPLETON AND COMPANY.